STAGE KISSES ON HALFPENNY LANE

HALFPENNY LANE
BOOK 2

CLODAGH MURPHY

Balally Books

A NOTE ON NAMES

Some of the characters and places in this book have Irish names that might be unfamiliar. Here's a quick guide to pronunciation.

Aoife
    Pronounced: EE-fa

Sive
    Pronounced: SYVE (rhymes with 'Five')

Ranelagh
    A Dublin suburb
    Pronounced: REN-el-a

1
___

Life didn't get much better than this, Mimi thought, practically bouncing with each step as she weaved through the crowds of tourists on the narrow, cobbled streets of Temple Bar. It was a warm May afternoon, the first dry day after weeks of solid rain, and she was on her way to Halfpenny Lane, the little theatre founded by their great-aunt Detta and now owned by her and her sisters. Thanks to a successful crowdfunding campaign last year, they'd managed to save the rundown building and fulfil their childhood dream of owning their very own theatre. They were still poor, of course, but blissfully happy with it, like three charming orphans in a storybook.

She was cast to play Amanda in their upcoming production of Noël Coward's *Private Lives* – one of her favourite plays and a role she'd long coveted – and today she was sitting in on the auditions for the part of her ex-husband Elyot. All was right with her world.

As she passed The Halfpenny Place, the little bakery and café at the end of the lane, she waved to Chloe, the owner, standing behind the counter. She paused for a

I

moment by the entrance to the theatre, turning her face to the sun and soaking up the warmth of its rays. Then she pushed through the stage door and took the narrow stairs to the backstage area two at a time.

'Good afternoon!' Sam greeted her outside the green room with a cheery grin.

'Hi, Sam.' She returned his smile. Though he'd been responsible, in a circuitous way, for them almost losing Halfpenny Lane, she couldn't find any resentment in her heart today even for him. It was no thanks to Sam that everything had worked out in the end, but he'd proved himself a cheerful and willing worker since they'd hired him to work at the theatre, and his dedication to Half-penny Lane couldn't help but endear him to Mimi and earn him her grudging respect.

'Nina's in there,' he said, nodding to the door of the green room where they were holding the auditions. 'Can I get you anything? Tea? Coffee?'

'A coffee would be great, thanks.'

'Ready to find our Elyot?' Nina said, looking up as Mimi entered the room. She was seated on the threadbare velvet sofa, poring over headshots and resumes, a mug of coffee on the table in front of her. A tall, angular English-woman in her mid-thirties who now lived and worked in Ireland, Nina had a growing reputation as a creative and original director, and Mimi was thrilled they'd been able to sign her on for *Private Lives*.

'Can't wait!' Mimi sat beside her, and Nina handed her an audition schedule. Mimi wouldn't normally be involved in casting, but *Private Lives* was such an intimate, sexually charged piece, it was essential that the two leads had the right chemistry together, so Nina wanted her to read with all the actors trying for the part of Elyot. Mimi was excited about being on the other side of auditions for a change and seeing the process from a different perspective. She also relished the opportunity it gave her to work more closely with Nina and learn from her.

She ran her eyes down the list of names, some familiar and others new to her, but there was no one she'd worked with before. Sam brought in her coffee and announced that the first candidate had arrived.

'Great,' Nina said. 'Send him in.'

'Well, that was … unusual,' Mimi said in a low voice, turning to Nina as the door closed behind Tim, the last actor on their list for the day. Mimi had struggled to keep a straight face when he'd chosen to play Elyot as a depressive, delivering all his lines in a flat monotone and sucking every ounce of humour from them. She'd felt like she was wading through mud, throwing her witty lines into the air only to have them land with a dull thud at his feet. When Nina had gently reminded him that it was a comedy and suggested he try it another way – perhaps make it more light-hearted and try to find the humour in the piece – he'd simply added a lisp. Which granted, was funny, but not in the way Tim intended. 'Do you get many like that?' she asked.

'There's always one.' Nina rolled her eyes. 'They take the advice to make bold choices too much to heart and feel they have to avoid the obvious reading at all costs. So they add some element out of left field, no matter how incongruous it may be. They're desperate to show you something you haven't seen before, so that they'll stand out.'

'He certainly achieved that. I won't forget Tim's name in a hurry.' Mimi sighed and leaned back against the sofa. She looked down at the audition schedule in her lap, her notes scribbled next to each name.

'What did you think otherwise?' Nina asked, studying an identical list in her hand.

'There were a couple of possibilities, but—'

'No one great.'

'No.' Apart from the hapless Tim, they'd all been professional, competent and engaged. One or two had brought an interesting nuance to the reading, and any of them could be trusted to give a decent performance in the role. But none had felt quite right and there was no one Mimi was excited about working with. 'Well, here's hoping for tomorrow.'

'Don't give up on today just yet,' Nina said with a little smile.

'But there's no one else to see today.' Mimi frowned, studying the schedule once more. They'd definitely seen everyone.

'I have a hunch you're going to like this next one,' Nina said. 'I didn't want to tell—'

She was interrupted by a soft knock on the door before it opened and Sam stuck his head around. 'Ready for the next one?'

'He's here?'

There was something significant about the look Sam gave Nina as he nodded, wide-eyed, eyebrows raised. He seemed ... excited? Surprised?

'Great. Send him in.' Sam disappeared and Nina grabbed Mimi's schedule from her, adding another name to the bottom. 'My wild card,' she said, handing the page back to Mimi with a flourish.

Mimi bent her head to the list, her eyes blurring as she read the name written there: Rocco Agnew. Her chest cavity seemed to freeze, making it impossible to breathe, while her heart was racing so fast she feared she might pass out. The schedule shook in her cold, clammy hand. All she wanted to do was run away, but at the same time she didn't trust her legs to hold her up.

Too soon, the door opened again and Sam was back, announcing Rocco – and suddenly there he was in front of her, large as life and ten times as beautiful. His skin tanned a light gold from the California sun, Rocco stepped into the worn and shabby backstage room like a creature from another world.

She was hardly aware of what was happening as Nina stood to greet him and proceeded to introduce them.

'Hi, Mimi,' Rocco said. 'It's been a long time.'

'Oh, you two know each other?'

Just in the biblical sense Mimi wanted to quip, but she clamped her mouth shut.

'You've worked together before?' Nina asked, turning to Mimi, still frozen in place on the couch. 'I didn't realise.'

'We were at acting school together,' Rocco explained, his familiar deep baritone sending a thrill through Mimi. The things he'd said to her in that voice, the words he'd whispered in her ear …

'Yes!' She shook herself out of her reverie and stood, taking Rocco's extended hand. 'It was a long time ago.' She was hardly able to speak, her throat was so dry. Rocco smiled and shook her hand as if they were old acquaintances. Nothing more, nothing less.

'Great! Well, why don't we do a little reading and see how we get on?' Nina waved Rocco to the sofa, seemingly oblivious to the tension in the room. Mimi felt there should be oxygen masks dropping from the ceiling. She struggled to drag air into her lungs as Rocco sat down beside her.

She tried to pull herself together as Nina engaged him in some preliminary discussion of the play and his ideas about the role of Elyot. If she could just pretend it was any other actor – anyone but him – maybe she could get through this without embarrassing herself. That was as much as she could hope for. She already knew she'd be so stilted and awkward, the reading would be a disaster, and Nina would decide to either ditch her or look for another Elyot.

But as they began to read the audition scene, her acting instincts took over and she lost herself in the script. It was as if a switch had been flipped and it was no longer Rocco sparring with her in a tatty backstage room, but Elyot, her ex-husband, exchanging barbs with her across adjoining balconies at a glamorous hotel in Deauville.

She and Rocco fell into step together as easily and instinctively as they had in their first weeks of acting school, and it was a wonderful feeling. They'd always brought out the best in each other, and it was no different today. It was as if the years apart had never happened.

Nina saw it, of course. She was beaming at them delightedly as they finished. 'I love what you did with that last line,' she said to Rocco as they stood. 'Thanks for coming in. We'll be in touch.'

Rocco thanked them both, and he was all smiles as they shook hands. Mimi couldn't look him in the face, afraid of what she'd see there if she did. She felt wobbly again now that the scene was over and she was back to herself. She nodded to him stiffly without making eye contact, while hating herself for being such a coward. It wasn't like her.

'Wow, that was *hot!*' Nina said, fanning herself with her schedule as soon as the door closed behind Rocco and they were alone again. 'How did you feel?'

Befuddled was how Mimi felt. 'Um … yes. He was great,' she mumbled incoherently.

'You were wonderful together.'

Mimi's frazzled brain scrambled for something negative to say to put some doubt in Nina's mind about casting Rocco. Maybe she could voice some misgivings about his ability to adapt to the discipline of stage work, having been away from it for so long; or she could say she didn't feel they had the right dynamic together. But there was no denying their chemistry, and any doubts she might have cast on Rocco's professionalism or capabilities would have been a lie. She knew he was the best person for the role, the best thing for the play, and she couldn't bring herself to suggest otherwise. Damned integrity!

Besides, they couldn't afford to turn down the opportunity to have Rocco playing at Halfpenny Lane. Apart from the prestige it would bestow on their little theatre, it would be a huge money-spinner. They'd managed to avoid having to sell up last year thanks to their fundraising campaign, but now they had to make it pay. They were receiving funding from the Arts Council, but they still needed to be commercially successful and turn Halfpenny Lane into a viable, profitable business. None of them wanted to get the begging bowl out again.

'Fancy a drink and a debrief?' Nina asked as she gathered up her things, jolting Mimi out of her trance.

'Oh, thanks, but I have a … thing with my sisters.' She glanced at her watch. 'Gosh, is that the time?' She leapt up from the sofa, cringing at the unoriginality of the line. 'Sorry, but I have to dash. We'll talk tomorrow, yeah?'

'Sure. See you then.'

Mimi raced from the room, breezing past Sam, who was about to launch into a chat, with a quick 'Sorry, can't stop' and didn't look right or left as she made her way out of the theatre.

What kind of cruel joke was this, she fumed as she stomped through the streets, fuelled by fury, hugging her cardigan to herself against the cool evening air. Of all the actors in all the theatres in all the world, Rocco had to come clomping into hers in his size twelves. It wasn't fair! Tears smarted her eyes as she came to a halt at the tram stop and swiped her travel card, all her pent-up emotion overwhelming her and finally spilling out.

Why could nothing go right for her? She'd been so excited this morning; everything had seemed to be going her way. She couldn't get her head around how suddenly it had all turned sour. She was like some cursed child in a fairy-tale, doomed to have bad luck her whole life.

Obviously Nina would want Rocco. She'd been delighted with his audition. So unless Mimi wanted to spend the next three months working alongside the man who'd abandoned her and broken her heart, she'd have to step down. She couldn't bear the thought of giving up the part she'd dreamed of playing, but she couldn't see any other way out. Damn Rocco to hell!

It was chilly now that the sun had gone in, and her rage was the only thing keeping her warm as she hopped from foot to foot, wondering if the tram was ever going to come. With her luck, probably not.

2
___

Mimi slammed the door behind her and raced down the hall as if she were being pursued by a bear.

'Oh my god, oh my god, oh my god,' she chanted under her breath as she burst into the kitchen.

Aoife and Sive were standing by the hob, presiding over bubbling pots and pans, and looked up, startled.

'What?'

'What's happened?'

Her sisters dropped their wooden spoons and turned to her simultaneously, their eyes wide with alarm.

Mimi flung herself into a chair at the table and put her head in her hands, trying to steady her breathing. She was aware of them crossing the kitchen to join her and lifted her head with a groan. 'My life is over! Not wanting to be dramatic about it, but——'

'That ship has sailed,' Aoife said with a wry smile. 'But go on.'

'You won't think I'm over-reacting when you hear what happened.'

'Was it the auditions?' Sive asked as they pulled out chairs and sat on either side of her.

'Did they not go well?' Aoife asked.

Mimi gave a harsh shout of laughter. 'That's an understatement. It was a nightmare. You will not *believe* who turned up to audition for Elyot.'

'Who?' Sive asked, agog with curiosity.

'Only the worst possible person in the entire world.'

'The worst person in the world … and he's an actor,' Sive said thoughtfully, a little frown of concentration between her brows, as if she were trying to solve a crossword clue. 'Oh! I know! Mel Gibson!'

'No! Of course it's not Mel bloody Gibson,' Mimi said scathingly.

'Oh, yeah. He'd be too old for Elyot.'

'And too famous for Halfpenny Lane,' Aoife said.

'Well … you'd think that, but—'

'So it's someone famous?' Sive gasped.

'Yes.'

'Do we know him?' Aoife asked.

Mimi nodded miserably. 'We do.'

Sive narrowed her eyes. 'Wait, is he just famous in Ireland or proper famous?'

'Proper famous. Like Hollywood famous.'

'Rafe Bradshaw!' Aoife guessed.

Mimi shook her head. 'No.'

'Anyway, Rafe's lovely so it couldn't be him,' Sive said. 'Proper famous and we know him … but he's the worst person in the world,' she mused, tapping her fingers on her chin. 'Oh, I give up. The only other real star I can think of who we know is—' She broke off with a gasp. 'Oh my God, it's not—'

Mimi nodded, her lips pursed. 'Yes. *Him.*'

'Oh for goodness sake!' Aoife huffed. 'Who the hell are

you talking about? Stop playing this stupid guessing game and just tell us.'

Mimi turned to her. 'Rocco,' she said, her voice flat, as if she were delivering the punchline to some awful joke.

Aoife's jaw dropped. 'No! Rocco Agnew?'

Mimi was gratified that at least both her sisters grasped the full horror of the situation and were gaping at her in dismay. 'How many Roccos do we know?'

'And he's auditioning for *our* theatre?' Sive's eyes lit up with glee, all her concern seeming to vanish. Maybe she didn't get what a disaster this was after all.

'Yeah. He wants to play Elyot.'

'But … that's brilliant!'

'It's not brilliant,' Mimi snapped. 'It's a disaster!'

'Was he no good?' Sive asked, wrinkling her nose.

Mimi sighed defeatedly. 'He was perfect.'

'But … there was no spark between you?' Sive asked tentatively.

'What do *you* think? We were a bloody fire hazard.'

'Well then. That's … good, isn't it?' Sive looked to Aoife for back-up.

Aoife grimaced and threw a wary glance at Mimi. At least she knew better than to start throwing her hat in the air.

But Sive was right. It *should* be a good thing. It would be beyond their wildest dreams to have a star with Rocco's pulling power playing at Halfpenny Lane, and if he were anyone else in the world, she'd be breaking open the champagne right now and wondering how they'd got so lucky.

Aoife put an arm around her, and Mimi leaned into it gratefully. She normally detested people feeling sorry for her, but it was comforting that Aoife understood how she felt.

'I know it'd be difficult for you to work with him,' Sive said, 'but—'

'I can't!' Mimi wailed, sitting up straight. 'There's no way I can work with him. So that's it, isn't it? I'll have to bow out.'

'No, you can't do that,' Aoife said.

'Well, I'm sure Nina will want Rocco. And I don't blame her. He was definitely the best person we've seen. He's perfect for the role.'

'But so are you.'

'I know.' Comedy was Mimi's forte and the part of the witty, waspish Amanda was exactly suited to her talents. 'It's not fair!' she fumed. 'This was supposed to be *my* play. Why did he have to come along and spoil it?'

'We could veto him,' Sive said. 'It's our theatre. And I'm sure Nina can find someone just as good who you'll have chemistry with.'

'And who you don't want to murder,' Aoife said.

'But she'll never find someone who can get that many bums on seats, will she?' Mimi said despairingly. 'Imagine what a coup it'd be for Halfpenny Lane to have Rocco playing there. Tickets for the show would sell out as soon as we put them on sale. There'd be queues down the street every night for returns. And think of the publicity!'

'It *would* be amazing,' Sive said.

'I can't believe he even *wants* to be in our show,' Aoife said. 'It's such small potatoes for him.'

'Me either.' Rocco was a Hollywood star now. He worked on big budget movies, not stage plays in tiny, obscure Dublin theatres. It didn't make any sense.

'How did it even happen?' Aoife asked. 'And why didn't we know about it before now? I didn't see his name on any of the audition schedules.'

'It wasn't. Nina wanted it to be a surprise.' Mimi

smiled wryly. 'It was that all right.' If only she'd had some warning. If she'd had time to compose herself, she could have played the part of a woman completely over her ex to perfection. She was an actress, after all. She'd have been cool and calm, totally unaffected by seeing Rocco for the first time in years – instead of the flustered, blindsided mess she'd been, stuttering and scrabbling for breath. 'I didn't know until about two seconds before he walked in the door.'

'Oh no! Poor you.' Aoife rubbed her shoulder consolingly. 'That must have been such a shock.'

'Nina was so pleased with herself, as if she'd just presented me with the most amazing gift. Which it should have been, in fairness. She wasn't to know.' Mimi huffed a laugh. 'It was like when Marlowe brings in a mouse and drops it at my feet, all proud, expecting me to be thrilled with him.'

'Still, she might have told us.'

'I think she was half afraid it wouldn't happen – that Rocco wouldn't turn up, or it'd be some other Rocco Agnew.'

'Because that name is so common,' Aoife said.

'Anyway, it's taken,' Sive said. 'Equity rules – there can't be another Rocco Agnew.'

No, Mimi thought, there could never be another Rocco Agnew. She took a deep breath. 'Anyway, it's an amazing opportunity for us and I know we can't afford to turn it down. Don't worry, I'm not stupid.'

'It *would* be a lifesaver,' Aoife mused. 'It'd really put Halfpenny Lane on the map. I'm sure Rocco's fans would come from all over the world to see him live on stage.'

Mimi nodded. 'So my life may not be over, but my part in this play is. I'll have to take one for the team – fall on my sword for the good of Halfpenny Lane. I'll tell

Nina I can't work with Rocco and she'll have to recast Amanda.'

'No!' Sive exclaimed. 'You can't do that. This is your moment in the spotlight. Don't let Rocco stand in your way.'

'That role is perfect for you,' Aoife said, 'and you've always wanted to play it. We really would nix Rocco if you say so, despite his star power.'

'I doubt the board would be unanimous on that,' Mimi said wryly.

'Leave the other board member to me,' Aoife said. 'I'm sure I can bring him around if he needs persuading.'

'Anyway, he'd be outvoted,' Sive said. 'If it's you or Rocco, we pick you. No contest.'

Her sisters watched her carefully, and she could practically feel the tension of their held breath. If she said yes, they'd do it. They'd ditch Rocco, just like that, and pass up this once-in-a-lifetime opportunity for their embattled little theatre. She blinked tears from her eyes, touched by their unflinching solidarity.

'I know you would, and I love you for it. But let's not be ridiculous. It'd be commercial suicide. This is our chance to strike box-office gold. It'd be madness not to take it. And speaking as a director of the theatre myself, I'm appalled you'd even suggest it.'

'But we'd hate to see you giving up this part,' Aoife said. 'You were so excited about it.'

'I was.' She heaved a sigh. 'But you must see how hard it would be for me working with Rocco, especially in this play. It's a tiny cast, and such an intimate piece. There's nowhere to hide.' There were only five characters in the play, and the size of the cast had been one of the deciding factors in choosing *Private Lives* over *Much Ado About Nothing* for their next production because it meant fewer actors to pay. Ironically, with Rocco on board, they could afford a cast of thousands – and she'd be happy to pay them if it meant she could get lost in the crowd.

'We totally understand it'd be tough,' Aoife said.

'But you're an actress.' Sive stroked her arm. 'You can rise above it.'

'I'll just have to if I want to do the play. But the show must go on, with or without me. If it comes down to me or Rocco, we have to choose him. If I can't handle it, I'll step down. There's no way we can say no to Rocco. We all know that.'

Sive and Aoife nodded, their expressions glum.

'Besides, we kind of owe him. He really helped with raising the funds for the theatre. We can't very well turn around now and put an embargo on him appearing there if he wants to.' It was largely thanks to Rocco that their crowdfunder to save Halfpenny Lane had been such a success. He'd put his weight behind it and rallied support for the campaign among his famous, influential friends and their collective fan bases.

'That's true,' Aoife said. 'If it hadn't been for Rocco, we probably wouldn't still *have* Halfpenny Lane.'

'Anyway, it's not the end of the world if I have to back out,' Mimi said briskly. 'It's just one play. There'll be other parts. But we're not likely to get another opportunity like this for Halfpenny Lane.'

'Well, don't make any rash decisions,' Aoife said. 'You're bound to be flummoxed, having it sprung on you like that. Why don't you sleep on it and see how you feel tomorrow? Maybe it won't seem so bad when you've had time to take it in properly.'

'Good idea,' Mimi said. It had been such a shock, suddenly being confronted with Rocco, she hadn't had a chance to consider it rationally. She'd been entirely focused on trying to behave normally and get through the audition with some degree of dignity.

'Besides, auditions aren't over yet, are they?' Sive said.

'No, we still have a couple of people to see tomorrow.'

'Maybe Nina will find someone she prefers.'

'Unlikely. But I suppose you never know.'

'Or maybe Rocco will get a better offer,' Sive said.

'Which would be pretty much any offer,' Aoife said wryly.

'Oh, that's true. Maybe the money will put him off,' Sive said. Mimi was touched by how hopeful she sounded.

'I'm sure he'll already be aware of the pay rates – which makes it even more baffling why he wants the part.' Still, maybe he'd think twice when he was faced with the reality of it. She was guiltily cheered by the idea. There was no way she could be responsible for turning him down, but it would be an enormous relief if he were to back out himself.

'We won't find anyone who's a bigger draw, anyway,' Aoife said, looking at Mimi carefully.

'No. It's a great thing for our little theatre,' Mimi said with a determined smile. 'Now, what's for dinner? I'm starving.'

'Pasta fagioli,' Sive said, larding on the Italian accent.

'Beans again?' They seemed to live on beans these days. They were more skint than ever since Aoife had quit her accounting job and enrolled in acting school. Not that they grudged it to her for a moment. It was what Mimi had wanted her to do for years, and it was lovely to see her so happy and excited. But it had been a hit for the finances of their little household. Now they were all getting by on what they could scrape together from part-time and freelance jobs between acting gigs that never paid enough even when you had one.

'Fancy beans, though,' Aoife said, as she and Sive stood and returned to the pots on the hob.

'It sounds better in Italian,' Sive said, stirring the sauce.

'Hey, I'm not complaining.' But her gut might. It could do with a break from beans. Which was yet one more reason they couldn't turn down Rocco. 'When Rocco comes and lays the golden egg, we can have something different.' She stood and joined her sisters at the stove.

'We shall live on lobster and caviar,' Sive said gaily.

'And in the meantime, this smells scrummy.'

Mimi was grateful that Rocco wasn't mentioned again throughout dinner, even if it was painfully obvious that they were all studiously avoiding the subject. He'd taken up his old position as the elephant in the room, a firmly established role since he'd moved to LA almost four years ago and left Mimi broken-hearted. Her sisters had become so accustomed to pretending he didn't exist, she supposed it was easy for them to slip back into their old routine – swerving away from any mention of his name, deftly steering the conversation in a different direction if it started to stray down that forbidden path. She almost forgot all about Rocco as they chatted and laughed over the pasta fagioli, which really was delicious.

But that night in bed, she gave in to fretting again, calculating exactly how many days, hours and weeks she'd have to spend with Rocco if she did the play. There'd be six weeks of rehearsals followed by tech week, and then a two-month run of the show to get through. Could she handle spending that much time working so closely with him – closeted together in rehearsals day after day, playing lovers on stage with him night after night, touching him, kissing him …

She couldn't sleep now for fretting about it, her mind whirring. Why on earth did Rocco choose their tiny little theatre anyway? If he wanted to test out his acting chops on stage, he could have his pick of roles on Broadway or in London's West End. Any theatre would be thrilled to have him – and they'd pay a lot better to boot. Even if it had been a different play, it wouldn't be so bad. But it was such a sexually charged piece, and it felt too close to the bone for her and Rocco to play Amanda and Elyot – a divorced couple who meet up again when they're both on honeymoon with new partners, only to discover they're still madly in love with each other.

And then there was Act Two, and all that kissing ... could she cope with that? She tried to ignore the little shiver of excitement she felt at the thought of kissing Rocco again, even if they were only stage kisses. It thrilled and scared her in equal measure.

Well, so much for sleeping on it. She sat up and turned on the light. Maybe if she read for a while, she could quiet her mind enough to drift off. As she picked up her book, Kit Marlowe, her cat, nudged his way through the door and padded across the room. He leapt onto the bed and kneaded the duvet beside her, purring loudly.

Dropping her book again, Mimi picked up the big ginger tabby. 'Oh Marlowe,' she said, burying her face in his fur, 'what am I going to do?'

3

MIMI AND ROCCO had met on the first day of acting school. It had been the happiest time of Mimi's young life, even before Rocco showed up. She'd been a difficult teen, going off the rails after the death of their parents when she was fifteen. She'd chased trouble with grim intent, piling a lot of stress and worry on Aoife who, as the eldest, had tried to step into the role of parent. Even though Mimi knew she should be pulling together with her sisters in their shared bereavement, she couldn't seem to help herself. The urge to rebel was too strong, though she couldn't have said what she was rebelling against – the unfairness of life, perhaps. She'd bunked off school, drank too much, used fake IDs to get into places she had no business being and made a beeline for boys who might as well have had 'trouble' tattooed across their foreheads.

There'd been little joy in it, nothing to ease her wild, insatiable grief – just too many hangovers, a lot of unsatisfactory sex and a constant background hum of fear and self-loathing. And she'd been vile to Aoife. She was deeply ashamed now of what she'd put her through, taking it out on her as if it was her fault when she'd been trying her best to hold everything together. She hated to think how hard and lonely it must have been for her, and she bitterly regretted not having been more supportive. She'd have given anything to be able to go back in time and do things differently.

Thankfully she'd sorted herself out in her last year of school and got through her final exams with respectable results. More importantly for her, she'd passed two rounds of auditions and been accepted into the Gaiety School of Acting, Ireland's leading drama school.

Acting school had been her salvation. The course was full-on and all-consuming – as well as early starts and long days, there was classwork to be continued at home, mandatory weekly theatre visits to fit in, and occasional rehearsals on evenings or weekends. It was demanding and exhausting, but it had been inspiring to work with such wonderful teachers and to be surrounded by people who were as devoted to the craft as she was. The discipline of it had been good for her, and she'd learned valuable lessons about collaboration and teamwork that she'd channelled into other areas of her life. Almost overnight, everything had changed. She focused all her energies on her studies, throwing herself into the course with a dedication and passion she'd never applied to anything else. It had given her somewhere to pour all her restless energy, a safe earthing for her unruly grief and anger.

Meeting Rocco had completed the transformation. They'd been thrown together in an improv class, and it was immediately apparent that there was something special between them. *This guy*, she'd thought, excited by how good they were together. She was already confident about her own ability, but with Rocco there was an ease and lightness to it that she hadn't felt before, something extra that was more than the sum of their parts. In a word, it was chemistry – and it was addicting.

Rocco evidently felt the same way and they sought each other out whenever they were allowed to choose partners for a scene or workshop. They were so in sync it was as if they were two halves of a whole, anticipating one another's moves with uncanny precision and delighting in spontaneously vibing off each other. Even unrehearsed, their choreography together was flawless.

Though Rocco was ridiculously good-looking and hugely popular, Mimi never had a moment's doubt that they would be together. They quickly became inseparable in class and out of it, and without any serious discussion or conscious decision on the part of either of them, it was understood that they were a couple.

Within a few weeks they'd moved in together, renting a top floor flat on Dame Street in the city centre. Even though she'd tingled every day with the heady excitement of being in love, Mimi had felt more grounded than ever before. Being with Rocco had steadied her, giving her a sense of calm and security she'd been missing since her parents died. She was no longer interested in partying and clubbing, even if there had been time for it in their hectic schedule. All she wanted to do was go to class and stay home with Rocco. When she wasn't studying acting she was kissing Rocco, talking to Rocco, or just sitting quietly beside him while they read or watched TV. Simply knowing he was there was enough, and she'd felt a sense of peace and contentment she'd never experienced before – like sliding into a warm bath. At some point in their first blissful weeks together she'd realised with a sort of delighted astonishment that she was happy – truly, bone-deep happy.

After graduating, they both worked part-time jobs

while attending auditions – Rocco in a spit-and-sawdust pub near their flat and Mimi in a club on Leeson Street. After long late shifts they'd crash into bed exhausted, but still somehow find the energy to make love. When they'd landed their first professional stage roles – Rocco as Corporal Stoddart in *The Plough and the Stars*, and Mimi as Ophelia in an inventive production of *Hamlet* – they celebrated each other's successes with cava and takeaway pizza.

They threw proper grown-up dinner parties, too many people crammed around their tiny rickety table, and spent long, lazy Saturdays in bed drinking coffee, reading the papers and having sex until hunger finally drove them to get up and go out for food.

On summer Sundays they lay in bed, the peal of bells from Christchurch and St Patrick's Cathedrals drifting through the open window, sporadically interspersed with snatches of commentary from passing tour buses – always the same line about City Hall floating up from the street. On St Patrick's Day they had a bird's eye view of the parade, and they threw parties for their friends with green food and cocktails – pasta alla genovese, grasshoppers and mojitos – taking turns to squeeze onto the tiny balcony two at a time to watch the parade.

They took long walks around the city, exploring the hidden lanes and back streets of the Liberties, sunbathing in St Patrick's Park in the summer or strolling through town to picnic in the Iveagh Gardens. They drank in the oldest pubs in Dublin and ate in the newest hipster cafes, talking endlessly about the future over bottomless cups of coffee – a future they'd both assumed they'd share.

They had been the happiest years of Mimi's life. Then Rocco had got an audition in LA for the lead in a new movie franchise. He didn't get it, but he'd come home full of Hollywood enthusiasm and ambition, and suggested they move there together. It was the first time they weren't perfectly in tune with one another, and it came as a shock to both of them.

'Don't you think we should stay here for a while?' Mimi said. 'Get some more experience under our belts first, build up our resumes?'

'It's where we're heading anyway, isn't it? Why wait?'

'Is it?' Mimi wasn't so sure. Even if Hollywood *was* their ultimate destination, she didn't think they were ready for it yet. They'd have a better chance of booking professional acting jobs in Ireland and working their way up to showier roles. Going to LA would feel like starting from scratch all over again.

'Don't you want to take Hollywood by storm?'

She gave a nervous laugh. 'I'd rather take Dublin by storm first. I quite fancy the idea of being a big fish in a small pond.'

'Really?' Rocco appeared baffled as the realisation that they weren't of one mind about this sank in. 'You haven't been thinking all along that this would be our next move?'

'No, I haven't.' But he had. She saw that the idea was fixed in his head and he'd assumed it was another unspoken decision they'd made together. It seemed when their synchronicity broke down, it did so spectacularly – devastatingly.

'What have we got to lose?' he said. 'We've both got a bit saved up and we can get jobs out there while we go to auditions. We could give it a year and really go for it – and if nothing happens, we can come home again with our tails between our legs.'

Mimi wasn't thrilled by the image of herself as the archetypal wannabe waiting tables in LA while hoping for some producer or casting director to pick her out from among the thousands of other hopefuls who congregated in that town. It wasn't what she'd spent two years training for. She was enjoying being able to put all she'd learned into practice and she had no desire to go back to square one.

'We could go to London?' she offered hopefully. She'd always dreamed of making a name for herself in the West End. The stage was where her heart truly lay, and it had always been the focus of her ambitions. She'd fantasised about winning Tonys rather than Oscars, and if she thought about making movies, it was something she saw happening later in her career, after she was firmly established as a stage actor.

'Hollywood's where it's at,' Rocco said, shaking his head. 'I met with an agent while I was over there and he's interested in representing me.'

'You've already spoken to someone?' She hated how hurt she sounded. But she felt so totally blindsided. How could he not have discussed this with her?

'He seems great. I'm sure he'd take you on too.'

'Really? As a sort of job lot? Sign up with me and I'll throw your girlfriend in for free?'

'No, of course not.' Rocco's eyes were flinty with annoyance. 'Look, I didn't want to say anything until it was a done deal because I didn't want to jinx it. But I thought you'd be excited.'

'This is coming totally out of the blue for me, Rocco. You've obviously thought about it a lot. It sounds like you've been planning it for quite a while. But this is the first I'm hearing of it and it's now how I expected the next couple of years to pan out. So forgive me if I'm not jumping up and down, waving my pom-poms. Give me a minute and I'm sure I'll be excited for you, but—'

'For *us*!' He raked a hand through his hair exasperatedly. 'I thought we'd do this together.'

'But you didn't think to tell me about this plan?'

'I just *did*!'

She gaped at him in horror. 'You mean just now? When you said, "let's move to LA" like you were saying "let's try the new Italian place for dinner"? What did you expect? That I'd just say "Yes, lets. Why not?" and that would be that? We'd pack up our stuff and off we'd go?'

'Honestly? Yeah, I did.' He sighed.

They gazed at each other in silence and a cold dread settled in Mimi's stomach as reality nudged its way into their idyll. She was aghast at the sinkhole that was suddenly opening up between them and helpless to do anything to stop it. Had they been fooling themselves all along, she wondered, leaving so much unspoken between them. Was it too late now to go back and thrash out their differences, state their terms, negotiate a compromise? She'd thought there was no need to discuss the big decisions because they wanted the same things. Clearly Rocco had thought the same. They'd both been wrong.

'And what about Kit Marlowe?' She waved at the ginger tabby happily stretched out in a patch of sun in the middle of the floor. 'Did you even think about what's to become of him if we go haring off to LA?'

'Your sisters would take him. You know they would.'

'But I can't just abandon him!'

'Come on, Mimi. It's not fair to use Marlowe as a pawn like that. You know he wouldn't care where he lives or who with as long as there's a steady supply of Dreamies.'

'That's not fair. Marlowe's a lot more sensitive than he lets on. He's got hidden depths.'

Rocco glanced sceptically at Marlowe who was now

contorted into a knot of limbs, giving his arse a thorough licking. 'I'll take your word for it.'

'Besides, Aoife would never let me run off to LA with you.'

'Aoife!' he fumed. 'Was Aoife okay with it when you were staying out all night? When you were drinking too much and getting wasted all the time? No, but you did it anyway. Stop blaming your sister for everything, Mimi. You do what you want – you always have. If you wanted to come with me, you'd come, and nothing would stop you.'

He was right, she realised, stunned into silence. She was a risk-taker, and she went after what she wanted, cut her own path. She'd go with him if it was what she really wanted. It was a truth she couldn't bear to face. Because if they broke up over this, she'd be miserable without him and she'd have no one to blame but herself.

'That may be true, but I'm trying to be less selfish these days,' she said stiffly. 'And I couldn't do that to Aoife – not after everything I've already put her through.' She was doing her best to make it up to her for how rotten she'd been. It wouldn't be fair to abandon their little family now, just when she was finally pulling her weight. 'I can't just ditch her and Sive.'

'They're grown women Mimi. I'm sure they'll cope.'

'Well, I'll think about it,' she said finally, because it was a rare day off together and she didn't want to ruin it.

But it was already ruined. They both tried to brush off the argument and enjoy the rest of the day, but they were both too shaken by their unaccustomed friction.

Over the following weeks, Rocco talked up LA, while Mimi tried to convince him of the benefits of staying in Dublin.

'I'm going to LA,' he told her finally over Sunday dinner in their favourite pub.

'Don't let me stop you.'

'But you won't come?'

'No,' she said quietly. 'I won't.'

He nodded, his jaw hard, and a coldness came over his face. 'So you're breaking up with me?'

'No, you're breaking up with *me*.'

'I'm asking you to come with me.'

'And I'm asking you to stay.'

They were both heartbroken, yet neither was willing to budge. And just like that, they were over – everything they'd shared come to nothing in the end. Mimi was dazed, reeling from the suddenness of it. She felt raw and disoriented as if her skin had been peeled off and she'd been dropped into a cold, alien world. It seemed impossible after what they'd had that their break-up could be so final, so bitter. But the intensity of their relationship had been matched by the brutality of its ending.

She'd expected Rocco to keep in touch, to update her about his adventures in LA and continue trying to persuade her to join him. But the calls never came, and the more time passed, the more impossible it seemed for her to contact him. He clearly wanted a clean break. They were done and he'd moved on. She had to accept that she was no longer a part of his life.

She'd felt as if she was going mad in those days. She was sure her sisters had feared for her sanity. She was restless, agitated, unable to settle to anything because what was the point? Nothing she could do would make any difference. She'd had the best thing life had to offer and she'd lost it.

Despite her sisters' best efforts, news started to filter back to her about Rocco's growing success, and she'd tried to be happy for him. But to her it just meant that he wasn't coming back and she was heartbroken. Every lead role, every accolade he got seemed to pull him further away from her and was another blow to her shattered heart. She could feel the lure of sliding back into her old ways – drinking too much, sleeping around, channelling her misery into every risky and destructive behaviour she could think of.

But instead she'd pulled herself together. She decided she wasn't going to let it break her and take anything more from her than it already had. She may have lost her trust, even her capacity for love, but she still had her health and her talent, and she wasn't going to languish on the sofa like some tragic Victorian heroine.

So she'd thrown herself into work, desperate to prove herself – not just for her own sake but to show Rocco that you didn't need to go to LA to be successful, that they could have made it in Ireland. She'd realised too late how rare what they'd had was, and she wanted him to see that he'd thrown it away for nothing. It was the waste of it that killed her more than anything, and she wanted him to feel it as keenly as she did. She wanted it to eviscerate him.

It hadn't quite worked out that way, of course. She'd done okay. She'd steadily built a career and earned a reputation as a reliable, talented actor, professional to the tips of her toes. She wasn't out of work often, and she'd won an Irish Times Theatre Award last year for her role as Polly in *The Threepenny Opera*. She was making a name for herself in Dublin theatre. But she wasn't exactly setting the world on fire, and compared to Rocco's success, her achievements seemed paltry. She doubted he was regretting his decision to leave her behind for the bright lights of Hollywood.

Still, the work was reward enough in itself – it made

her happy and fulfilled, and as the months passed and her grief and desire for revenge faded, she realised she was content with the life she had. Saving Halfpenny Lane last year had been the final stage in her recovery. She'd thrown herself into the campaign with every atom of energy she possessed, and was so absorbed by it that she'd find she'd gone whole days, weeks even, without thinking of Rocco at all. She'd been reinvigorated along with the ramshackle theatre. She'd even started dating again, trying to do that 'moving on' thing that people talked about.

It was ironic that it was Halfpenny Lane that had brought Rocco back into her life. If she was the fanciful sort, she might suspect Detta had had a hand in it. She'd always been rooting for them. But Detta would never play such a cruel trick on her … would she?

4

'I THINK you'll agree we've found our Elyot,' Nina said to Mimi the following day. They'd held the final auditions in the morning and had gone to a nearby cafe for lunch.

Mimi schooled her expression and nodded. 'Rocco?' There was no use pretending Nina might be talking about anyone else.

'There's no contest, is there?'

'No,' Mimi admitted. They both knew they were just going through the motions in this morning's auditions. Even taking his star power out of the equation, Rocco had nailed it. 'It's quite the coup for our little theatre. Clever old you! How did you pull it off anyway?'

Nina gave a self-deprecating shrug. 'I can't take the credit, I'm afraid. His agent put him up for it – said he was in town, and he wanted to come in and read. To be honest, I wasn't entirely sure it wouldn't turn out to be one of my mates pulling a prank.'

'Hence why you didn't say anything until he turned up.'

'Yes. I hope you didn't mind me springing it on you like that. I thought it'd be a nice surprise.'

Mimi was saved from having to respond by the timely arrival of the waitress with their food. She set down a bowl of Greek salad in front of Mimi and gave Nina a steaming dish of linguine.

'I didn't realise you two knew each other,' Nina said when the waitress had gone. She ground black pepper onto her pasta. 'I mean, it was very flattering what he said about admiring my work and everything, but I did wonder … It makes more sense him wanting the part if you're old friends. He hadn't told you he was coming in?'

Mimi concentrated on mixing dressing through her salad and tried to ignore the stab of pain in her gut. Rocco had been in Dublin seeing his family and presumably looking up old friends … and Mimi wouldn't have known anything about it if Nina hadn't brought him in for an audition. He'd have come and gone without her hearing so much as a whisper.

'No, I hadn't seen him.' She shrugged. 'I suppose he wanted to surprise me too.'

'I should have realised there was some connection. When I thought about it afterwards, I remembered he was involved in your crowdfunder for Halfpenny Lane, wasn't he?'

'Yes, he was a big help.' Mimi watched as Nina twirled linguine around her fork. 'When he asked to audition … did he know I was cast as Amanda?'

'Yes, he did. He was very complimentary about you, it seems. His agent said he's a big fan.'

'Oh?' Mimi brightened a little. 'That was nice of him.'

'So you're friends from acting school?'

Mimi swallowed and took a sip of sparkling water before answering. 'Not exactly. I mean yes, that's where we met. I hadn't seen Rocco in ages until he turned up at the audition. But we used to be … together.'

'Oh no!' Nina gasped, clapping a hand to her mouth. 'I feel like such an idiot. He's your ex?'

Mimi nodded stiffly.

'I'm so sorry. God, I really shouldn't have put you on the spot like that.'

'It's fine,' Mimi said, hastening to reassure Nina. 'It's ancient history.'

'Will it be a problem for you working with him, though? It's not too late to cast someone else. I haven't offered him the part yet. I wanted to run it by you first. Thank goodness I did.'

Mimi shook her head. 'I'm fine with it, honestly. Besides, who else would you cast?'

'Well, let's not forget Tim.'

'Oh, please lets!' Mimi laughed. 'Tempting as that is, I think we're going to have to go with Rocco. Apart from the fact that he's by far the best person for the part, it's the right decision from a commercial point of view.'

'You're sure you're okay with it?'

'Absolutely,' Mimi said with more conviction than she felt. 'It was ages ago. We were young.'

'Ah, first love!' Nina sighed wistfully. 'No wonder you had such great chemistry.'

Mimi was irrationally irritated by how quickly Nina had cheered up. She'd have liked her sympathy to last a *little* longer.

'Well, I'll give his agent a call this afternoon and offer him the part,' Nina said, forking an olive.

'Great!' All Mimi could do now was cross her fingers that Rocco would get a better offer in the meantime.

· · ·

Mimi arrived home later that afternoon to find Aoife and Sive in the kitchen, busy preparing for this evening's board meeting. Aoife was seated at the table doing theatre admin on her laptop, while Sive stood beside her making scones.

'Nina offered Rocco the part and he's accepted,' she told them, tossing her phone onto the table. Nina had called with the 'good news' while Mimi was on the tram.

Aoife shot her a sympathetic look, while Sive's floury fingers paused over the mixing bowl.

'It's okay, you can be happy about it,' Mimi told them grumpily.

'What are you going to do?' Aoife asked. 'Have you decided?'

Mimi gave a jerky nod of her head and lifted her chin defiantly. 'I'm not letting Rocco screw up my life again. I'm doing the play.'

'That's great,' Aoife said, finally allowing herself to smile.

'Yay! *Now* I'm happy about it.' Sive beamed.

'Are you sure you're going to be okay, though?' Aoife asked. 'Working with him?'

'It'll be fine.' She stiffened her jaw, trying to convince herself as much as anyone. 'Torture, of course,' she admitted. 'But fine.'

'You don't have to do it,' Sive said. 'If you need to back out, we'll understand. You have to take care of yourself.' She looked to Aoife, who nodded in agreement.

Mimi smiled. 'Thanks. But we're both professionals. It really will be fine, honestly.'

They were both still regarding her dubiously.

'Come on, cheer up! This is a great day for our theatre. And it's not just about Rocco being a cash cow. He'd be the right choice even if he wasn't such a big star.' Rocco hadn't coasted to the top on his good looks and charisma. He was a wonderful actor. 'We're very lucky to have him. We should be celebrating.'

'If you're sure,' Aoife said.

'I'm probably crazy. But, you know, the show must go on.'

'And the show must go gangbusters!' they all chorused.

Mimi flopped into a chair at the table as Sive resumed mixing her dough. 'I just wish you two were doing the play with me. Or at least one of you.'

'It would have been fun to play Sibyl,' Sive said. They'd originally thought she might have that part, but then she'd been offered a recurring role in a TV drama series that would begin shooting in the middle of the run. 'But that would only leave the part of the maid for Aoife.'

'I wouldn't mind playing the maid,' Aoife said. 'But it's better for us to earn some outside income when we can.' She was still doing some freelance accounting work from home in between taking as many acting classes and work-shops as she could afford in preparation for starting acting school in the autumn. 'Besides, we don't want the three of us in every production, do we? How narcissistic would that look?'

'And it's nice to be able to spread some work around,' Mimi said. It was one of her favourite things about owning the theatre, that they could give opportunities to other actors, as well as directors, designers and tech crew. It was in keeping with Detta's legacy, and she liked to think they were carrying on her tradition.

'We could have done an all-female production,' Sive said, her eyes lighting up at the idea. 'Then you could play Victor, Aoife – or Elyot.'

Mimi smiled. 'That would be interesting. But we can't afford to be experimental with our more commercial shows. This is supposed to be one of our crowd-pleasers.

Besides, I may not relish the idea of playing love scenes with Rocco, but I definitely don't want to play them with my sister. No offence, Aoife.'

'None taken. I feel exactly the same.'

After dinner they set up the table in the dining room for their board meeting, laying out four sets of notepads, pens and water glasses. They took the business of running the theatre seriously and had a formal meeting once a month to go over everything from finances to programming. The board consisted of the three of them plus Sam's brother Jonathan – Detta's godson, and now Aoife's boyfriend.

Detta had left Jonathan a share in the theatre along with the three sisters, and they'd had to buy him out to avoid selling. But to their surprise he'd still wanted to be involved, and when they'd invited him to join them on the board, he'd agreed readily. So now he was fully on board with Halfpenny Lane – literally. It was useful having someone more objective and business-minded involved in the management of the theatre, and he'd proved to be a valuable addition, especially when it came to financial and legal issues, and making hard-headed commercial decisions.

To her surprise, Mimi found she enjoyed the business side of running the theatre. She'd thought she'd resent letting commercial concerns influence their artistic direction, but instead she found it interesting, and the limitations it imposed challenging rather than restricting. It was gratifying to see programming decisions justified by receipts or a marketing campaign paying off in ticket sales.

Keeping the theatre afloat was a constant struggle, however. They'd filled the theatre every night for their inaugural run of *Three Sisters*. But that wasn't saying a lot when it seated less than a hundred and fifty people, and what they could make in box office returns and Arts Council grants would barely cover their running costs. They didn't care about making big profits, but they didn't want to end up so far in the red that they'd risk losing Halfpenny Lane. So it was essential to make it pay.

At seven, they seated themselves around the table with a pot of coffee and a plate of Sive's cranberry scones. They tried to run their monthly meetings in a business-like and professional manner, like the board of a proper company – albeit with more homemade cake and a chummier atmosphere.

When the doorbell rang, Aoife went to let Jonathan in. Sive and Mimi sat patiently waiting, listening to their muted voices in the hall punctuated by silences they knew were filled with kisses. So much for keeping it professional, Mimi thought wryly. She didn't suppose most board meetings began with two of the directors canoodling in the hall.

Aoife looked flushed and happy when she came back into the room, followed by Jonathan. Sive poured everyone coffee while Aoife handed around copies of the agenda she'd printed out, and after a little chit-chat, they got down to business.

They went through the accounts, the budget for the next few months, and the cost of the recent renovations. After a successful run of *Three Sisters*, they'd closed the theatre for a few months to get some more work done with what money was left from the crowdfunder. There were new seats and curtains, and the flies and lighting system had been upgraded.

'So, next up is *Private Lives*,' Jonathan said, moving on to the next item on the list. 'How's that going?'

Mimi felt her sisters casting wary glances her way.

'It's completely cast now,' Aoife said. 'Mitch will play Victor, and Andrea Long is playing Sibyl. You know the play, don't you?' she asked, looking at him adoringly.

Jonathan nodded. 'I've seen it, but it was a long time ago. What about the other part … who is it?' He frowned, trying to remember.

'The maid, Louise?' Aoife said. 'It's a young actress called Orla Balfe. It'll be her professional debut.'

'But I saw her graduation play and she was really good,' Sive said. 'Sam did pitch us for it, but—'

'No, I meant the leading man. I can't remember his name.'

'Elyot,' Sive said. 'That's the exciting news.'

'Oh?' Jonathan turned to her, eyebrows raised, inviting her to go on.

'Rocco,' Mimi told him, annoyed that her voice came out as a croak. She took a sip of coffee and cleared her throat. 'Rocco Agnew.'

Jonathan reared back in surprise, eyebrows raised. 'Rocco Agnew? Really?' A slow smile spread across his face.

His first reaction was pure excitement, but then he threw Mimi a cautious look, and she could tell that he was aware of her history with Rocco. No doubt Aoife would have told him.

'That's …'

'It's brilliant,' she said firmly. 'Obviously it's an amazing coup for Halfpenny Lane.'

'Yes, obviously. But, um … are you okay with it?'

'Of course I am. Why wouldn't I be?'

She saw Aoife frantically trying to send him warning signals with her eyes.

'Er … no reason, I suppose.'

'It'll be amazing for ticket sales. And the publicity will be off the charts.'

'Of course.' He nodded.

She was touched by his concern, but she didn't want anyone pitying her. She sighed. 'Look, obviously you're aware that Rocco and I used to be an item. But it's all water under the bridge. Working together won't be a problem.'

'You're sure?'

'Honestly, if people couldn't work with their exes, very few Hollywood films would ever get made.'

'Right. Well … excellent.' Jonathan tapped a pen on his notepad. 'What about understudies?'

'We've got two recent graduates – Caroline and Ben,' Aoife told him.

'But they won't end up playing the leads?'

'Not unless the whole cast is wiped out. If Rocco's off sick, Mitch will take over his role and the understudy will play Victor. Same with Mimi – Andrea would play Amanda and the understudy would play Sibyl.'

'Great. Well, we should get a casting announcement out as soon as possible.'

'I'll post it on our Facebook page tomorrow,' Aoife said. 'And I'll organise a press release.'

'And I'll do Twitter and Instagram,' Sive said. 'If only we had a bigger theatre … we could sell any number of tickets with Rocco on board.'

'Could we extend the run?' Jonathan asked.

'We could,' Mimi said, 'but I doubt Rocco would be available beyond what he's already committed to.'

'And there's not much point in extending it if we had to replace him,' Sive said.

'We can do matinees,' Aoife suggested. 'It's not much, but it'd give us a few extra shows.'

'Good idea,' Mimi said, making a note on her pad. 'Wednesdays and Saturdays? We'll have to square it with everyone, but I'm sure it'll be fine.'

'They'll be glad of the extra work,' Sive said. 'Oh! Why don't we do a live stream performance, like we did for *Three Sisters*?'

'Of course!' Jonathan said. 'That's a great idea.'

Mimi nodded. 'There'd be almost no limit on the number of virtual tickets we could sell – and Rocco's fans will want to see it, even if it's not their usual cup of tea. They'd pay to see him reading the IKEA catalogue.'

'I'll get quotes for filming it tomorrow,' Aoife said. 'And I'll coordinate with Cara about the logistics.'

'Well, it'll certainly be good for the coffers, and we could do with the boost,' Jonathan said. 'The renovations went over budget …'

To Mimi's relief, they moved on to more neutral topics as they discussed the finances of the theatre.

'How's Sam doing?' Jonathan asked when they'd concluded their business.

'Really well,' Sive said, with a little more enthusiasm than Mimi would have liked.

As if sensing Sive's bias, Jonathan looked to Mimi for confirmation.

'He is,' she said. 'Cara can't praise him enough, and Nina loves him.' A wannabe actor, they'd hired Sam as an usher on the understanding that on top of his official duties, he'd muck in and help out wherever he was needed. Mimi couldn't deny that he'd since proved himself an indispensable member of the Halfpenny Lane team, adopting the role of assistant stage manager to Cara, single-handedly running the front of house, and acting as PA to Nina, while educating himself in all aspects of theatre management and production along the way.

'He certainly loves it. I hardly see him these days. He practically lives in the place.'

'We really should be paying him more,' Aoife said. 'But I don't think we have the budget for it at the moment.'

'Don't worry about that,' Jonathan said with a wave of his hand. 'He's getting free training, and it keeps him off the streets. Besides, I think he'd be happy to do it even if you weren't paying him anything at all.'

'Don't give us ideas,' Mimi said wryly.

5

The following day, Mimi was booked to record a voiceover for a commercial.

'Sorry I can't help with the social media stuff,' she said to her sisters at breakfast. She drained the last of her coffee and stood up from the kitchen table.

'Don't worry about it,' Aoife said.

'Anyway, you're the star of the show,' Sive said, smiling at her. 'So you get a free pass. We may be bootstrapping it at Halfpenny Lane, but we don't expect the talent to get involved in the admin and marketing.'

'Thanks.' Mimi grinned as she gathered up her bag and jacket. She had to admit she was glad to have a break from thinking about *Private Lives*, and something to take her mind off the Rocco situation. She had the whole weekend to fret about that. 'This will probably only take a few hours anyway, so I can do my bit later on.'

'There's no need to rush home,' Aoife said. 'We've got it covered. Sive doesn't have anything on today and I've just got the dentist in the afternoon.'

'Problems?' Mimi asked.

41

Aoife shook her head. 'Just a check-up.'

'Go watch a movie or something if you're free for the afternoon,' Sive told her.

'I might just do that.' The idea was tempting – it would be another distraction. 'Well, have fun. And good luck at the dentist,' she said to Aoife on her way to the door.

Mimi took her sisters at their word and gave herself a day off. Her recording session was finished by midday, and afterwards she treated herself to lunch and a movie. She loved going to the cinema in the afternoon – it felt like such an indulgence – and it was good to switch off completely and focus on something other than Halfpenny Lane. The theatre took up so much of her time and energy, it was hard to remember sometimes that there was life beyond it.

The movie she chose was an entertaining romantic comedy, with comfortingly formulaic and predictable tropes, and she felt relaxed and refreshed as she made her way home.

She found Aoife and Sive still at the kitchen table, where she'd left them this morning, but now it was covered in papers and laptops. Their heads were bent together over a magazine, but as Mimi entered, Sive shut it quickly and shoved it under a pile of papers.

'There's no dinner,' she said to Mimi. 'We didn't have time. We thought we'd get a takeaway.'

'Suits me. How did you get on at the dentist?' Mimi asked Aoife.

'Fine. I didn't need anything done.'

She was aware of Aoife and Sive giving her an odd look as she took off her jacket and hung her bag on the back of a chair.

'What's this?' she asked, leaning across the table and reaching for the magazine they'd been reading. Sive snatched it away, but not before Mimi caught a glimpse of the *Wow!* magazine masthead.

'It's nothing … just something I picked up at the dentist,' Aoife mumbled.

'We weren't sure if we should show you.' Sive clutched the magazine to her chest.

'What? Mimi asked impatiently. 'Stop being so annoying and just let me see.'

Sive lowered the magazine slowly and slid it across the table to Mimi as if it were a loaded gun.

At first all she saw was the photo from the wedding of some minor royal that took up most of the cover and the sticker from the dentist's office saying that the magazine wasn't to be removed from the surgery. But then she saw the picture of Rocco in the bottom left corner, his arm around Willow Bell, the co-star of his latest movie *Waterfall*. 'Willow and Rocco: Hollywood's newest golden couple make it official' the headline read.

'Oh.' She swallowed hard, her stomach lurching. Rocco was *engaged*?

'You didn't know about this?' Aoife asked.

'No.' Her sisters had shielded her from any news about Rocco. A certain amount still filtered through about his career, but she knew nothing about his personal life, and she'd had no idea he was with Willow Bell. 'You?'

Sive and Aoife shook their heads.

'First we've heard of it.' Sive gave her a solicitous look.

'Sorry,' Aoife said. 'Drink?'

'Yes, please. Just a large one,' Mimi said absently as she thumbed through the index and turned to the feature about Rocco and Willow Bell. It was a double page spread, the gushing interview accompanied by photos of the happy couple posing in Willow's beautiful home, strolling along the streets of Los Feliz hand-in-hand, and posing together on the red carpet at the Golden Globes. Mimi really didn't want to look, but at the same time, she couldn't tear her eyes away, and she drank in every excruciating detail.

There was a brief history of their whirlwind romance. They'd met on the set of *Waterfall* and apparently 'romance had blossomed' over the course of filming. Mimi's stomach turned over as she read about how they'd clicked from the first day working together; the evenings they'd spent in each other's trailers eating pizza and talking long into the night; how they'd cemented their friendship over their shared passion for books. Here the interviewer noted that Willow – a beloved child star who'd won an Oscar at the age of eight – had taken time out from her film career to go back to college and earn her degree in English literature.

But as Mimi combed the article, she was relieved to find that there was no mention of an engagement. It tran-spired that 'making it official' simply referred to the couple confirming they were together after months of denials when they'd insisted they were just friends. The writer, clearly smug about having nailed this exclusive, commented that it was unlike Willow to talk so openly about her personal life. She was notoriously private and was known to veto questions in interviews about who she was dating. Asked why she and Rocco had decided to open up about their relationship now after keeping it secret for so long, Willow replied: 'Filming is such an intense experi-ence, and you often form very close friendships with the people you meet on set. But they can fizzle out just as quickly once the director calls it a wrap on the final shot. We needed some time to figure out what this was without the added complication of public scrutiny. It puts too much pressure on a relationship, especially when it's new. Now we're sure this is real, and we don't care who knows it.'

'Ugh, pass me a sick bag,' Mimi said.

'This'll have to do instead.' Sive handed her a gin and tonic.

'Thanks.' Mimi took it from her and took several long slugs, downing half the glass in one big gulp.

'He looks such a prat, doesn't he?' she said, jabbing a finger at a photo of Rocco standing with his arm around Willow in the garden of her 'stunning Spanish-style home'.

Sive leaned over to peer at the photo. 'Very puffy. He looks like he's not getting enough sleep.'

'Hmm. I don't imagine he is,' Mimi said sourly.

'Oh God,' Sive put a hand over her mouth. 'I didn't mean it like that.'

The truth was, Rocco was as beautiful as ever. Her gaze lingered over his thick black curls, that heart-stopping grin that transformed his whole face. Her heart twisted at the way he was looking at Willow; there was such tenderness in his soft brown eyes. He used to look at *her* like that.

'I suppose it's not really a huge surprise, is it?' she said, closing the magazine.

'It's not?' Aoife raised her eyebrows. 'I thought you hadn't heard anything about it?'

'Not about Willow Bell specifically. But it's only to be expected. I mean, it's been four years. I kind of figured he hadn't joined a monastery.'

Aoife laughed. 'True.' Mimi could tell she was relieved by how well she was taking this.

'What I'm really surprised about is this.' Mimi pointed to the label on the cover. You stole a magazine from the dentist's! I'm so proud of you, finally making up for your misspent youth. I mean, a lippy from Boots is more traditional, but given your lack of experience, I'll allow it.'

'I didn't steal it! I asked the receptionist if I could take it.'

'Aw.' Mimi smiled fondly. 'Of course you did. I should have known you'd ask permission before nicking something.'

Aoife gave her a playful shove. 'Shut up and let's order pizza. I'm starving.'

Aoife and Sive had spent the day getting the word out about Rocco and they filled Mimi in over pizza that they ate straight from the box. They'd made the casting announcement on social media, and the news had spread quickly.

'I've never seen so many comments on our Facebook page,' Aoife said. 'And we've got over a thousand new followers on Instagram.'

'And my tweet went viral,' Sive said excitedly. 'Half-penny Lane is trending in Ireland. So there's no backing out now. Rocco's fans would have our guts for garters.'

'Of course we're not backing out,' Mimi said, nettled. She'd thought she'd done such a good job of putting their minds at rest that she was fine about it. 'Why would we want to do that when we've hit the jackpot?'

'Well, because …' Sive trailed off.

Aoife was eyeing her with concern. Mimi knew it shouldn't get her back up, but she couldn't help it. She couldn't stand being pitied, and she didn't want anything to stop them enjoying the excitement of having Rocco in their show.

'If you're worried about me, don't be,' she said firmly. 'I'm a professional, not some hysterical teenager. I can work perfectly well with Rocco.'

'It's not that we doubt your professionalism,' Aoife said,

and Sive nodded vigorously in agreement. 'We just don't want you to put yourself in a situation that makes you miserable.'

'I won't be. Honestly.' She leaned across the table earnestly as she spoke, eyeballing them both. 'I've decided it's actually a good thing – not just for the theatre, but for me.'

She'd been fretting about it again last night, turning it over in her mind. But then she'd decided to look at it rationally. She and Rocco were simply two people who used to be an item and weren't any longer. It was so mundane, it was ridiculous to be melodramatic about it. They'd both moved on. She was dating, wasn't she? Okay so she wasn't making a great fist of it, but she was trying. And apparently Rocco was with Willow Bell now. They were both grown-ups, and they could be around each other without the world burning. Maybe they could even be friends.

'It's silly the way we've all been tiptoeing around the idea of Rocco. I know you were only thinking of me, but it's not helpful anymore. Making him a taboo subject has only built him up into this big scary behemoth. But it's just Rocco.' She smiled at her sisters. 'You know, Rocco who used to come to Sunday dinner with us at Detta's? Rocco who played charades with us and helped us run lines and came to your transition year play, Sive, and led the standing ovation?'

Aoife and Sive smiled fondly.

'He was your friend too,' Mimi said, and her sisters nodded. 'So we can all be friends again, can't we?'

'It *will* be nice to see him again,' Aoife said.

'It'll be lovely,' Sive said. 'Oh! We should invite him to Sunday dinner. It'll be like old times.'

'Yes, exactly,' Mimi said firmly. She could do this. She wasn't quite there yet, but she'd fake it till she made it.

6

For all her brave words, Mimi was sick with nerves on Monday morning, the day of the first table read. She hadn't seen Rocco since the audition, but the news of his casting had lit up every corner of the internet over the weekend, and the papers had taken up the story of the homecoming hero treading the boards in their humble little theatre.

'They really make it sound like he's slumming it,' she'd complained to Aoife yesterday, tossing a Sunday supplement away from her in disgust.

'I suppose when you think about what he's used to now, he kind of is …'

Now, as she got ready, she felt the kind of jitters she hadn't experienced since her first day of acting school, and she cursed herself for her bravado. What had she been thinking, imagining she could handle this? She ran through some lines from the play as she applied her make-up, and it only increased her panic. How could she possibly play that part night after night – hearing Rocco telling her he still loved her and wanted her back more than anything? Telling him that she felt the same? She should have backed out when she had the chance.

Pull yourself together, she told herself crossly as she leaned closer to the mirror and applied a final coat of mascara. You're an actress; you can totally do this. She frowned at her reflection, tossing the mascara wand onto the dressing table with a sigh. The trouble was, it would be all too easy to get into the character of Amanda – freaking out about being thrown together with her old flame, realising she was still in love with him. The part could have been written for her. She'd hardly have to act at all.

Could it be the same for him, she wondered, finally acknowledging the little voice in her head that secretly questioned Rocco's motives. After all, if he wanted to flex his acting muscles, why pick Halfpenny Lane? He was guaranteed box office, and any producer or casting director in the world would be falling over themselves to book him.

She tried to be sensible and tell herself it was just one of those quirky moves Hollywood actors liked to make from time to time. But there was no denying it was an odd choice when his career was at an all-time high. Late at night she couldn't quite silence the voice in her head that whispered he was doing it to get close to her again … that maybe he wanted her back. Her wayward heart skipped with hope as she brushed her eyebrows and checked herself one last time in the mirror.

'Wish me luck, Marlowe!' she called to the mound of ginger fur sleeping on the bed as she picked up her bag and made for the door.

. . .

Sive walked into town with Mimi, mumbling something about needing to collect costumes from the theatre. But Mimi suspected she really wanted to chat up Sam, who was helping set up for today's table read. The idea didn't please her. Sam was sweet and a diligent worker, but it was thanks to him they'd almost lost Halfpenny Lane. They'd had to raise the money to buy Jonathan out so that he could pay off his brother's debts. Sam had overcome his gambling addiction and seemed to be a reformed character, but Mimi still wouldn't trust him as far as she could throw him – which wasn't far, given his penchant for bench pressing. The sooner Sive's boyfriend Ben got back from his travels, the better.

Nevertheless, she was grateful to have Sive keeping up a steady stream of chatter as they made their way to Halfpenny Lane, distracting Mimi from the nerves fluttering in her stomach. If she'd been alone, she'd have been sorely tempted to turn and run.

'Good morning!' Sam greeted them with a cheery smile that widened into a grin when he saw Sive. 'They're all in there,' he said to Mimi, jerking his head to the door of the auditorium. They didn't have a separate rehearsal room at Halfpenny Lane, so they were doing the table read on the stage. All rehearsals would be held there too, to save on the cost of renting a space.

'Thanks.'

'I was just going to go to the Halfpenny Place to get pastries,' Sam said to Sive. 'Want to come with? You can help me choose.'

'Sure.' Sive beamed at him.

'Maybe one of you should stay here and man the fort, in case we need anything,' Mimi said.

'Everything's set up, and we won't be long,' Sam told her, already heading for the door.

Mimi didn't have the headspace to worry about that anymore as she watched them go. She took a deep breath and walked into the auditorium. A large round table had been placed in the centre of the stage and everyone was milling around drinking coffee and chatting as she walked down the aisle. She felt that magnetic pull immediately, her eyes automatically seeking out Rocco. Her heart skipped a beat as her gaze settled on him, and she was so over-whelmed by the emotions that surged up inside her, she felt she might cry.

A thousand memories flickered through her mind at the sight of him. The chill of his naked body against hers when he climbed into bed after a night shift. The tingle of his chilli-hot tongue in her mouth after an evening at the Mexican restaurant downstairs from their flat. The soft-ness of his hair against her fingers and the weight of his head in her lap when they lay on the couch together running lines. The glorious sound of his full-throated laughter. That devastating smile that could melt hearts and light up a room. The softness in his eyes that was just for her.

He glanced at her for a moment as she climbed the steps to the stage and gave her a quick nod and a smile, then turned back to Nina beside him. It was a perfectly friendly greeting, but still Mimi struggled not to flinch. She had to admit it hurt that he could be so casual and detached when she was reeling from the shock of seeing him again.

Rocco was already the centre of attention, of course – drawing everyone to him with his irresistible combination of magnetism and good looks. Orla, Andrea and the two understudies Caroline and Ben formed a little circle around him vying for his attention, their eyes glittering with excitement. Even no-nonsense Cara seemed a little starstruck. He charmed everyone with such ease, it was nauseating.

She left them to it, busying herself with getting coffee.

'I don't know how you did it, but props for pulling this off,' Mitch said, sidling up beside her and nodding to Rocco.

Mimi smiled, glad to see there was at least one person who wasn't worshipping at Rocco's feet. Mitch was a good friend. A wonderfully versatile actor, he'd been in their opening production of *Three Sisters*, and was committed to becoming a regular member of Halfpenny Lane's budding repertory company.

'I can't take the credit,' she said with a shrug. 'He put himself up for it.'

'Curioser and curioser.' Mitch took a gulp of coffee. 'Well, let's just hope he doesn't get sick during the run. Just imagine people's disappointment if they come expecting Rocco Agnew and get me.'

'They'd be lucky to have you. I just hope he doesn't prove too much of a distraction,' Mimi said, glancing over at the group around him. 'Have you worked with Andrea before?'

'No. But I'd watch your back if I were you. I'm getting strong *All About Eve* vibes from her.'

Mimi laughed. 'Thanks for the warning.'

'Well, not to be all fanboy about it, but I'd better go and say hi.'

As Mitch drifted off, the group around Rocco broke up and Mimi went to introduce herself to the understudies and Andrea.

'I'm so excited to be part of this!' Andrea said, shaking her hand. 'I'm such a fan.'

'Oh! Thank you, that's—'

'Oh gosh,' Andrea giggled, clapping a hand to her mouth. 'I meant of Rocco's.'

'Oh, of course. Silly me.'

'But I love your work too,' she said, giving Mimi a consoling pat on the shoulder. 'Big admirer here.' She pointed to her face.

'I couldn't be more thrilled to hear it.' *You'd better be a bloody good actor*, Mimi thought, fighting the urge to kick Andrea.

There was a distinct buzz in the air as they all settled around the table – an extra layer of excitement that Mimi knew was all about Rocco. Sam had done a good job setting up, and each place at the table was set with a printout of the script along with pens, a bottle of water and a glass. The seat to Rocco's right was left empty, obviously meant for her. As the two principals, they would naturally sit next to each other.

'Hi Mimi,' Rocco turned to her as she took the seat beside him. 'It's good to see you again.'

'Hi.' She gave him a stiff smile. 'It's great to have you here.'

'You look well.'

'Thanks. So do you.'

'Sorry we didn't get a chance to talk the other day,' he said ducking his head and lowering his voice. 'Nina just told me you didn't know I was auditioning. I didn't realise. I hope you didn't think I was trying to blindside you.'

Mimi glanced around the table. Everyone was chatting and getting settled, pouring water and flipping through the scripts. No one was paying attention to them. She lowered her voice just the same. 'It's fine. I can't say it wasn't a surprise. I mean, this isn't really your speed nowadays, is it?'

He shrugged. 'Like I said at the audition, I've been wanting to do some stage work for a while. It's good to mix things up every now and then.'

'Keep your adoring fans on their toes?'

'Bring my adoring fans to Halfpenny Lane.' He grinned, knocking her off balance. 'I think it's great what you've done with the place.'

'Thanks. It's largely down to you we were able to keep it. Your appeal was what made the crowdfunder such a success.'

'You know me – always happy to whore myself out in a good cause.'

'We're not a charity,' she said primly.

'I didn't mean it like that,' he said, his smile fading. 'I really like what you're doing here. I'm just excited to be part of it in some way.'

'Well, we're very happy to have you here,' she said, mollified. She was proud of that *we* – keeping it impersonal, speaking on behalf of Halfpenny Lane.

'I'm really looking forward to this,' he said, nodding at the script in front of him.

They were saved from further conversation by Nina calling everyone to attention. She made a brief introductory speech, thanking them all for being there, saying how excited she was to get started and outlining her vision and ideas for the show. She said the play was one of her favourites, and she thought they could do something special with the production. Mimi felt a little queasy when she talked about emphasising the powerful sexual attraction between the two main characters and going full throttle on the Act Two love scene.

'Let's not forget that when the play was first produced,

it was considered so risqué, it was almost censored,' she said. 'Obviously, we can't hope for that kind of reaction in this day and age, but we can certainly ramp up the sex and give the audience a real sense of the heat between this pair.'

When she was finished, everyone introduced themselves and their role, ending with the stage manager Cara, who was seated beside Nina. As well as reading the stage directions, she'd be timing the read-through to get a rough estimate of the running time of the show.

'Right, let's get to it,' Nina said, and everyone opened their scripts.

Act One began with a scene between Rocco and Andrea, and Mimi was glad it gave her a bit of time to relax and watch their performance before it was her turn. It didn't surprise her that Rocco was funny, already inhabiting the role of Elyot and making everyone laugh. But she was impressed with Andrea, who held her own with him and brought a lightness of touch to the insipid Sybil, squeezing her lines for every drop of humour she could wring from them. She may not have a talent for diplomacy, but she was going to be great in the play.

Some of Rocco's lines were so close to the bone, Mimi couldn't help feeling as if he were speaking directly to her, and it was almost unbearably poignant. She had to swallow a lump in her throat when Sibyl said Amanda had been a fool to lose him, and Rocco replied that they'd lost each other, his voice laden with regret.

But once she started to read and get into character, she almost managed to forget that it was Rocco beside her. The old chemistry with him kicked in, working its magic, and for a glorious couple of hours they were Amanda and Elyot, alternately bickering and sniping, and making love to each other. She began to enjoy herself, and she felt a rush of pleasure when she made the rest of the cast members laugh. It was a huge relief that any awkwardness she may feel around Rocco wasn't going to affect her performance.

Thankfully it was just a table read and they didn't have to actually kiss, Cara simply reading the stage directions briskly in a flat tone. They didn't even face each other some of the time, concentrating on reading from their scripts, but they did occasionally get into their characters with long, loving gazes into each other's eyes.

It was hard having Rocco looking at her in that intense way, as if he was completely captivated by her, while he said how much he loved and wanted her. It stirred up old feelings, a sense memory of when he used to look at her that way for real, and Mimi wasn't sure her poor heart could take it. How would she cope when they were doing it night after night, and kissing for real?

'Well done, everyone,' Nina said, clapping when they got to the end. 'That was great.'

Mimi was jolted by how quickly the light went from Rocco's eyes as soon as the read-through ended, and he reverted to being nothing more than a friendly colleague. It was a stark reminder to her not to get carried away by the fantasy that any passion between them was real.

After Nina had run through her notes, the meeting broke up. There was a general hubbub as everyone started gathering up their stuff and chatting to each other. Rocco turned to Andrea, who'd shot straight over to talk to him. She was giggling like a schoolgirl within seconds, twirling a strand of hair around her finger as she gazed into the depths of his warm, brown eyes.

Mimi was aware of Mitch standing on her other side. 'We're all going to the pub for a drink,' he said to her as she stuffed her things into her bag. 'You coming?'

She glanced at Rocco and Andrea. Was he flirting back? She wasn't sure. It occurred to her that he might be doing it on purpose, to punish her. He was behaving amicably towards her on the surface, but perhaps he was still harbouring some bitterness about their break-up. She had no idea how he felt about her now, but she knew he'd been angry with her when he left – and resentful enough not to contact her once in the last four years.

'I can't, sorry.' She couldn't bear to spend the evening sitting in a pub watching Rocco flirting with Andrea. It would be torment enough having to spend her days with him. She didn't need to have her nose rubbed in it in her free time too.

'Oh, pity. Next time?'

'Yeah.' She smiled at him vaguely. 'Hopefully. Although I'm kind of busy at the moment. Not much time for social-ising.' She thought it would be useful to establish an alibi upfront.

Mitch nodded, looking disappointed, and Mimi felt like a heel. But she was disappointed too.

She gathered up her bag and jacket and headed for the door. She was aware of Rocco and the others filing out behind her as she walked downstairs, but she didn't turn around. She pushed open the door and they all streamed out onto the street. 'See you tomorrow,' she said, turning in the opposite direction.

'You're not coming for a drink with us?' Rocco looked surprised.

'No. I can't.' Ha! There go your plans for performative flirting with Andrea to make me feel like crap, she thought. 'I'm … meeting someone.'

'Ah, pity. Well, have a good night.'

'Yeah, you too.'

It wasn't fair, she thought, as she walked away – even

Sam and the understudies were going to the pub, but not her. She hated missing out on a bonding session with the cast and crew. They'd already be a tight-knit unit by tomorrow and she'd be the odd one out. Worse than that, they'd all think she was a stand-offish cow if she kept refusing to socialise with them. Rocco was going to ruin this whole experience for her.

7

Mimi didn't want to go straight home and eat dinner with her sisters like it was any ordinary day of the week. It would be too much of an anti-climax after the high of the table read. On her way out of the theatre she decided to text her friend Catherine and ask if she was up for a drink. She could give truth to her lie about meeting someone, and she wouldn't mind so much missing out on all the bonding and camaraderie the rest of the cast were enjoying if she had someone to go out on the razz with her. Catherine was back in Dublin for a short break having recently finished filming a movie in Hollywood.

Almost as soon as she'd sent the text, her phone rang. She cheered up considerably when she heard her friend's voice.

'You must be psychic! I was just about to call you and suggest the same thing. Where are you?'

'I'm just leaving Halfpenny Lane.'

'I'm in town too. I've just been in with my agent. Where will we meet?'

'The Reading Room?'

'Sounds good. See you there in ten.'

She smiled to herself as she ended the call, her spirits lifting as she walked through Temple Bar, the narrow streets thronged with tourists and roving hen parties. Groups stood on the pavement outside pubs clutching pints, making the most of the early evening sunshine, while live music spilled out through the open doors, traditional folk ballads and amped-up renditions of recent pop hits mingling incongruously in the air.

Things were looking up. It was a glorious summer evening, and she was looking forward to spending it with her friend. Catherine was always up for a good time. They'd met at the Gaiety and quickly bonded over a mutual love of improv and taco fries. Mimi was instantly drawn to Catherine's forthright attitude and big, raucous laugh, and they shared the same snarky sense of humour.

As she made her way uptown, Mimi was focused on the night ahead, her angst about Rocco forgotten for the moment. She called Aoife to let her know she wouldn't be home for dinner.

'How did the table read go?' Aoife asked her.

'Great! I'll tell you all about it later.' That was another reason she didn't want to go straight home. Her sisters would naturally be curious, but she couldn't face them quizzing her about it just yet. It was different with Catherine. She wouldn't feel the need to pretend she was cooler than she was about the whole thing with her.

The Reading Room had been a favourite haunt of theirs since college. A hidden gem tucked away down a lane and up a narrow flight of stairs, it was beloved of locals for its squashy sofas, cosy fires, and almost complete lack of tourists. Its hushed atmosphere was in keeping with its name and had made it a favourite meeting place for book clubs and study groups.

When she made it up to the first floor bar, Catherine was already sitting at a large wooden table under the window. She waved as Mimi entered, and Mimi did a double take.

'I like the hair,' she said as Catherine stood to give her a hug.

'Do you?' Catherine gave an affected toss of her head as she sat down again. Her formerly mousy brown hair was now a glossy, razor-sharp brunette bob with golden high-lights framing her face. 'Rodeo Drive, darling!'

'Get you! It seems to be my fate to be surrounded by pretentious LA types these days.' She grinned as she took a seat opposite Catherine. 'Still, it's so good to see you, I'll forgive you for going all Hollywood on me.'

'I got us wine,' Catherine said, lifting the bottle of red on the table. 'That okay for you?'

'Perfect. You're definitely forgiven.'

'Cheers!' Catherine clinked glasses with Mimi and took a sip, making a show of savouring the taste. 'A plucky little Zinfandel with a cheery demeanour and ideas above its station,' she said. 'Very appropriate.'

Mimi laughed.

'So, tell me everything!' Catherine said, relaxing back against the sofa. 'I couldn't believe it when I heard the news about Rocco. How come you didn't tell me?'

'Because I didn't know myself until he showed up at the audition.'

'What!' Catherine gaped in shock.

'It was a surprise. Nina didn't tell me he was coming in.'

'Oh my god! That's—' Catherine seemed lost for words, which didn't happen often.

'I know.'

'You should have her struck off! Can you do that to directors?'

Mimi smiled, cheered by her friend's outrage. 'She's very nice actually. She thought I'd be thrilled – understandably.'

'Hmm,' Catherine said, lips thinned in disapproval. 'In fairness, I suppose it *is* a good thing for Halfpenny Lane.'

'Exactly. It's going to do wonders for our finances.'

'That's true enough. But what's it going to be like for you, working with him?'

'Judging by today, I'd say … agonising.' Mimi lifted her glass of wine and took a deep gulp. 'But bearable.'

'God, poor you!'

'Well, the only alternative is to bow out, which I'm not willing to do.'

'I should think not.'

'Apart from the kudos, we really need the money, especially since Aoife quit her job.'

'How is Aoife? And Sive?'

'They're great. Aoife aced her auditions for the Gaiety and she's starting there in October. And she's all loved up with Jonathan, of course, so we don't see as much of her these days.' She smiled fondly. It was great to see Aoife so happy, finally following her heart. She'd been so tightly wound for years, holding everything together, afraid to let go. Now it was as if she was uncoiling and spreading her wings for the first time.

'And Sive?'

'She's good … I think. You know Sive, she's always cheerful. Ben's coming back from his travels soon, so that's good. She's missed him a lot.'

'And you're going to be working with Rocco – in *Private Lives* of all things.' Catherine ran a finger around the rim of her glass and eyed Mimi thoughtfully. 'You're not over him, are you?'

It was barely a question. 'No, of course not.' It was freeing to be honest about it. 'But that's just between us. No one need ever know.'

'You don't think …' Catherine bit her lip, seeming reluctant to say whatever she was thinking.

'What?'

Catherine shrugged. 'Just … him coming to Halfpenny Lane to do this play. No offence, but it's kind of an odd move for him, isn't it?'

'I doubt his agent has the bunting out.'

'Exactly. With all due respect to Halfpenny Lane, it's not exactly a great career move for him.'

'So what's your point?'

'Don't you think … maybe it's all about you? That he's not over you either?'

Naturally it had occurred to Mimi – not that she'd admit it to anyone. She'd barely acknowledged the thought to herself. But it was gratifying to hear someone else say it out loud. It made her feel slightly less deranged for having entertained the idea, however fleetingly, and she couldn't deny the warm glow it gave her that Catherine saw it as a possibility. 'Do you think?'

'It seems like the most reasonable explanation, doesn't it?'

Even as she tried not to get her hopes up, she had to allow that it was possible. But then she remembered that magazine feature. 'What about Willow Bell, though? You know they're together?'

Catherine snorted. 'Willow Bell! Is she even a real person? If you ask me, she sounds like some woodland creature from a Disney cartoon.'

'Looks like one too,' Mimi said broodingly. 'A doe-eyed fawn lost in the forest.'

'Anyway, I'd heard something about them dating, but are you sure they're still together?'

Mimi shrugged. 'As far as I know.' The issue of *Wow!* magazine that Aoife had picked up at the dentist was six months old, so they might have split up since.

'Why don't you ask him?' Catherine said.

Mimi gave her friend a crooked smile. Of course, that was what Catherine would do. She sighed. Life would be so much simpler if everyone could be as straightforward and upfront as her. 'I can't just come out and ask him.'

'Why not?'

'Because … it'd look like I'm still hankering after him … hoping to get back with him.'

'You are, though, aren't you?'

'Maybe. But he doesn't have to know that.'

'So you're going to pretend you don't have feelings for him anymore?'

Mimi nodded. 'That's the plan.'

'Well, it's a shite plan, if you ask me.' Catherine leaned forward and topped up their glasses. 'Maybe coming to Halfpenny Lane was his grand gesture and he just needs some signal from you that you're open to it. I mean, you could be with someone else for all he knows.'

'That's true.' Maybe she should work it into the conversation that she was single the next time they spoke – give him an opening.

'Has he asked you if you're seeing anyone?'

Mimi grimaced sheepishly. 'I haven't really spoken to him much so far. We just had the table read today and I left immediately it was over.'

'And came to meet me?'

Mimi nodded. 'Everyone else was going out for drinks, but I couldn't face it.'

Catherine gave an exasperated sigh. 'Honestly! You should get in there, girl – get your man.'

'Rocco's not my man, though, is he? Not anymore.'

'That's defeatist talk if ever I heard it. Look, you know I don't believe all that fated lovers nonsense, but if ever there were two people who were meant to be together it's you and Rocco.'

Mimi smiled, pleased with the idea. If even her unsentimental friend saw them like that … Maybe Catherine was right, and they were both acting cool around each other when they felt anything but.

'But one of you will have to break cover and admit how you feel.'

'I'd rather it was him, though' Mimi said petulantly.

'Maybe he has the same fears as you about looking pathetic and getting rejected again.'

'What do you mean "again"? I didn't reject Rocco. *He* dumped *me*.'

'He didn't, though, did he? He asked you to go with him.'

'And I asked him to stay.'

'Right. So it was a mutual decision to split up. No one got dumped.'

Mimi pondered this. She'd never looked at it that way before. Had Rocco been as hurt by their break-up as she'd been? Had he felt as abandoned by her as she had by him? Maybe they'd lost each other, like Amanda and Elyot.

'You could end up circling around each other forever,' Catherine continued. 'And it could be he thinks he's already made the first move. He's come all the way here to work in Halfpenny Lane – with you. Maybe he just needs you to meet him halfway.'

Was that all it would take? Some signal from her? But what if Catherine was wrong and Rocco no longer had feelings for her. She'd make a complete fool of herself.

'He's not going to be here forever,' Catherine said. 'You've only got him at Halfpenny Lane for a few months. You have to grab the bull by the horns and go for it while you have the chance – if you want him back, that is.' She sighed. 'It's a pity I'm not in this play with you. I could knock your two heads together.'

'Oh, I wish you were! It would be such a laugh to do something together.' She couldn't imagine Catherine playing the coquettish, bubbly Sibyl, though. Tall and solidly built, she tended to get cast as stern nuns, hard-nosed detectives and thuggish matriarchs.

'Maybe next time,' Catherine said. 'So, how did the table read go?'

'It was great.' Mimi felt sad that she couldn't have enjoyed it more. Everyone had been so funny. They'd riffed off each other brilliantly and made each other howl with laughter. Today should have been a great day. She'd be on a total high about it if it weren't for Rocco.

'Anyway, enough about me and my woes. Tell me all about Hollywood. Have you met Meryl Streep yet?'

8

MIMI FELT MORE positive as she made her way to the theatre the next day for the first rehearsal. She was glad she hadn't had any more to drink after they left the bar last night. She didn't want to start today with a hangover. Seeing Catherine last night had been a tonic. After the bar, they'd gone for pizza – Catherine's treat – and laughed and gossiped the night away. It had been just what she'd needed, and she'd woken up this morning feeling optimistic, with a fresh perspective on her situation.

She had a lot to feel good about. It was a warm sunny day, and she was going to spend it doing what she loved. She had her dream part in one of her favourite plays; she was working with talented, creative people; and there was just a glimmer of hope that Rocco wanted her back.

She tried not to set too much store by what Catherine had said last night, but she couldn't help the rush of pleasure it gave her to think that Rocco might have ulterior motives for doing the play. However, she wasn't going to let herself get caught up in fretting over it and allow it to sour this experience for her. She'd focus on the show, and if something should happen between them, well … that would be a bonus. She didn't need Rocco – or any man – to make her happy. The work was enough, and she was determined to enjoy every precious moment.

She threw herself into the rehearsal with a new energy and enthusiasm, and the hours flew by. Nina was a dream to work with, truly collaborative and open to suggestions and insights from every member of the cast. Mimi loved these early rehearsals when they were still feeling their way into their characters and were free to explore the play without the need to lock in choices yet. They could play around with ideas, try different approaches, even go wildly off piste when there was nothing at stake. It was when the dynamics of the ensemble started to gel.

In the first break, Mimi saw Rocco glancing her way, and she was sure he was about to come over to talk to her. But then Andrea made a beeline for him and monopolised him for the rest of the break. Mimi was probably the only person in the room who could tell that he was itching to get away. He was being his usual charming, smiling self and seemed entirely focused on Andrea as she blabbered away. But Mimi saw the tell-tale tapping of his fingers on his folded arms and the way his smile didn't quite reach the corners of his eyes.

He was wearing a sky-blue T-shirt that set off his golden tanned skin, and she couldn't help noticing how it clung to the taut muscles of his stomach. He was leaner than he'd been when she'd lived with him, his jawline sharper; but every line of his body, every gesture and expression was still achingly familiar.

She was sitting on the floor at the side of the stage drinking green tea when he approached her in the next break.

'Mimi,' he greeted her, sliding onto the floor beside her, clutching a cardboard cup of coffee.

'Rocco.'

'So, we haven't had much chance to chat yet. How've you been?'

'Fine. Great.'

'Good night last night?'

'Yeah, it was fun.' Mimi smiled, glad she didn't have to lie. 'You?'

'Yeah. Pity you weren't able to join us.'

She wondered was he fishing, trying to find out if she'd been on a date. If he was, she could put him out of his misery. 'I was meeting Catherine.'

'Ah, Catherine!' His face creased in a smile. 'How's she doing?'

'Great! She's just finished filming a new movie.'

'Yeah, I heard about that. Good for her.'

'So you're not the only Hollywood star in town.'

Rocco laughed. 'You should have brought her along to the pub – we could have swapped notes.' He drained his coffee and put the empty cup on the floor. 'So what have you been up to for the past four years?'

'Oh, you know – this.' She waved to the auditorium.

'And I saw you won an Irish Times Award for *The Threepenny Opera*. Congratulations.'

'Thanks.' She felt a flush of pleasure that he'd been following her career.

'I'd love to have seen it. What else have you been doing?'

'Just the usual,' she said airily. 'Working, eating, sleeping.'

'With anyone in particular?'

'What?' she frowned, startled by the suddenness of the question. Okay, that was definitely fishing.

'Sorry,' he said, shaking his head before she could formulate an answer. 'None of my business.'

'It's fair enough, I suppose. I mean, I don't have to ask who you're seeing,' she said, neatly deflecting his question and doing a little fishing of her own.

'Been googling me, have you?' He grinned, seeming amused by the idea of her stalking him online, still obsessing over him.

'Don't flatter yourself. It's hard to avoid. I'll be trying to watch a YouTube tutorial about cleaning out the washing-machine filter or looking through a photo gallery of former hotties who've gone to the dogs, when up pops a story about you and your latest squeeze.'

'Well, as long as I'm not in the photo gallery ...' He smirked. 'Anyway, haven't you heard we're living in a post-truth world? You shouldn't believe everything you see on the internet.'

'So you're *not* stepping out with America's sweetheart?' She knew she should play it cool, feign disinterest, but her curiosity was piqued, and the question was out of her mouth before she could stop herself.

He frowned. 'You mean Willow?'

'Yes, your deep, dark secret that you're with Willow Bell. Why all the cloak and dagger about it? You've nothing to be embarrassed about. I mean she's not exactly Quasimodo.'

'She just doesn't want people prying into her relationships. She's a very private person.'

She noticed he didn't say 'our' relationship, but she tried not to read too much into that.

'You can tell me. I won't run off to the papers with the story. Anyway, it's old news. I saw your interview in *Wow!* the last time I was at the dentist. So the genie's out of the bottle.'

His eyes took on a cornered look and she got the sense he was uncomfortable with the topic.

'Unless you've split up since then …'

He shook his head. 'No, we're still together.'

Huh! That was the trouble with fishing. You might not catch what you were hoping for. So much for Catherine's theory about him coming here to win her back. Despite her best efforts, it had worked its way into her head and taken root there. At least she hadn't shown her hand and declared her feelings.

'That's good,' she said. 'I mean she seems lovely.'

'Yeah, she is.' Rocco's smile warmed every inch of his face, his eyes crinkling deeply at the corners. Mimi felt a pang of loss – which was ridiculous, she chided herself. She'd lost Rocco years ago. He wasn't hers to lose anymore – he hadn't been for a long time.

'Anyway, how are you finding this so far?' she asked, waving to encompass the stage. She was desperate to change the subject.

'It's great.' He grinned. He seemed pleased with the change of subject too, visibly relaxing. 'I've missed this so much. Making movies is cool, but there's nothing like the energy of live theatre,' he said, his eyes sparkling. 'I'd forgotten how much I love it. It's kind of scary, but exhilarating, you know?'

'Yeah, I know.' God, we're so well suited, Mimi thought longingly. 'Nina's great, isn't she?'

'She's amazing. And we're brilliant, of course.'

'Of course,' she said with a light laugh.

'I hadn't forgotten how good we are together.' His eyes met hers and suddenly all the humour was gone from his face. His eyes burned into hers with an intensity that took Mimi's breath away, and she knew he wasn't just talking about their performance.

'We did always have great chemistry,' she said, annoyed to find her voice shaky.

For a moment as they gazed at each other in silence, everything else seemed to melt away. Then Nina clapped her hands, calling everyone back to rehearsal, and the moment passed.

Once again Mimi turned down an invitation to go for post-rehearsal drinks. She needed headspace and time alone to decompress, and she tried to sort out her feelings as she walked home that evening. She still felt a warm tingle from Rocco's flirting. But she was confused, and cross with him too – because he shouldn't be flirting with her when he was in a relationship with Willow. He never used to do that when they were together. She'd seen him around other women all the time, but it had never given her a moment's concern. Could he want her back after all? Maybe he was planning to break up with Willow …

She shook her head impatiently, annoyed with herself. This was exactly what she'd resolved not to do. She wasn't going to waste any more time or energy obsessing over Rocco. He was a colleague now, nothing more. Starting tomorrow, she'd treat him as such and enjoy the opportunity to work with such a fantastic actor. Tonight she'd allow herself to feel deflated and lick her wounds, and then she'd put it behind her and move on.

9

Mimi went to the theatre early the following morning, almost a full hour before rehearsals were due to start. So she was surprised when she entered the green room to find Rocco already there.

'Hi, Mimi.' He was pouring himself a coffee.

'Morning.' She slung her bag onto a chair and joined him at the coffee machine. 'Good night last night?'

'Yeah, it was fun,' he said.

I bet it was, she thought sourly, wanting to howl at the unfairness of it. It should have been *her* out having fun with the others last night. They were *her* tribe, not his. He got to swan around in LA, going to swanky parties and hobnobbing with the rich and famous. Why did he have to have this too? He'd made his choice and he'd left all this behind – left *her* behind.

'Pity you couldn't make it,' he said. 'What were you doing? Hot date?'

Rocco knew it wasn't like her to miss a night out. 'I had … things to do.' It was as close as she'd come to telling him it was none of his business.

'Ah, things.' He nodded understandingly. 'You're getting a bit of a reputation for being up yourself – just so you know.'

'No, I'm not!' She frowned.

'You are, though – stand-offish, unfriendly. Ask anyone.'

'I'm not up myself,' she protested, not bothering to hide her upset.

'I know you're not,' he said, his tone gentle. 'But what are people supposed to think when you keep refusing to come out with us? I've heard murmurings that you think you're above everyone else.'

Mimi fumed silently. That was so unfair!

Rocco sighed, dropping his gaze to the floor. 'Look, I hope it wasn't anything to do with me, you not being available for drinks last night.'

'Everything isn't about you, you know – despite what they might tell you in Hollywood. It was nothing to do with you.'

'Anyway, I was hoping we'd get a chance to talk properly, just the two of us. Maybe we could get together another time soon?' He took a sip of coffee.

'What do you want to talk to me about?' she asked, narrowing her eyes at him.

He laughed softly. 'Don't look so suspicious. I just thought we could get together and discuss the play a bit, one on one.'

She searched his face but there was no hint of mischief, no indication that he was insinuating anything more than a meeting to discuss the work.

'Shouldn't we do that here, with Nina?' she said primly.

He sighed. 'I think we need to talk properly, without other people around – to clear the air.'

She bristled, her heart rate picking up at the thought of

having such a conversation with him. 'I don't think that's necessary, do you?'

'I didn't. But I get the feeling you're avoiding me. Look, we're going to be working closely together for a while. Can't we be civil to each other?'

'Have I been uncivil?' she said stiffly.

'Friendly, then.'

'You can't stand for everyone not to be your friend, can you?'

'I can't stand for *you* not to be my friend.'

Mimi was shocked by the sincerity in his tone. It put her on the defensive. 'And whose fault is it that we're stuck working together? What's the deal, Rocco? What are you even doing here?'

'Is it so strange? I'm an actor. This is what I do.'

'But why Halfpenny Lane?'

'Why not?' He huffed a laugh. 'Everything isn't about you, you know,' he said, throwing her own words back at her. 'You think I have some hidden agenda? And what would that be?'

She flushed, feeling foolish and exposed. 'I have no idea. It just seems odd, that's all.'

'Maybe I was nervous about getting back on the stage, and I wanted to do it somewhere small, so at least if I failed, it wouldn't be in front of an audience of thousands.'

'Come on. You must know that nothing you do will languish in obscurity.'

'Sure, I knew people would be watching and I might get panned by the critics. But I still didn't think that many people would actually see it. I didn't know you were going to do the live stream.'

'Oh! Do you not want to do it?'

'No, it's fine. Anyway, that's not the reason. Honestly, maybe it *is* about you.'

'Oh?' Her heart rate quickened.

'Watching your production of *Three Sisters* made me realise how much I missed the buzz of live theatre.'

'You saw it?'

'Of course.'

'Oh.' It was weird to think of Rocco sitting in his living room in LA, watching them all … watching her. Or maybe it was Willow's living room and they'd watched it together.

'Plus I really admire Nina and I was excited about the opportunity to work with her.'

She nodded, but she still wasn't quite satisfied by his answer. She sensed there was something he wasn't saying.

'And besides—' He broke off, hesitating.

'Yes?'

'Watching *Three Sisters* reminded me how much I loved working with *you*.' He shrugged. 'I missed it. We always were good together, Mimi.'

'Yeah,' she said shakily, his words hitting her like a punch. They'd been so good together – on stage and off. 'We had something.' Her voice sounded faint and far away to her ears.

'Still have. We haven't lost the old spark, have we?'

'No.' She shook herself out of her daze. Of course he was just talking about work. 'No, not at all. We're still pretty awesome.'

He glanced towards the door as it swung open, and Andrea walked in.

'Good morning!' she called cheerily. 'Look at you two huggermugging. You're in early.'

They both turned to her and smiled as she poured herself coffee.

'Don't mind me. I'm not here. Carry on plotting world domination or whatever it is you're doing.' She threw herself onto the sofa and pulled a magazine out of her bag.

'So, friends?' Rocco asked, lowering his voice. 'No more avoiding me like I'm dog poo?'

Mimi gave him a reluctant smile, masking her disappointment. 'Sure, friends.' It looked like that was the best she was going to get.

In the first break in rehearsals she sought out Mitch, still nettled by what Rocco had told her.

'We missed you last night,' he said as she joined him by the craft services table in the wings. He grabbed a Danish pastry and took a big bite.

'Do people think I'm up myself?' she asked him without preamble. 'Because I don't go out drinking with you all after rehearsal?'

Mitch chewed and swallowed before answering. 'No, of course not,' he said, but his face told a different story, his eyes sliding away evasively.

'You can tell me the truth. I can take it.'

He shifted his gaze to her. 'Obviously *I* don't think that. But I have heard a few whispers. Andrea was bitching you up last night,' he said, lowering his voice. 'She reckons that because you own the theatre, you think you're too important to mix with the likes of us mere players.'

Huh! She might have known it was Andrea. She was starting to take a strong dislike to that girl. It was bloody ungrateful too, biting the hand that was feeding her. There were hundreds of other actresses who'd have killed for her role and the opportunity to work at Halfpenny Lane.

Still, clearly she'd have to make more of an effort to be sociable if she didn't want people to think Andrea had a point. She also knew she couldn't avoid having a proper chat with Rocco, not when they were working so closely together. He was right – they needed to clear the air. If there was any tension or awkwardness between them it would detract from the show.

So when he asked her to go for a drink with him that evening after rehearsal – just the two of them – she said yes. For the sake of the play, she told herself.

10

THEY WENT to an old pub near Christchurch that they used to frequent when they lived on Dame Street. It was Rocco's choice. Mimi would have picked more neutral ground, but she was trying to be amenable. A wave of melancholy washed over her as they stepped out of the warm evening sunlight into the cool darkness of the pub. She hadn't been here in years, not since Rocco had left and she'd moved back to Ranelagh. A few heads turned as they entered, and she noticed the barman give Rocco a discreet nod, but this place didn't attract the sort of clientele that was impressed by celebrities.

They found an empty table in a little snug at the back, and Rocco went to order drinks at the bar, chatting to the barman while he waited for his pint of Guinness to settle. Mimi felt a pang of nostalgia as she watched them laughing and chatting casually. Rocco had always been so gregarious and easy with people – he could talk to anyone and leave them feeling like they were old friends after a few minutes' conversation. It was one of the things Mimi had always loved about him.

Rocco carried the drinks to the table and settled beside her on the worn leather banquette.

'Well, *sláinte*,' he said, lifting his pint.

'Cheers.' She picked up her gin and tonic and crashed her glass against his.

Rocco took a sip of his pint, leaving a Guinness foam on his lip that Mimi suddenly had images of licking off. 'God, that's good.' He sighed. 'I miss proper Dublin Guinness.'

'What else do you miss about Dublin?' she asked.

He leaned back against the seat, running his finger around the rim of his glass thoughtfully. 'Pubs like this,' he said, looking around. 'Tayto crisps.'

'Obviously.'

'A decent cup of tea. And just the craic, you know.'

'You don't have the craic in LA?'

'Nah. People are too busy for the craic.'

'So, how are you liking it so far, working in theatre again?'

'I'm loving it!' Rocco beamed. 'It's brilliant, isn't it? I have that edgy feeling back – you know? Kind of terrified, but excited at the same time?'

She nodded. She knew that feeling well. 'It's the best.'

'I'm just having so much *fun*. It hardly feels like work at all, does it?'

She loved his unabashed enthusiasm. 'No. Sometimes I can't believe I get to do it as my job.'

'So, tell me about you,' he said after a pause.

'There's not much to tell. Halfpenny Lane takes up most of my time lately. It turns out it's a full-time job running a theatre.'

'What about boyfriends? You never answered my question the other day.'

She reminded herself they were friends now and tried

not to take umbrage. It was a normal thing for a friend to ask. 'Nothing newsworthy,' she said evasively. 'Unlike you.'

Something flickered across his features at her oblique reference to his girlfriend.

'So, you're not with anyone at the moment?' He took a deep swig of his pint.

'What makes you think that?'

He frowned. 'You just said.'

'I said nothing newsworthy. There is someone, as it happens.' He didn't need to know that her love life was so barren it would give the Atacama Desert a run for its money.

'Oh. Right.' Was that disappointment in his face? 'What's his name?'

'It's early days, but—'

'He hasn't told you his name yet? Call me psychic, but I don't think that's a good sign, Mimi.'

She cast around for a name. 'Sam.' She blurted out the first one that came into her head. That'd show him. He wasn't the only one who could move on.

'Really?' Rocco's eyebrows shot up. He had the effrontery not to hide his astonishment.

'There's no need to look so surprised,' she snapped, annoyed with herself more than him. 'You're not the only man on the planet. Did you think you'd come back and find me still here crying into my beer because my man done left me?'

'No, of course not.' He played with his beer mat, turning it over and over in his hand. 'You don't even drink beer,' he murmured, and they both laughed. 'I just didn't realise ... I hadn't heard any mention of it before, that's all.'

'We haven't been dating long. Besides, you're not the only one who likes to keep your private life private.'

'Fair enough.' He nodded broodingly.

Mimi's eyes dropped to his hands, still toying with the coaster, remembering how they'd felt on her skin, how their lightest touch could set her on fire. They were sitting so close their legs were touching, and it would be the most natural thing in the world to take his hand, to lay her head on his shoulder, to nuzzle into the warmth of his neck and run her fingers through his wayward curls.

She dragged her eyes away, rousing herself from her reveries. 'What's Willow like, then?' she asked, forcing herself to sound casual. 'In real life?'

He smiled, a genuine warmth flooding his face that knocked her back and made her sorry she'd asked. 'She's great. Very—'

'Please don't say down to earth,' she scoffed.

Rocco laughed. 'She is, though. Not up herself at all.'

'Unlike me,' Mimi said tartly.

Rocco smiled. 'She's probably the kindest person I've ever met. She doesn't have a bitchy bone in her body. But I think you'd like her, all the same,' he said with a mischievous grin.

'So why all the secrecy about your relationship? It's nothing to be ashamed of, you know – going out with a hot movie star.'

'Tell *her* that – I mean, look at me!' He spread his arms. 'She should be taking out a full-page ad in the *Times*.'

Mimi laughed and gave him a playful dig with her elbow.

'I told you, she's a private person. So am I, as it turns out. We just didn't want to deal with all the media intrusion before we knew if it'd even last, you know?'

She nodded. 'Yeah, I get that. It must be hard having people poking their noses into your life all the time like that.'

'It's not my favourite.'

'Do you hate it? Being famous?'

He paused, considering. 'I like being famous for the work. The recognition is nice, and it's good to know that if I do something I'm proud of, it'll get a fair shake. And of course, I love the awards and the adulation.' He grinned.

'Obviously,' she said dryly. They were both the most appalling applause junkies.

'You never get enough of that. But all the crap that comes with it … yeah, I could do without that. I'd like if Rocco Agnew the actor could be famous, but not me personally.'

'But you can't have one without the other.'

'No. That's the pact you make with the devil.'

'Still, I suppose it's useful for getting into restaurants and stuff. And you can use your power for good – like you did with our crowdfunder.'

'True.' He took a long gulp of his pint. 'I was sorry to hear about Detta,' he said softly.

'Thanks. Your letter was lovely. We all appreciated it.'

When Detta had died, Rocco had sent a sympathy card and written a lovely letter that had made them all cry. He'd known Detta – it was one more thread tying him to Mimi. Detta had been such an important part of her and her sisters' lives, it seemed wrong that any future boyfriend she might have would never have met her.

'I can't believe she's gone,' he said, smiling fondly. 'She was the sort of person you thought would live forever.'

'She was.' Mimi smiled. 'She was very fond of you, you know.' Detta had been gutted when Mimi and Rocco had broken up. She'd couldn't resist a man with a mischievous smile and a twinkle in his eyes, and she'd always had a soft spot for Rocco.

'It was mutual.' He ran a finger along his glass,

collecting the condensation dripping down it. 'What about everyone else?' he asked, lifting the mood, which had become sombre. 'What have your sisters been up to?'

'They're great. We've all been busy with the theatre, of course. Aoife's starting at the Gaiety in October.'

'That's great. I'm glad she's finally doing it. She was terrific in *Three Sisters*.'

Rocco knew Aoife had given up her acting dreams to become the breadwinner of the family after their parents died.

'She's so talented. And Sive's … well, you know Sive – steady as they come.'

'Ah, little Sive.' He smiled fondly.

'She's the same as ever. Still working, still with Ben … you remember Ben?'

'Mountainy Ben? Silent-Bob Ben?'

She laughed. 'That's the one.' Sive's boyfriend was a man of few words.

'They're still together?'

Mimi nodded. 'Not that he's around at the moment. He's been travelling, but he'll be back soon.' She took a sip of her drink. 'She's got a part in a new TV series coming up. That's why she's not doing this play with us. She was originally going to play Sybil.'

'That would have been fun.'

'Yeah. Bit weird, though, maybe? Given our history.' Rocco may not have, but she'd have found it unsettling to have her sister playing his bride. It was probably just as well how things had turned out.

'She'd have been great, though.'

'She would. What do you think of Andrea?'

'She's very good, isn't she?'

'Yeah, she is.' Mimi nodded, quick to agree. If she'd been

hoping to lead him into bitching up Andrea, she was clearly going to be disappointed. In fairness, Andrea promised to be excellent in the show. Mimi couldn't fault her acting.

'Bit of a pain in the arse, though,' Rocco added.

'Yes!' Mimi pounced on this with a relieved hoot of laughter. 'Exactly. She's a giant pain in the arse. She treats poor Caroline like she's her personal slave. She seems to think she's just there to fetch and carry for her.' Being an understudy was a thankless enough task without being treated like a gofer.

'Yesterday I overheard her quizzing Cara about how things work with her girlfriend – who's the "man" in the relationship, how they decide who does what in bed …'

'Oh God, seriously?' Mimi giggled. 'Poor Cara.'

'And the other day I heard her giving Mitch tips on how to deliver some of his lines. She was talking to him like he was her straight man, and he was just there to make her look good.'

Suddenly they were laughing and bitching together like old times.

'Mitch thinks Andrea has her eye on my role and wants to scupper me.'

'Well, Orla might take her out first. She's ambitious and she strikes me as the proactive type.'

'You mean …'

'I'm just saying if Andrea should happen to, say, fall down the stairs and Orla had to go on, it wouldn't exactly be a three-pipe problem.'

'That would leave Caroline playing the maid. At least all her training as Andrea's lackey would be good for something.'

They finished their drinks and Rocco went up to the bar for another round.

'How's Marlowe?' he asked when he was sitting down again.

'He's great. Not pining for you either, in case that's what you're worried about.' Marlowe was originally Mimi's cat, but she'd adopted him while they were together, and he'd lived with them in their little eyrie on Dame Street. Rocco had adored him.

'I wouldn't have thought it for a minute.'

'He got over you remarkably quickly – insultingly so, if you're inclined to take offence.'

'I'm not. Marlowe and I have an understanding. I'd love to see him, though.'

'I'm sure he'd like that. You should come round.' Damn! What was she saying? Still, if they were friends, she'd ask him over.

'I'd love that.'

'Great!' She forced a smile. 'We'll arrange something.'

'It'd be great to see Aoife and Sive again too.'

'What about your family?' Mimi asked, glad they were moving on to less personal topics.

'They're all fine. Mum always asks after you, whenever I'm home. And Gabbi, of course – she's your biggest fan.'

Mimi smiled. It hurt to think how many times he must have been home in the last couple of years, visiting his family and friends, and never once contacted her. If it had been the other way around, she didn't think she could have stayed away.

'She goes to see you in everything you do, you know.'

'Really?' Mimi frowned.

He nodded. 'She was at the opening night of *Three Sisters* – so was Mum. They said you were marvellous.'

'Oh, I wish I'd known. They should have got in touch.' She shouldn't be so surprised really. He'd made a very public appeal on behalf of Halfpenny Lane's crowdfunder.

It made sense that his family would support a cause he was championing.

'I think they were afraid you'd find it weird.'

'I'd love to have seen them.' She'd adored Rocco's big boisterous family. But maybe it *would* have been weird.

'Francesca and Charlie had a baby,' Rocco told her, his face softening. 'So I'm an uncle.'

'Oh wow! Congratulations!'

'Thanks.' He grinned. 'Though I can't take much of the credit.'

'Boy or girl?'

'Boy – Marco. He's one.'

It was so strange to think there was another whole person in Rocco's family who she'd never met. She drained her drink with a rattle of ice cubes.

'Another?' Rocco nodded to her empty glass.

Mimi glanced at her watch. 'I'd better not. Rehearsals in the morning.' It was only nine, but she was worn out from the effort of acting cool around him, and she'd had enough for one evening.

'Just one more? I haven't told you my real reason for coming to Halfpenny Lane yet. I need a bit more Dutch courage to work up to it.'

'So there is something else?' Mimi's heart fluttered with a dizzying blend of hope and fear. Was he going to confess that it was all about her after all? That he still wasn't over her?

'All the stuff I said about missing the theatre and wanting to work with you again is true. But yeah, there's something else.'

'Okay, then,' she said. 'I'm intrigued. But I'll get this one.'

She was glad of the breathing space as she stood at the bar, trying to calm her racing heart as her head spun with ideas about what Rocco could want to say to her.

'Okay, spill,' she said, when she'd returned with the drinks and was sitting beside him again. 'I'm all ears.'

He took a sip of his pint and leaned back against the cushion of the banquette. 'So, the thing is, I'm thinking about moving back to Dublin.'

'Oh, really?' Whatever Mimi had been expecting – hoping for –it wasn't that.

'Yeah. I never meant for LA to be permanent.'

'Right.' She nodded stiffly. Had he known that at the time? Had he said it? Surely she wouldn't have thrown away everything they'd had for the sake of a few years. 'What about your film career?'

'They know where to find me. Now that I've established myself and I'm in demand, I can live where I like. Obviously, I'll still have to go away a lot for work, but I want my permanent home to be here in Dublin. I miss it. I hate not being near my family and ...' He broke off. 'Anyway, I wanted to get a feel for it – working here, living here. And what better place to start than Halfpenny Lane?'

He took a long swig of Guinness and brushed foam from his upper lip. 'And you were right that it was about you too.' He turned to face her fully, his expression serious. 'I wanted to see you again and make things right between us. I'm sorry for the way things ended.'

Oh god, they were going to have *this* talk? If she'd known, she'd have ordered something stronger – like a triple tequila. 'It wasn't your fault. We were both to blame.'

'I was a hot-headed idiot.'

'So was I.'

'But I shouldn't have expected you to up stakes and follow me to LA, just like that. You were grieving.'

She reared back, eyebrows arched in surprise. 'Hardly. My parents died when I was fifteen.'

'You were still grieving.' His tone was soft but firm.

She nodded, blinking away tears as she realised he was right. 'I suppose I was. I was getting over it, though – healing. You helped.'

'And then I ran out on you.'

'You asked me to go with you.'

'And leave your sisters and Detta.' He shook his head. 'I should never have asked that of you.'

'Well, what's done is done. And it turned out all right in the end, didn't it?'

He frowned questioningly.

'You don't regret it, do you – going to LA?'

He watched his thumb rubbing against the pint glass. 'I regretted losing you. Every second of every day. You?'

'Same. I was a mess.'

He dropped his gaze to the table, watching his finger trace patterns in the gnarled wood. 'Do you still regret it?'

She thought about it. She'd never considered it that way before. She always went back to how she'd felt then, wild with grief, that tearing wrench in her gut whenever she thought of him. But she realized now those feelings had calmed, abated. They hadn't been there in years.

Right here, right now, did she regret not going with him? She thought of everything that had happened in the intervening years, all she'd have missed if she'd been in LA. She wouldn't have been involved in Halfpenny Lane with Aoife and Sive. She'd have missed the last precious years of Detta's life. Then there were her sisters, how they'd supported each other and the fun they'd had. She'd loved the three of them living together. She wouldn't have done *The Threepenny Opera*, the role that won her an award. More importantly than the award, Detta had got to see her in it. Would she have given all that up for the sake of waiting tables and playing bit parts in Hollywood, even with Rocco?

'No,' she said with a conviction that surprised her. 'I don't regret it anymore.' When she thought about it now, it felt lonely. Yes, she'd have had Rocco – and the thought that she'd lost him was almost unbearable. But here she had her whole family, what was left of it, and she wouldn't have missed the time she'd spent with them for anything – not even him.

'Me either,' he said.

She couldn't help flinching.

'I wish it had been different, but career-wise, I'm where I want to be. I've done work I'm really proud of.'

'So have I.'

'It was the right thing for me at the time.'

'And staying here was the right thing for me. If we'd gone to LA together one of us would have been compromising. There'd have been resentment. It probably would have broken us up anyway.'

He gave a crooked smile. 'We weren't great at compromising, were we?'

'No.' She smiled sadly. Because they'd had no practice. The one time they'd needed to, it had turned out to be a deal-breaker. 'Anyway, it probably worked out for the best. Who knows where we'd be now if we'd stayed together? You mightn't be a Hollywood A-lister. I mightn't be running Halfpenny Lane with my sisters. You wouldn't have met Willow Bell.'

'It was Willow who persuaded me I should come here, actually – to make my peace with you.'

'You were talking about me to Willow?'

'Yeah.'

'Okay, here's a tip – don't talk about an ex to your current girlfriend. It's considered bad form.'

He shrugged, a fond smile creeping onto his face. 'It's fine. Willow's cool.'

Of course she was, Mimi thought sulkily – because no one was a threat to America's sweetheart.

'It really helped, talking to her. She's surprisingly insightful.'

'For one so young and beautiful?'

'It was her who made me see that you were still griev-ing,' Rocco continued, ignoring her snark, 'and how callous it was to expect you to uproot your whole life to go to LA with me.'

Mimi swallowed hard, touched despite herself.

'She saw I had ... unfinished business with you,' he said as if he was picking his words carefully, and Mimi felt there was something else behind them, something he wasn't saying. 'So that's the main reason I'm here – why Halfpenny Lane. I hate not having you in my life.' He looked across at her. 'So, what do you think? Can we start over – as friends? Clean slate?'

Mimi considered. It would be nice to have Rocco in her life again. And Willow was right – they had unfinished business. She'd never had closure because they'd ended so abruptly. They hadn't fallen out of love or slowly drifted apart; there'd been no months of bickering before finally calling it quits. They'd had one difference of opinion about what to do next and then suddenly he was gone and it was over. No wonder it had shaken her so badly.

If he was back in her life, maybe she could finally move on and learn to see their relationship as simply a wonderful phase of her life that was over now, and to make peace with that. Wasn't it true that it was better to have loved and lost than never to have loved at all? If she could go back in time now and change anything, she wouldn't have missed a single moment with Rocco, however excruciating the pain of losing him had been. Wouldn't it be better to have him in her life in any capacity than not at all? She realised she wanted that. Apart from anything else, she still liked him so much.

'Yes,' she said. 'I'd like that.'

He grinned and gave a sigh of relief. 'Here's to old friends,' he said, lifting his almost empty glass.

'Old friends.' Mimi raised her glass, then tossed back the rest of her drink. 'Well, old pal, I'd better be getting home.'

'Where are you headed?' Rocco asked as they both stood and started pulling on jackets.

'Ranelagh. We're still living in the old house.'

'We?' He frowned, something flicking across his features that Mimi couldn't quite make out.

'Me, Aoife and Sive.'

'Oh.' His face relaxed. 'I'm renting a place in Ranelagh too, so we can get the tram together.'

Mimi felt a little shaky, getting a strong sense of déjà vu as they left the pub and walked towards Stephen's Green. They'd walked this route together so often in the past.

'The old neighbourhood,' she said softly as they turned onto Dame Street. Her throat felt tight as memories came flooding back. It was where they'd lived when they'd moved in together in their first year of drama school. Rocco came to a halt outside their old building.

'Our little garret,' he said, gazing up at the top window where their flat used to be. There was a juice bar at street level now. It had been a Mexican cafe when they'd lived there.

'I wonder who lives there now,' Mimi said, looking up at the windows. And if they're as happy as we were, she thought. A wave of longing to be back in that flat, in that time, swept through her, so strong it could have knocked her off her feet. She had an overwhelming urge to push through the door, run up the stairs and walk back into their living room, with everything just the same as it had been then.

It had been such an exciting time in her life, she still felt a little breathless just thinking about it. It had been her first time living away from home – and living with a boyfriend. She'd been dizzily in love and she couldn't believe that she got to live with this beautiful man who felt exactly the same way about her as she did about him. She'd never had to wonder or worry about how Rocco felt. He was demonstrative, openly affectionate, and never reticent to talk about his feelings. He told her he loved her often, but she didn't even need the words – she could feel it; she could see it in his eyes every time he looked at her.

'I wonder if they ever fixed the damp on the ceiling,' Rocco murmured. It had been covered in black mould that they constantly complained about to the landlord, who'd promise to take care of it. Eventually they'd give in and clean it off themselves, leaving all the windows open and escaping downstairs to the Mexican to get away from the bleach flumes. It would creep back over the weeks when they'd begin the futile complaining/cleaning cycle all over again.

'I don't suppose the same couple still live next door.'

'Shaking the walls with their Sunday morning bonk.' Rocco laughed.

'I pity whoever lives there now. All they've got is a lousy juice bar. No excuse for Friday night tacos, when you're too tired to go further than downstairs.'

'We got a much better deal,' Rocco said. 'I miss that old place.'

They were standing side by side, still looking up. But Mimi felt Rocco's fingers brush against hers. She took his hand and he clasped it.

'Me too.' But it wasn't the grotty flat she missed. It was that time, that life; it was their love.

'This is what I miss the most about Dublin,' Rocco said softly.

Mimi turned to him. 'That old kip?'

He shook his head, his gaze shifting from the rooftops to her. 'You.'

Her breath caught at the intensity in his eyes.

'This.' He squeezed her hand. 'Being here with you.'

'Rocco, you can't say things like that to me.' She dropped his hand like it was on fire. 'What happened to friends?'

'Sorry.' He gave her a shaky smile. 'Just overcome by nostalgia for a minute there.'

'Come on.' She turned back to the street. 'Let's go home.'

11

MIMI WAS anxious going into rehearsals the next day. She and Rocco had travelled to Ranelagh on the Luas together last night mostly in silence. They'd parted ways at the station as they were both going in opposite directions. Rocco had given her a quick, chaste peck on the cheek before turning away. She hoped things weren't going to be awkward between them now.

She was relieved that he seemed to have shaken off the intense, broody mood of last night and was back to his friendly, affable self, chatting casually to her like any other member of the cast. Mimi loved working, and she was glad that having Rocco around didn't change that. In fact, it only made it more invigorating because they were so good together. She could feel her performance reach new heights when she was playing opposite him.

She was secretly a little hurt that Rocco only seemed to feel that chemistry between them when they were performing. Whatever he'd been feeling last night had been a fleeting mood brought on by a blend of Guinness and nostalgia. But it had clearly passed. Once they finished a

95

scene, it was as if he flicked a switch to turn off the electricity that fizzed between them.

'I'm having a bit of a party at my place on Saturday,' he told her during a break when she joined him at the water dispenser. 'Just a get-together for the company. Everyone's invited.'

'Even me?' she asked archly.

'Of course you.' He frowned. 'Will you come?'

'Sure. I'd love to.' Mimi couldn't think of anything she'd like less. But she had to get used to being around him as a friend. It would be good practice.

'My family will be there too. Bring Sive and Aoife, if they're free. It'd be great to see them.'

'Thanks. I'll ask them.'

'Sam's already said he'll come,' he said, his gaze flicking to the door as Sam came in to restock the tea and coffee supplies.

'Oh. Right. That's … nice.' Why did he think she was interested in whether Sam was going or not? Then it hit her, and she had to suppress a gasp. 'Oh, *Sam*! My boyfriend!' When she'd told him her fictitious boyfriend's name, he'd assumed she was talking about Sam Hunt. No wonder he'd been so surprised.

'Your boyfriend, Sam, yes,' Rocco said with a bemused smile. 'I asked him if he wanted to check with you, in case you had plans, but he said he could make a unilateral decision.' Rocco smirked. 'His exact words were "Mimi isn't the boss of me on Saturday night".'

'Right, but he's not—' She was about to explain that she hadn't been talking about Sam Hunt, when they were interrupted by Nina calling everyone to attention.

She'd just have to explain later. But damn it! Now she had to come up with another 'Sam' before Saturday. Or she could just make up some excuse. Maybe her Sam could have gone on a business trip ... or fallen down a well. She'd think of something. Then again ...

'Okay, if you have any plans for next Saturday night, cancel them,' Mimi told her sisters that night at dinner.

'What? Why?'

'We're going to a party at Rocco's.'

Aoife and Sive exchanged a look.

'Yeah, I don't like it any more than you do,' Mimi told them. 'But if I don't go, it'll look like I'm avoiding him because I'm not over him.'

'Well ... you're not, are you?' Aoife said cautiously, as if afraid she'd get her head bitten off. 'Over him?'

Mimi sighed and pushed her plate away. 'Maybe not, but I'm working on it. And in the meantime, he doesn't have to know about it. I don't want to look like I'm still pining after him like some poor loser puppy.' She made big sad puppy-dog eyes.

'Aw, that's adorable,' Sive said. 'And there's no such thing as a loser puppy.'

Mimi rolled her eyes. 'So you two have to come. I need all the buffers I can get. Please? You can bring Jonathan, Aoife.'

'I'd love to, but are you sure it's a good idea?'

'It's short notice,' Sive pointed out. 'It's perfectly believable that you'd have other plans.'

Mimi shook her head. 'No. I'm going. I've already told him I would. Anyway, we're going to be friends now, so I have to get used to seeing him flirting his arse off with other women and practise not caring. I'm going whether you come or not.'

'Of course we'll come,' Aoife said, turning to Sive, who nodded.

'I have a square dance class, but I don't mind cancelling. I still have the bruises from last week's swing-your-partners pile-up.'

'Good. And don't look so glum. It's a party. It'll be fun,' she said unconvincingly. 'Now, one more thing. Aoife, invite Jonathan round for dinner tomorrow. And get him to bring that delinquent brother of his. I've got a proposal for him.'

12

'YOU'RE PROBABLY WONDERING why we asked you here today, Sam,' Mimi said as she moved around the table pouring wine. It had been a gloriously sunny Sunday, so they'd decided to have dinner outside, and they were seated in the partial shade of the mature olive tree at the end of the garden. Golden rays of sunlight filtered through its branches, throwing shifting patterns across the slatted wooden table that Sive had upcycled and painted a soft, dusky blue. A large dish of lasagne sat in its centre, alongside a basket of garlic bread and a bowl of crisp dressed salad. The early evening sun was still hot, but there was a light breeze gently rustling the tree's silvery leaves.

'Er … no, I can't say I am, really.'

'No? Why do you think you're here, then?' She took a seat opposite him, flapped her napkin open and placed it in her lap.

'Well, you said dinner. So I assume eating, drinking, pleasure of my company … that sort of thing. It didn't strike me as mysterious.'

'That's a bit presumptuous. We've never invited you to dinner before, have we?'

'No. But if the scran's good, I won't hold it against you,' Sam said cheerfully. 'And it smells great.' He helped himself to a big wedge of vegetable lasagne, the delicious aromas of garlic, tomatoes and Italian herbs rising in the air. 'Anyway, I'm practically family now, thanks to these two.' He tilted his head to Jonathan and Aoife.

'There's a bit more to it than that,' Mimi said as she passed the basket of garlic bread to Jonathan. She waited until she'd loaded her plate before speaking again. 'So here's the thing.' She rested her chin in her hands, facing Sam squarely across the table. 'You know the way you want to be an actor?'

'Yeah?'

'Well, I've got a part for you.' Out of the corner of her eye she saw Aoife and Sive exchanging worried glances.

'Oh? Really?' Sam beamed eagerly.

Mimi took a sip of red wine, deliciously warmed by the sun. 'Yes.' She put down her glass and picked up her knife and fork. 'I want you to play my boyfriend.'

'I'm in. Sounds great. In what?'

'Sorry?'

'What would I be playing your boyfriend in?'

'In real life,' Mimi said as if it was obvious.

Sam frowned in confusion. 'Real Life? I haven't heard of it. Who's it by?'

'It's not *by* anyone. It's not a play. I want you to pretend to be my boyfriend in real life.' She gave an exasperated sigh. 'How hard is it to understand?'

'Oh! Right. Like …' Sam trailed off, seemingly lost for words, taking refuge in a big gulp of wine. 'Sorry, maybe I'm being a bit thick,' he said with a self-deprecating laugh. 'How would that work exactly?'

'We pretend we're dating and you convince everyone that we're madly in love and you're besotted with me.'

'I think you've already blown our cover,' he said with a laugh, looking to either side to indicate the others.

'Oh, these people don't matter,' Mimi said with a dismissive wave of her hand. 'It's all to the good that they're in on the act. They'll be our supporting players. So what do you say?' She forked up a piece of lasagne.

'I don't know …'

'You want to act, don't you? Come on, it's the role of a lifetime.'

'It is?'

'Consider it an ongoing audition. A chance to prove your acting chops. If you can do a convincing job of making everyone think you're mad about me …'

'Well, that sounds like an easy job. I mean, you're so pretty, and—'

'Relax,' Mimi said wearily, rolling her eyes. 'You're not on the clock yet.'

'But no one will know I'm acting, will they? So I don't see what good it'll do me career-wise. I could give the performance of my life and no one would know except you lot.'

'Well "us lot" do have some influence. Have you forgotten we own a theatre?' Mimi put down her cutlery and folded her arms on the table. 'Okay, how about this? If you agree to be my pretend boyfriend, you can have a part in *A Christmas Carol*.' They'd already decided the Dickens classic would be their show for the festive season.

'Really?' Sam's eyes widened and he leaned forward eagerly. 'What part?'

Aoife and Sive were shooting Mimi horrified looks, but she ignored them.

'Tiny Tim,' she said.

Jonathan spluttered on a mouthful of wine.

'But … isn't he, like … a little kid?'

Mimi nodded. 'You can do it on your knees,' she said briskly, picking up her fork again. 'It'll be fine.'

Sam shook his head. 'I want Bob Cratchit.'

Mimi narrowed her eyes at him. 'Do you know *A Christmas Carol?*'

'Yes, of course!'

'Apart from the Muppets version?'

Sam looked shamefaced. 'Well … no.'

'But the Muppets version was really good,' Sive murmured.

'Very faithful to the material,' Aoife agreed.

'A modern masterpiece,' Jonathan said.

'Well, then you know Tiny Tim has the most important line in the play.'

'God bless us, every one,' Sam said.

'See? You know the part already.'

'But we can't have a grown man playing Tiny Tim on his knees,' Aoife protested. 'We'll be laughed out of town.'

'And someone would have to carry him on at the end,' Sive said. 'It'd look ridiculous!'

'Not to mention giving some poor actor a hernia,' Aoife added.

'Okay then. What about Ferdy?' Mimi said to Sam.

'Ferdy?' Sam screwed up his face. 'I don't even remember him.'

'Or Fred?' Sive suggested, smiling at him kindly. 'That's a nice part. And it's much more in your age range.'

'Sive's right,' Mimi said. 'You're too young and … hearty for Bob Cratchit.'

'I've seen what you can do with make-up.'

'There are limits. Anyway, Mitch will be playing Bob

Cratchit. He's perfect for it. He has that gaunt, half-starved look about him already.'

Sam sighed. 'How about young Scrooge, then?'

Mimi glanced at her sisters. 'Okay, what about this? If you impress me in the role of boyfriend, you can *audition* for young Scrooge. But I can't promise anything. We'll put you forward for it, but the director has the final say on casting and I'm not going to interfere.' Aoife and Sive nodded their approval.

'You weren't going to make me audition for Tiny Tim.'

'Oh, that's such an unimportant role,' Mimi said airily. 'We'd just tell the director you were already attached to the project.'

'What if I don't get young Scrooge?'

'Then you can have Ferdy, okay? You'd have a speaking part, even if it is only one line.'

'Okay, deal.' Sam held out his hand to Mimi and they shook on it.

Mimi wondered what she was letting herself in for.

'What do you need a fake boyfriend for anyway?' Jonathan asked, a perplexed frown furrowing his brow.

'I told Rocco I was going out with someone, and he's invited us all to a party at his house next week – you too, Jonathan. So I need someone to back up the lie.'

'Ah!' Sam nodded. 'That explains why he asked me if I wanted to check with you first when he invited me.'

'But why lie in the first place?' Jonathan asked.

'Because …' Mimi flailed around for an answer. It had made sense at the time, but now she wasn't sure why herself. 'Because he has someone – he's going out with Willow Bell.'

'But just because he's going out with someone doesn't mean you have to. It's not a competition, is it?'

'Of course it's a competition! Everything's a competition.'

'I'm sure Rocco won't think less of you for going solo,' Sam said. 'He's a great bloke – really sound.'

'Yes, he's real salt of the earth.' Mimi stabbed her fork into a tomato with such force it burst open, spraying juice onto her top.

'Anyway, I'm sure there'll be lots of other people there without dates,' Sam said.

'Not ex-boyfriends who are currently dating Hollywood royalty.'

Sam's eyes widened. 'You and Rocco—'

'Yes, we were in a relationship.' She'd forgotten Sam wouldn't be aware of their history. 'Now he's moved on, so I want him to see that I have too. Hence the fake boyfriend.'

'Well, I'm flattered you picked me,' Sam said with a grin.

'Don't be. I panicked! I just said the first name that came into my head and it happened to be Sam. I wasn't even thinking of you.' If she'd had time to think about it, she'd never have chosen him as her fake boyfriend. He was handsome enough in a fresh-faced boyish sort of way and really quite sweet once you got to know him. But sweet and boyish was so not her type.

'Ah, that's why I love you, Mims.' He sighed, placing a hand on his heart. 'You always know just what to say to make me feel special.'

'Knock it off, this is not a joke,' she said crossly. 'And you *never* call me Mims.'

'Whatever you say, sweetheart. Light of my life.' Sam bent his head over his plate, hiding his chuckles, but she saw his shoulders shaking.

This was going to be torture.

13

Rocco's PRESENCE at Halfpenny Lane was causing quite a stir, and not just among the company – the whole of Dublin was abuzz with excitement that he was in town. There was always a crowd of fans now waiting outside the theatre to watch him coming and going from rehearsals, mobbing him for selfies and autographs when he finally appeared. Word spread quickly on social media if he was seen in one of the local cafes or pubs and his devotees would converge on the place in droves. The local businesses were delighted.

Online magazines and newspapers were awash with photos of him 'spotted out and about' doing perfectly normal things like a regular human being – shopping on Grafton Street, strolling through Temple Bar, or having coffee at The Halfpenny Place (a grainy shot through the glass of the front window) – and turning them into click-bait 'stories'. A photo of him going for a swim at the Forty Foot had gone viral and was shared countless times on Twitter and Instagram. Adoring fans pulled him into selfies and recounted their tales of bumping into him, gushing about how friendly and approachable he was – so 'down to earth'. Mimi tried not to resent it, but she couldn't help it – it was infuriating.

'Down to earth!' she ranted to her sisters. 'He's a person, for goodness sake, not a god or something. What do they expect?'

'I know he's just Rocco to us, but he is super famous now,' Sive said reasonably. 'You can't blame people for being a bit starstruck when they meet him.'

'And he *is* very friendly,' Aoife added. 'He's really nice to his fans.'

Mimi had to concede that point. Rocco didn't seem to mind how long he spent taking photos and signing autographs. His fans were always rewarded for their patience, and he'd wait until every one of them had got their picture or declared their undying love or whatever it was they wanted to say to him.

'But how is this a "news" story?' she raged, pointing at her phone. 'Man drinks cup of coffee?'

Aoife shrugged. 'The photo's what sells papers, or whatever the internet equivalent is. Page views? I suppose they have to put something with it to make it look like there's more, so people will click.'

Print media ran more in-depth features about him. Mimi affected disinterest, but when no one was looking, she devoured his interviews, mining them for clues, particularly when journalists asked him why he'd chosen a tiny Dublin theatre for his first foray onto the stage since leaving Ireland for the bright lights of Hollywood. But there was nothing in his bland answers to give her ridiculous heart hope – just a lot of guff about taking risks and keeping it interesting and blah, blah, blah …

Inevitably, of course, there was speculation about his love

life, every article working in some mention of Willow Bell. There were no direct questions about their relationship, however, and Mimi wondered if he'd vetoed them. Unfortunately, word had somehow got out that *she* was an ex-girlfriend, and now almost every piece written about Rocco included a mention of that fact while noting that they would be starring opposite each other in *Private Lives* – Nöel Coward's sexy play about a divorced couple reigniting their tempestuous relationship – with the oblique suggestion that perhaps it was art imitating life. It was terrific publicity for the show, of course – and for Halfpenny Lane in general – and Mimi had to admit she rather liked the image it painted of her as a cool, mature professional, still on friendly terms with her ex.

'Rocco Agnew was in yesterday,' Chloe, the owner of The Halfpenny Place told her when she went in to get a coffee and croissant on the way to rehearsals. 'He's lovely, isn't he?'

Mimi gritted her teeth and forced a tight smile. 'Yes, so friendly and down to earth.'

'That's what I said!' Chloe turned to her assistant, who nodded. 'It must be amazing to work with him.'

'Yes, brilliant,' Mimi said, as Chloe placed the paper bag containing her croissant on the counter alongside a cardboard cup of coffee. 'Lucky me!'

'That's on the house,' Chloe said as Mimi rummaged in her bag for her purse.

'Oh, that's really kind, but I couldn't—'

'It's nothing,' Chloe said, waving away Mimi's protests. 'Thanks to your theatre, business is booming. We've never been so busy.'

Rocco was doing wonders for the theatre too. *Private Lives* had sold out for its entire run within an hour of tickets going on sale, almost crashing their website, and they were having no trouble drumming up publicity for the show.

Mimi and her sisters were bootstrapping the theatre as much as they could, which included taking care of the marketing themselves, thus avoiding paying a dedicated marketing manager or hiring publicists ad hoc. That task had never been so easy, and Rocco and Mimi had a busy press tour booked for the next couple of weeks, with a full schedule of TV chat show appearances, radio interviews and newspaper features. Everyone wanted a piece of Rocco.

Halfpenny Lane was Mimi's happy place, and she went in well before rehearsals were due to start, so she could have the place to herself for a while. She enjoyed having some quiet time alone to enjoy her morning croissant and coffee, just absorbing the atmosphere before everyone else arrived. So she was surprised when she pushed open the door of the green room to find Andrea already there on the couch drinking coffee, a newspaper open on the low table in front of her.

'Morning!' Mimi swallowed her annoyance as she flopped onto the sofa beside her.

'Morning,' Andrea murmured without looking up.

Glancing across at what she was reading, Mimi saw that it was an article about Rocco. The girl was clearly besotted. When she wasn't fawning over him at rehearsals, she was fangirling over articles about him. Mimi took the lid off her coffee and took a sip.

'Is that from Halfpenny Place?' Andrea asked with a sidelong glance at Mimi as she took a bite of croissant, laying the brown paper bag in her lap to catch the crumbs.

'Mmm,' Mimi mumbled through a mouthful.

'Have you any idea how much butter they put in those things?' Andrea asked, her eyes still on the newspaper.

'It's delicious, so I'm guessing lots.'

'I don't think you'd be eating it if you saw how it was made.'

'It would still taste just as good,' Mimi said and took a defiant bite.

'Just saying,' Andrea murmured. 'I keep telling Chloe she'd do a lot better if she provided a few healthier options.'

'I think The Halfpenny Place does very well.' She wanted to add that Chloe didn't need an actress telling her how to run her bakery business, and how would Andrea like it if Chloe gave her advice on how to play her role – but she kept her mouth shut for the sake of diplomacy.

'Gosh, it says here you used to go out with Rocco,' Andrea said as Mimi licked buttery crumbs off her fingers and wiped her hands on a napkin.

'I suppose it must be true, then,' Mimi said archly.

'I didn't know you two were in a relationship.'

'It was years ago,' Mimi said, aiming for super casual.

'Well, I hope I haven't stepped on anyone's toes.' Andrea finally lifted her gaze from the paper and looked at Mimi. 'If I'd known, I wouldn't have—I mean, I'd have asked for your blessing at least. Sistas before mistas and all that, right?'

'What?' Mimi frowned irritably. What was the bloody girl going on about?

'Anyway, I hope you don't mind …'

'Mind? About what?'

'About, you know, me and Rocco.'

It still took Mimi a moment to realise what Andrea was trying to say, in the most oblique way possible. 'Oh! You mean, the two of you …'

'We're sort of an item, yes. I thought everyone knew?' She looked deflated, obviously disappointed that news of her triumph hadn't travelled far and wide and reached the ears of all Rocco's exes.

'No. At least, it's news to me.' She strongly suspected it would be news to Rocco too. How had Andrea got the idea in her head that they were going out? She knew Andrea never missed an opportunity to flirt with Rocco, but unless she'd missed something, Mimi wasn't aware of them spending any time together without the rest of the cast.

'So …' Andrea looked at her expectantly, eyebrows raised.

'Oh god, no! Of course I don't mind. Like I said, it's ancient history. It's nothing to do with me who he goes out with.' She laughed. 'God, if I had every little starlet in Hollywood calling to ask for my permission when they wanted to go on a date with him—' She broke off, aware that Andrea's face had frozen. Ugh, she was being mean. The fact was the thought of Rocco going out with someone else nettled her. It was different when he was thousands of miles away in LA, but it was another thing if he was doing it here in Dublin, right under her nose, when he might just as easily have gone out with her.

'Sorry. My point is – no, I don't mind.'

'Right. Thanks.' Was it Mimi's imagination or was Andrea blinking back tears?

'I mean, I know he's probably dated a lot, but I think what we have is really special, you know?'

'Do you?' Seriously? Had they even been on a date? And besides, what about Willow Bell? Didn't Andrea read any magazines? Look at celebrity gossip on Twitter? Maybe it'd be kinder to give the girl a hard dose of reality. 'Well, you have my blessing, for what it's worth.'

'Thanks.' Andrea smiled.

'But Willow Bell might have something to say about it. Perhaps she's the one you should be asking.'

'Oh, I don't believe all that about them being together, do you?'

'I've no reason not to. Have you?'

'I think it's all just a publicity stunt,' Andrea said confidingly. 'I watched a whole TikTok about it the other day – and there was a thread on Twitter too by a fan account, laying out all the evidence why it's not true.'

'Evidence? Good lord!'

Andrea nodded. 'It was very convincing.'

'I suppose people believe all sorts when they want to,' Mimi murmured, then felt mean. Maybe that was too harsh.

Andrea gave a nonchalant shrug. 'Anyway, even if their relationship is real, that doesn't mean it'll last. And when the cat's away …' she added with a smirk.

If the mouse is going to play with anyone, it should be me, Mimi thought.

'Wow!' Sam's eyes widened gratifyingly as Mimi opened the door to him and Jonathan on Saturday night. 'You look amazing!'

'Thanks.' Mimi smiled, fiddling with the tendrils of hair framing her face. 'But save it for when someone can hear you,' she added, ushering them inside. She'd pulled out all the stops, though not for the benefit of her fake boyfriend. She was on a mission to bring her 'A' game tonight and show Rocco what he was missing. It seemed to be having the desired effect on Sam at least. She'd done her hair in a messy upstyle and had gone full-on vamp with dramatic eye make-up and bright red lipstick. Her black dress was simple but low-cut, a silver pendant necklace drawing the eye to her cleavage.

'You look pretty spiffing yourself,' she said, giving Sam a once-over. He did look handsome, in a fitted pink shirt and cargo pants, his short, top-heavy hair perfectly styled. But there was something irredeemably boyish about his fresh-faced good looks that just wasn't her style. Still, he'd have to do.

Sive and Aoife came downstairs and joined them in the hall.

'You look nice,' Sive said to Sam. 'That's a lovely shirt.'

Sam's face lit up as he turned to Sive with a bashful smile. 'Thanks. So do you.'

He had to stop looking at her sister like that, Mimi thought, irritated. 'Eyes on me, buster,' she said, giving him a little nudge. 'You're my boyfriend now, remember?'

'Sorry! Of course. I think we all look great.'

They gathered up bags and jackets, and walked together to the house that Rocco was renting in Ranelagh. Aoife, Jonathan and Sive walked ahead, and Mimi linked Sam's arm and hung back a little so she could brief him more thoroughly on his role.

'We haven't been together long,' she told him. 'Just a month or so.'

'But it's serious?' Sam asked.

Mimi considered. When she'd invented her fake boyfriend, she'd thought she'd only need him for a couple of months until Rocco returned to LA. It was only afterwards that he'd told her he was thinking of moving back to Dublin. She was sorry she'd started it now, but she'd just have to work with it. 'It's not going to last, obviously. But for now, it's … intense. It flared up quickly and swept us both off our feet.'

'Is that how it usually is for you?' Sam asked.

Mimi frowned. Was it? She had very little experience of relationships when she came to think about it. 'That's how it was with Rocco. How about you?'

Sam shrugged. 'Can't say, really. I've only had one proper relationship – long-term, that is.'

'Ah yes, Sophie Barron.' Sam had been engaged to Sophie, but she'd promptly dumped him when she discovered he was broke.

'That was more of a slow burn, I suppose. We'd known each other since we were kids.'

Mimi felt an unexpected pang of pity for Sam. 'Would you like to get back with her? Maybe I could help you with that when all this is over. We could make her jealous. Quid pro quo.'

'God, no! Thanks for the offer but splitting up with her was the best thing that ever happened to me. It was a huge part of my … recovery, I suppose you could call it.'

'From your gambling addiction.'

'Yeah. I'm not blaming her or anything,' he said emphatically. 'Not for a second. But she was very … demanding. It wasn't easy to be around her when you were skint.'

'Never mind; you've got me now,' Mimi said, giving his arm a squeeze. 'I wouldn't know what to do with someone who had money.'

'Is that why we're doing this?' Sam asked after they'd walked in silence for a few minutes. 'To make Rocco jealous? Because you want to get back with him?'

'No! Well, maybe to make him jealous a little, yes. But not because I'm expecting to get back with him. He's with Willow Bell now anyway.'

'You could totally take her,' Sam said with a grin.

'Thanks. I'll take that as a compliment to my fighting spirit and not the fact that I'm twice her size.'

'Only because she's minuscule! Anyway, that's not what I meant at all.'

'What did you mean, then?'

'Just that if it's you versus Willow Bell, it's no contest. People do break up, you know – when someone better comes along.'

Mimi smiled. Sam really could be very charming when he tried. 'It's not that, though. I just want to show him that

I've moved on too and I'm not still pining for him. And if he's kicking himself that he ever let me go, I wouldn't mind.'

'We'll make him rue the day!' Sam said with a grin. 'How long were you guys together?'

'Four years.' It was almost the same length of time they'd been apart now, Mimi thought sadly.

'So, um … you never told me how long this little ruse is going to last. I presume we break up at some stage?'

Mimi frowned. 'I'd thought until the end of the run, when Rocco goes back to LA. But it turns out now that may not be happening. Still, I suppose it can fizzle out as quickly as it started. Can we play it by ear for a bit?'

'Sure. Just let me know whenever you're ready to fizzle,' he said as they neared Rocco's house.

'My favourite weird sisters!' Rocco beamed as he threw open the door. It was how Aoife, Mimi and Sive often jokingly referred to themselves, and it was the name of their WhatsApp group.

'It's so good to see you again,' he said as he embraced Aoife and Sive in turn. He'd always got on well with them – which was just as well because Mimi's sisters were a deal-breaker.

Aoife introduced him to Jonathan, and they shook hands, while Sam got a matey clap on the shoulder.

'Well, come in.'

Mimi took Sam's hand, entwining her fingers with his as Rocco led them into a large living room, already full of people standing around in groups, drinking and chatting. The house was a typical upmarket rental with tasteful but inoffensively bland décor – white walls, wooden flooring, beige furniture. Twin console tables on either side of a large marble fireplace were adorned with tall vases of flowers, and double doors leading to the garden were thrown open to a paved terrace strung with lanterns and fairy lights. It was a lovely evening, and the party was already extending outside.

Mimi was pleased she knew most of the people in the room – that was her favourite kind of party. It meant you could mingle all night and be sociable, without the annoyance of making small talk and the pointless effort of chatting up people you may never see again. Rocco's sister Gabbi waved to her from across the room, and she spotted his parents, Bea and Ollie on the terrace talking to Nina. Out of the corner of her eye, she saw several people noticing her and Sam's joined hands as they moved through the crowd. Most of them looked away again hastily, not wanting to be caught gawking, but Andrea did a full-on jaw drop, her eyes popping cartoonishly.

Rocco got them all drinks and handed them around.

'It's good to see you,' Aoife said to him. 'You look well.'

'Thanks. So do you. Mimi tells me you're starting in the Gaiety this year.'

'Yes. I can't wait!' Aoife's face lit up as it always did when she was talking about acting school.

'You're going to love it,' Rocco said. 'You were amazing in *Three Sisters*. You all were.'

'Oh, you saw it?' Sive asked.

'Of course. Willow and I watched the live stream together.'

Mimi struggled not to flinch at the mention of his girlfriend's name.

'So you're Sam's brother,' Rocco said to Jonathan.

'For my sins.'

'Are you an actor too?'

'No, just a boring solicitor, I'm afraid.'

'Though he did have a brief moment in the spotlight when he went on as Vershinin in dress rehearsal,' Sive said with a mischievous smile in Jonathan's direction.

'Least said about that the better,' Jonathan said gruffly.

'You didn't get the acting bug, then?' Rocco asked.

'Definitely not. I think I can safely say it was the most excruciating half hour of my life. Never to be repeated.'

'It wasn't what you'd call a star-is-born moment,' Mimi said. Jonathan's performance had been toe-curling for all concerned.

'I'll stick to what I'm good at from now on.'

'And he's excellent at lawyering,' Aoife said proudly, 'He and a couple of friends have just set up their own firm.'

'Good for you. And well done to all of you on Halfpenny Lane,' Rocco said to the three sisters.

'Thanks.' Aoife said. 'We're very proud of it.'

'Congratulations on all *your* success!' Sive said to Rocco. 'We haven't seen any of your movies,' she announced gaily, 'but we've heard great things.'

'Really? You haven't seen any of them?' Rocco asked, aghast.

'Nope. Not one. Or your TV show either.'

'Gosh! Not even *Waterfall?*'

Sive shook her head. 'No. None of them.' She took a sip of her drink. 'We had an embargo on your movies in our house.'

Rocco gave a startled laugh. 'Wow, I don't know what to say. That makes me feel ...' He broke off, scratching his head.

'But I'm sure they're brilliant!' Sive continued. 'They get terrific reviews, and you're always getting nominated for awards and stuff. You're certainly very popular.'

'Um ... thanks.' Rocco said, bemused.

'I've seen *Waterfall*,' Jonathan piped up. 'If that's okay?' he added with a wary glance at Aoife. 'I didn't know about the embargo.'

'Of course it is.' Aoife smiled and rubbed his arm reassuringly.

'It's really good,' Jonathan said to Rocco.

'I think Aoife's secretly watched it too,' Sive stage-whispered to Rocco. 'In Jonathan's house, though, so I suppose it's allowed.'

'Well, I've seen *all* your stuff,' Sam said. 'I'm a huge fan.'

'Thanks, Sam,' Rocco said, raising a glass to him. 'It's nice to know *someone* appreciates me.'

His tone was light and jovial, but there was something in his expression as his gaze flicked to Mimi that she couldn't name. Was it hurt – or, god forbid, pity? She was annoyed with Sive for bringing up the subject. The ban on Rocco's movies had obviously been imposed for her benefit, to help her get over him, and it made her look pathetic.

'You've really never seen anything I've been in?' he asked her.

She was spared from having to answer by Andrea joining them. 'Rocco! Where have you been hiding?' She linked her arm through his. Mimi never thought she'd be so glad to see Andrea. 'And as for you two,' she said, her gaze flicking between Mimi and Sam. 'You're a right pair of dark horses! How long has this been going on, then?'

'Oh, not long.' Sam draped an arm casually around Mimi's shoulders. 'It's a whirlwind romance. Knocked us both off our feet.' He was good, Mimi had to give him that – he sounded completely natural. 'Mimi tells me the two of you used to be an item,' he said to Rocco.

'A long time ago,' Rocco said.

'Well, your loss is my gain.' Sam slipped his hand to

Mimi's waist, pulling her into his side. 'Can't imagine why you let this one get away,' he said, smiling at her adoringly, 'but I'm very glad you did.' His delivery was note-perfect, with just the right balance of swagger and bravado. So far, so good. 'I still can't believe my luck, to be honest.'

Mimi searched Rocco's face for some trace of upset or jealousy – but there was nothing. He smiled at Sam, his expression as open and friendly as ever.

As everyone chatted with Andrea, Mimi was aware of Rocco's mum glancing her way now and then. She'd known his family would be here, of course, and she'd been nervous about seeing them. She had no idea how they felt about her now, or what kind of reception she'd get from them. Were they angry with her for breaking up with Rocco? Or was she just a distant memory, someone they used to know, who they no longer had any feelings about one way or another?

She'd been close to his family when she and Rocco were together, but she didn't suppose she'd ever been as important a part of their lives as they'd been of hers. They had each other – a large extended family of siblings, aunts, uncles, cousins and grandparents. Girlfriends and boyfriends would come and go, bit part players drifting in and out of their lives over the years, but not leaving any lasting impression. She was probably no more than a distant memory to them now – just one of the ghosts of girlfriends past.

'Mimi!' Rocco's mum called from across the room, waving her over with a warm smile.

'Excuse me,' Mimi said to everyone. 'I'm just going to say hello.' She took a bolstering sip of her drink, then went to join Bea and Ollie.

'It's so lovely to see you,' Bea said, pulling Mimi into a hug. 'We've missed you.'

'Me too,' Mimi said, suddenly overcome with emotion as Ollie embraced her in turn. It had been so long since she'd had one of Bea's motherly hugs.

'You should have called round,' Bea said. 'Any time – you know we don't stand on ceremony.'

Rocco's parents had always operated an open house, constantly filled with their children's friends who'd often stay for impromptu meals and sleepovers. You never knew who you might meet around their kitchen table.

'We think it's marvellous what you and your sisters have done with Halfpenny Lane,' Ollie said. 'Well done.'

'Thanks.' Mimi smiled.

'We contributed to your crowdfunder,' Bea said.

'Oh, that was really good of you. Thank you.'

'Happy to help,' Ollie said gruffly. 'It's a shame to see beautiful old buildings like that getting turned into fast food restaurants and the like. You did a brilliant job. It looks fantastic.'

They couldn't have said anything that would please Mimi more, and she beamed at them like a proud parent.

'We went to see *Three Sisters*,' Bea said. 'Gabbi and I.' She nodded to Rocco's sister who was now chatting to Sam in the opposite corner of the room.

'Rocco told me. You should have said. You could have come backstage and said hello.'

'We didn't want to intrude. But it's lovely to see you now.'

'You wouldn't be intruding. In future, you must let me know if you're coming to the theatre.'

'Well, we'll certainly be there for the next one,' Bea said with a twist of her lips. 'How's Rocco doing?' she asked in an undertone, her eyes darting to him nervously. 'Is he coping all right?'

'Rocco? He's brilliant!'

'Really? You're not just saying that?' She frowned anxiously.

'No, of course not!' Mimi said, aghast. Was Bea genuinely nervous that Rocco was out of his depth? 'You must know how good he is?'

'I was just a bit worried, you know, that he might have bitten off more than he could chew. He hasn't been on the stage for quite a while. I thought he might have … gone off the boil.'

Mimi smiled. 'I suppose you never get over being an anxious parent, do you? But you needn't worry about Rocco. He's terrific! An absolute dream to work with.'

'A dream?'

Mimi turned to find Rocco joining them. 'I should eavesdrop more often. It's not true you never hear anything good.'

Mimi gave him a shaky smile, feeling caught out. 'Anyway, it's lovely to see you again,' she said to Bea and Ollie. 'I'd better go and say hi to Nina.' She peered over Bea's shoulder as she saw Nina going out onto the terrace. Really she just wanted an excuse to get away. 'Excuse me.'

'Oh, of course,' Bea said. 'Don't let me keep you. But I'd love to catch up properly. Why don't you come to dinner tomorrow?'

Um … so many reasons! Damn Rocco, if he hadn't interrupted their conversation this wouldn't have happened.

'I'd love to, but—' She racked her brain for an excuse and flicked a look at Rocco, expecting him to help her out.

'You should come,' he said instead.

'Please do,' Ollie said. 'It's been ages. It'll be like old times.'

That's what Mimi was afraid of. She thought longingly of Sunday dinner with Rocco's family – everyone crowded around the big kitchen table, all talking at once; his mum's amazing food, his father's terrible dad jokes, his siblings all ribbing each other good-naturedly. She'd loved being part of that. At the time, she'd thought it would go on forever – that one day she and Rocco would have their own baby sitting in a high chair between them, and their child would have doting grandparents and a bunch of adoring aunts and uncles fussing over them. She'd loved the idea of having lots of children and a big close-knit family just like Rocco's, with chaotic mealtimes and people always dropping in. She'd looked forward to it as if it was a sure thing. It would be bittersweet to be back there, but there was also a little part of her that wanted to go and relive those times, to be part of the Agnew clan again, even if it was only for a few hours.

'But maybe you're busy?' Ollie said.

'No. I don't have anything on.'

'Great. That's settled, then,' Bea said. 'We'll see you tomorrow. Say, six o'clock?'

Mimi looked at Rocco, but he didn't seem at all put out about her going to dinner with his family. 'Thanks. I'll look forward to it.' She drained her drink. 'Well, I'd better go and find Nina.'

She drifted out onto the terrace, but Nina had disappeared. Instead, she immediately bumped into Rocco's sister Gabbi.

'Mimi! It's so lovely to see you.' Mimi was engulfed by a warm wave of perfume as Gabbi threw her arms around her. 'You were always our favourite of Rocco's girlfriends, you know.'

Mimi had fully expected Gabbi to be her sister-in-law

one day, part of the big extended family she'd envisaged having with Rocco.

'Not that there were many,' Gabbi added hastily. 'Rocco's always been a one-woman guy.'

Mimi felt a pang that she was no longer that one woman. 'How about Willow?' she asked. 'Have you met her?'

'No, not yet. To be honest, we weren't even sure that was real at first.'

'Oh?' Mimi frowned, trying to batten down the hope that was springing in her chest.

'We saw the stories, of course, like everyone else. But we didn't know if there was any truth to them or if it was just stupid gossip. I mean, last year they had Rocco going out with Saoirse Ronan just because they were photographed together at some Hollywood party. But apparently that was the one and only time he's met her.'

'Didn't he tell you himself, though – about Willow?'

'No, he didn't say anything about it until recently – not until after they'd gone public about it. He still gets a bit prickly if we bring up the subject. He's playing his cards pretty close to his chest when it comes to their relationship.'

That was strange. Rocco was so close to his family, and he used to be such an open book. But maybe Hollywood had changed him.

'It's not like Rocco to be so guarded,' Gabbi said. 'I mean it's not as if one of us is going to blab to the press about them.'

'Maybe Willow's rubbed off on him.' Willow was notoriously protective of her private life, famous for nixing personal questions in interviews.

'Maybe.' Gabbi sighed. 'Anyway, I'm sure she's lovely,

but you'll still be my favourite. I always thought you and Rocco …' She trailed off.

You and me both, Mimi thought.

'You just seemed so great together. And you fit in so well with our lot. You were like one of us from the first day you came to the house.'

Mimi had felt the same. She smiled, remembering that day. She'd been right at home the moment she'd stepped into Rocco's parents' house and sat around the dinner table with his family. She'd felt as if she'd found the place she was meant to be all along, like a jigsaw piece slotting into place with a satisfying click. 'Well, I'll be there for dinner on Sunday. Your mum invited me.'

'Great! It'll be like old times.'

Mimi laughed. 'That's what your dad said.'

15

'Stop looking over there and focus on me,' Mimi hissed at Sam, tugging on his sleeve. 'Young Scrooge, remember?'

'Yes, sorry!'

As the night progressed, many of the guests had migrated out to the garden. Mimi followed Sam's gaze and spotted Rocco in conversation with Nina and Sive at the edge of the terrace.

'Let's dance,' she said, grabbing Sam's hand and pulling him into the middle of a group of couples swaying in time to the gentle notes of a jazz song emanating from the speakers. The low, sultry tones of Sade carried over the clink of glasses and the hum of distant conversations, enveloping the garden in a warm embrace.

'How am I doing?' Sam asked, gazing into her eyes as they shuffled around the terrace together.

'Not bad.' She flicked a glance over his shoulder to make sure Rocco was watching. 'But let's ramp it up a bit. Kiss me,' she hissed urgently.

'What, now?'

'Don't wait to be told twice,' she said crossly. 'You'll

have to learn to take direction if you want to be—' She was cut off by Sam's mouth clamping over hers in a very hard, closed-mouth kiss. Still, it would look convincing enough from a distance, she thought, cupping the back of his head and running her fingers through the short hairs at the nape of his neck.

'How was that?' he asked, lifting his head.

'Not bad,' she nodded, patting his chest in what would look like a loving gesture. Then she glanced to the edge of the terrace and as well as Rocco she saw Sive looking across at them, her face the picture of misery. Oh god, she really did have feelings for Sam, didn't she? Even though she knew this was fake, it must be hard to watch.

'Excellent work, Sam. Now maybe you can be a good boyfriend by being nice to my sister.' She nodded to Sive and Sam turned around to look.

'Absolutely. My pleasure.'

Mimi watched as he walked away. Sive's face lit up with pleasure as he approached. Damn! No good would come of that. She really shouldn't encourage it.

'I think Sive really likes Sam,' Aoife said, appearing at her side.

'I know.' She turned to her sister, who looked as concerned about it as she was. 'But it won't last, will it?'

Aoife shrugged. 'I don't know. You know what Sive is like. Once she gets an idea in her head, it's very hard to shift it.'

'She is very loyal. But what about Ben?'

'We can only hope he comes home soon. Even Sive has her limits.' Aoife sighed. 'So how's it going with you and Sam?'

'Fine.' Mimi glanced across the terrace. Sam was chatting with Rocco and Sive. As she watched, he said something that made Rocco throw his head back and roar with laughter. 'But I think I'm wasting my time.' She sank down onto a garden bench and Aoife sat beside her.

'I feel like such an idiot,' she said to Aoife. 'Coming here all got up like this.' She waved a hand to her face. 'Thinking I could show Rocco what he's missing; make him sorry he left me.' She rolled her eyes at her own folly. She was as deluded and lacking in self-awareness as Andrea. 'But he doesn't care. Why would he? He's got Willow Bell. He doesn't mind seeing me with Sam at all. Look at him there, chatting to my new 'boyfriend' – happy as Larry!'

'He just likes Sam. But of course he regrets losing you,' Aoife said, putting a hand on Mimi's shoulder. 'Who wouldn't? And not because you can rock a red lip or because of how hot you look in that dress – which is seriously, hot by the way—'

Mimi huffed a laugh.

'But because you're *you* – funny, clever, snarky *you*. That's what he lost – what he can never have with anyone else – and I guarantee you he regrets it, every single day. Twice on Sundays.'

Mimi sniffed, her eyes welling up. 'But he's moved on all the same.'

'I suppose he has. But—' Aoife hesitated, biting her lip.

'What?'

'He thinks you have too. Have you given him any reason to believe you're not perfectly happy with Sam?'

'No, of course not – quite the opposite. I mean, that's the whole point of Sam.'

'Well, maybe he's doing the same thing.'

'Pretending to be with Willow?' Mimi gasped, thinking of what Andrea had said the other morning. Could the whole thing be a publicity stunt? At the time, she'd dismissed the idea as a conspiracy theory cooked up by jealous, possessive fans. But if Aoife thought there might be some truth to it …

'Pretending he's over you.'

Mimi frowned. He *had* persisted in asking her if she was seeing anyone. She thought back to the other night when they'd stood outside their old apartment building, and Rocco had taken her hand. It certainly hadn't felt as if he was over her then. *This is what I miss the most … being here with you.* She was sorry now she'd been so quick to shut him down. She could have let it play out, see where it led …

'But one of you has to stop playing it cool and make the first move.'

'But why should that be me?'

'Why shouldn't it?'

'Because … I'm the girl?'

'Oh, come on!'

Mimi pouted. 'It's times like this I wish feminism had never been invented. Besides, what if he isn't pretending and he really is over me? I'd be making a complete fool of myself if I made a move on him. It'd be humiliating.'

'You don't have to make a grand declaration. You can be subtle. Just give him an opening.'

Mimi nodded, smiling. She could do that – allow Rocco to flirt with her, maybe flirt back a little. She could play the long game – concentrate on being friends with him for now, give him time to realise he was still in love with her, then ditch Sam after a decent interval and let Rocco know she was single again. Now that she knew he was moving back to Dublin, she had time. She also had hope because what were the chances of Willow moving here with him? It would probably split them up – if they were really together in the first place. Maybe she shouldn't have been so dismissive of Andrea's conspiracy theory.

Perhaps she should take a look at that 'evidence' for herself.

Later Mimi stood in a dark corner of the terrace, hidden in the shadows of the house, where she could watch unobserved. The sounds of the party flowed around her, music and laughter mingling together in the balmy night air. Aoife and Jonathan were wrapped around each other, swaying in a gentle rhythm under the twinkling fairy lights. Aoife was positively glowing with happiness.

'Dance with me?' The deep voice came from behind her.

She turned to see Rocco stepping out of the shadows, holding out a hand to her.

'Come on. For old time's sake.'

She smiled. 'Okay.' She took his hand and they stepped into the circle of light. He pulled her into his arms, and she buried her face against his shoulder, breathing in the delicious sandalwood and citrus notes of his cologne. It felt so right to have his arms wrapped around her, the rough bristle of his cheek against hers, and as they swayed slowly to the music, the years seemed to melt away. It was as if they'd never been apart.

'Why didn't you stop your mum from asking me to dinner?' she asked him, lifting her head.

'Why would I?' He frowned.

'Because … I'm sure you don't want me there.'

'Of course I do.'

'But I'm your ex. Won't it be awkward?'

'With Mum?' He laughed. 'Have you forgotten what she's like?'

Mimi smiled. She hadn't forgotten. Bea was so easy-going and friendly, it was impossible to be uncomfortable around her.

'Anyway, we're friends now, aren't we?'

'Of course,' she said staunchly.

'And it's not as if we split up because we were at war with each other. Or because one of us was cheating.'

'No.' They'd just wanted to live in different places, to have different career paths. It didn't seem like a good enough reason anymore. 'But it's one thing being friends. It's quite another having dinner with your family.'

'Isn't that what friends do?'

She narrowed her eyes at him. 'Are you angling for an invitation to dinner at our house?'

He grinned. 'You've already given me one, remember – as a guest of Marlowe's.'

'I think I said you should come round to visit him. I don't remember mentioning anything about dinner.'

'It was implied,' he said with a smirk. 'Anyway, I think we should do it for old times' sake – in honour of Detta. God, I miss those evenings at her place.'

Detta had often invited Rocco to join them for dinner at her little cottage in the Liberties. They'd spent long, lazy Sundays gorging on her wonderful food and watching old movies, while she shared bits of gossip about the stars and gave them all advice on their future acting careers.

'Are you friends with all your exes?' she asked, regretting it as soon as the words were out of her mouth. She didn't really want to hear about his other girlfriends.

He shrugged. 'Not so much. Anyway, there aren't as many as you seem to think. You're the only significant one really.'

'So I set the tone?'

'Exactly.'

'I suppose I'd better do a good job of it, then. Show Andrea how it's done,' she added with a little laugh.

'Andrea?' Rocco pulled back a little, screwing up his face.

'You know she thinks you two are an item?'

'What?'

Mimi nodded. 'I had her asking my permission to date you the other day. Apparently, that's one of the duties of an ex. Who knew? Anyway, I gave her my blessing.'

'Where on earth did she get the idea we're dating? And how come I don't know about it?'

'You haven't gone out with her?' Mimi asked, more invested in the answer than she cared to admit.

'No.' Rocco frowned, confused. Then his face cleared. 'Unless … I did go to that burrito place down the road with her the other day.'

'Just the two of you?'

'Yeah.'

'Bingo!' She pointed a finger at him. 'That'll be it then.'

'It was just lunch. She said she wanted to go over our scenes together, run some lines … She thought that was a date? Seriously?'

'I think she's probably expecting a proposal any day now. Just FYI.'

'If she thought a burrito sitting at the counter in a fast-food joint was a date, I hope she doesn't go to the papers with it. I'd look like a right cheapskate.'

Mimi laughed. 'We used to have dates like that. Burgers and tacos out of Styrofoam. Plastic cups of Coke.'

'When we were broke students. Believe it or not, I've moved on from that. It's a bit more sophisticated when I take someone out these days.'

'Really? How so?'

'There are real china plates. Glasses. Cloth napkins. Waiters who bring your food right to the table. The whole shebang.'

'Fancy!'

'I know.' Rocco gave her a crooked smile. 'Anyway, thanks for the heads-up, about Andrea.'

'I know she can be annoying but let her down gently.'

'Who says I'm going to let her down?'

'The woman you described as "a pain in the arse"?' She shrugged. 'I guess I just assumed. None of my business anyway.'

'She obviously thinks it is if she wants your permission.'

'I told her she should ask Willow. She has custody of you now.'

'Do you think she'll ask her for my hand in marriage?'

'You shouldn't mock. She's just young.'

'*We're* young!' He said indignantly.

'She's *younger*. Besides, we're old souls. Detta always said so.' In a rare burst of romanticism, Detta had in fact said that they were two halves of one soul that had been split apart and they needed to find each other again to feel whole. It was a lovely idea, but where did that leave them now?

'So how long have you been going out with Sam?' Rocco asked after a pause.

'Not long,' she said breezily.

'I'd never have known there was anything between you. No one else seems to have had an inkling either.'

'Oh, we keep it on the down-low at work. We don't want to be one of *those* couples.'

'We were one of those couples, weren't we?' Rocco said with a laugh.

'It's probably safe to say we were nauseating.'

'But you've decided to break cover now?' He glanced across the patio at Sam.

'You know how it is – we needed some time to figure out what this was. Now we're sure it's real and we don't care who knows it,' she said, quoting Willow's words from the magazine interview. Then she burst out laughing. 'Obviously I don't need to ask you anything about your romance with Willow – it's all there in *Wow!* magazine.'

'You might be surprised. *Wow!* magazine doesn't know everything.'

'Your meeting on set, the long nights spent huddled together in your trailers, the bonding over pizza and books – what else is there?'

'What would our story have said?' His voice was low, husky.

She looked at him carefully. There was a challenging glint in his eyes. Okay, she could play this game. 'We met at acting school and bonded over spice bags and our love of getting rat-arsed in the local pub.'

Rocco threw his head back and laughed, and Mimi felt a tinge of pride.

'We moved into a top floor flat in Dublin's historic city centre,' she continued, 'and our romance was played out against a backdrop of noisy drunks and ambulance sirens—'

'And the couple next door having their Sunday morning bonk.'

Mimi faltered halfway through a laugh. God, she missed those days. 'I think our story needs some work,' she said lightly. 'It's not very glamorous, is it?'

'It might not be *Wow!* material, but it's got real heart.'

'Yeah, your and Willow's story is sadly lacking in authenticity.'

'You have no idea,' he said enigmatically.

Mimi wondered what he meant by that, but she couldn't think of a casual way to pursue it.

'And we had our moments,' he said, a wistfulness in his tone that gave her a pang.

'We did. I guess nothing beats the romance of first love.'

'What about you and Sam? Do your *Wow!* story.'

'Hmm.' She decided it was best to stick to the truth as much as possible. 'We met when Jonathan inherited a share in Halfpenny Lane and needed to cash in because Sam had embezzled a load of money from him.'

Rocco gave a hoot of laughter. 'You're not serious.'

'I'm afraid I am. My boyfriend is a thief. Well, more of a con-man, I suppose, in fairness.'

'Is that better?'

'It's a higher calling.'

'If you say so.'

'You know I always liked the bad boys,' she said, then felt a stab of guilt for bad-mouthing Sam so cavalierly. 'That's not fair, really. He's a good guy. He had a gambling problem, but he's dealt with it. He's a reformed character now.'

'Thanks to the love of a good woman?' He nodded at her.

'I like to think so.'

'I'm glad. He seems like a good bloke.'

'He is.' Mimi smiled, but her heart was sinking as the music stopped and Rocco released her.

'Sorry,' he said, looking over her shoulder. 'I'd better go and talk to some of my guests.'

'Yes, go. I've monopolised you long enough.' She wrapped her arms around herself as she watched him walk away. There'd been nothing in his demeanour this evening to suggest he wanted them to be anything more than friends, no sign of the flirtatiousness that had surfaced the other night when he'd taken her hand on Dame Street. That had clearly been a momentary lapse. He talked about their past now with fond nostalgia, and wished her well in her relationship with Sam. Aoife was mistaken. He wasn't acting cool because he was afraid of being rejected. He was completely over her.

16

MIMI'S STOMACH fluttered with butterflies the following day as she made her way to Rocco's parents' house in Rathgar, and she cursed herself for not coming up with some excuse. Why was she putting herself through this? She didn't think she had masochistic tendencies. Last night she'd had some crazy idea that she could relive the past, but in the clear light of day, she realised that was impossible and it would only make her yearning for what she'd lost more acute.

'Mimi! Great to see you. Come in, come in.' Bea greeted her warmly with a hug and a welcoming smile.

As soon as she stepped inside the house, she knew she'd made a mistake.

'You've had work done, I see,' she said as Bea led her down the hall to the kitchen, their footsteps clicking on polished wooden floorboards that hadn't been there when Mimi was last in the house.

'Yes, we have – rather a lot of work. We're very pleased with it,' Bea said proudly as she led Mimi into a large living/dining room extension where the cosy kitchen used to be. 'What do you think?'

'It's lovely,' Mimi said, as she looked around in dismay. Nothing was as it used to be. But of course it wasn't, she chided herself. What did she expect – for time to have stood still? It was idiotic to think the past would be here waiting for her to step back into it. It was over four years since she'd been in this house, for goodness' sake. Besides, it was just some renovations and redecorating – nothing to get upset about. It wasn't as if anything fundamental had changed. Bea was still the same person – they all were. But she couldn't shake the feeling that the past had been erased – painted over and obliterated.

Delicious aromas of garlic and herbs permeated the kitchen. At least that hadn't changed. A long table of solid oak in the middle of the room was set for six, but there was plenty of room for double that – unlike the old IKEA one they used to all crowd around, their knees and elbows knocking together. The room was empty, and Mimi wondered where everyone was. She took the bottle of wine she'd brought from her tote bag and handed it to Bea.

'Thank you.' Bea glanced down at the label. 'Ooh, my favourite!'

'I remembered.' Mimi smiled.

'We're all outside.' Bea jerked her head to the door. 'It's such a nice day, we thought we'd have a drink in the garden first. You have to grab the opportunity when you can, don't you?'

'Good idea.'

'The weather's been fabulous the last few weeks, hasn't it?' Bea remarked as she led Mimi outside.

Ollie, Gabbi, Rocco and his younger sister Mia were sitting at a big garden table under a large red umbrella. The garden had been landscaped too. There were neatly edged borders and raised flowerbeds brimming with vivid colour, and at the far end there was a new sandstone patio, with a built-in barbecue and a set of chairs clustered around a fire pit.

'Mimi!' Mia beamed, jumping up and rushing across the garden to give her a hug.

'Hi, Mia.' Mimi squeezed her tight before letting her go. 'You weren't at the party last night?'

'No, I had something else on,' she said.

'She got a better offer,' Rocco called. 'Some guy she chose to hang out with over her own brother.'

Mia blushed adorably, her cheeks dimpling. Like Rocco and his older sister Francesca, she took after their Italian maternal grandparents with their dark colouring and olive skin. Gabbi was more like their father.

'I hope it was worth it,' Mimi said, smiling at her.

'It was. But I was sorry to miss you, so I'm glad you were able to come today.'

Rocco stood and greeted her with a kiss on the cheek, her senses tingling even from the brief brush of his lips on her skin.

'This is gorgeous,' she said, looking around the garden as she took a seat at the table beside Ollie.

'We love it,' Bea said, handing her a glass of cava. 'We can really make the most of days like this.'

'Rocco paid for it all,' his father said proudly. 'You'll notice a few changes to the place, I'm sure.'

'Yeah. Quite a lot of changes.' Everything was different, Mimi thought. Absolutely everything. What the hell was she doing here?

But the conversation flowed easily, and she began to relax as she sipped her drink and caught up with Rocco's family.

'Did Rocco tell you we're grandparents now?' Bea asked her.

'Yes,' Mimi nodded. 'You must be thrilled.'

'We are. Marco's such a cutie. It's a pity you won't get to meet him. They're on holidays in Crete at the moment.'

Mimi was secretly relieved she wouldn't have to witness Rocco playing the doting uncle. Today was overwhelming enough already.

Mia had just graduated from Trinity with a first in Art History, and Gabbi, a software engineer, had recently been laid off by one of the big tech companies and was doing freelance work while considering her options.

'I'm thinking about travelling for a while,' she said. 'Working remotely, being a digital nomad.'

'That sounds fun.'

Ollie and Bea had both retired. Bea had taken up golf and was loving it – 'I'm absolutely crap, and I don't have a competitive bone in my body, but I enjoy the social side of it' – and they were enjoying being doting grandparents to Marco.

'We spoil him rotten, don't we?' Bea said to her husband.

'We do.' Ollie smiled. 'But isn't that what grandparents are for?'

Bea got her phone out and pulled up some photos. 'That's Marco,' she said proudly, handing the phone to Mimi. There was a photo of a pink-faced new-born with a thatch of soft dark hair.

'Aw, he's gorgeous.'

'Swipe this way,' Bea said, indicating with her finger. 'There are some more.'

'There are about five thousand more,' Ollie said, laughing.

'We *are* a bit obsessed,' Bea admitted.

'Francesca and Charlie look so happy,' Mimi murmured, pausing on a photo of Rocco's sister and her husband with their baby. Ollie wasn't kidding, she thought as she scrolled on – every second of Marco's life so far seemed to have been recorded for posterity. Inevitably she came to several photos with Rocco, and she felt a pang as she lingered on an image of him holding his new nephew in his arms, smiling down at him adoringly. She scrolled through several more photos, making the appropriate cooing noises before handing the phone back to Bea.

'We're going to do more travelling now that we have the freedom,' Bea told her. 'We're planning to buy a camper van and drive across the States.'

'That sounds amazing,' Mimi said wistfully.

'I might hitch a lift,' Gabbi said.

'I suppose Rocco's told you he's moving back here?' Bea asked.

'Yes. You must be pleased.'

'We're delighted. It'll be great to have him home.'

'And hopefully it means we'll see more of *you*,' Gabbi said to Mimi.

'Though we're going to miss having somewhere to crash in LA,' Mia said.

'And there was I thinking you came because you wanted to spend time with me,' Rocco said, pressing a hand to his heart as if he'd been wounded.

'So what have you been up to?' Bea asked Mimi. 'Apart from the theatre? I'm sure that keeps you busy.'

'It's been pretty full-on. I haven't been doing much else lately, to be honest.' She wasn't about to fill Rocco's mum in on her love life – or lack thereof – and she willed her not to ask.

'Any boyfriend?' Mia piped up.

It was on the tip of Mimi's tongue to say no when she

remembered Sam. 'There is someone,' she said casually, 'but it's very early days.' She was grateful that Bea chose that moment to announce that the chicken would be rested, and they all began to gather up glasses and head inside.

Mimi excused herself to go to the loo before dinner. Upstairs, the layout of the house was unchanged, though the bathroom and landing had been redecorated. She resisted the temptation to sneak a look at Rocco's old bedroom, where they'd often crashed for the night after a boozy dinner or family celebration. Passing through the hall on her way back to the kitchen, her eyes fell on a framed photograph standing on the console table by the door. She stopped in her tracks, recognising it instantly. It was Francesca and Charlie's wedding, a group photo of Rocco's family, and she was there among them, Rocco's arm around her on one side, Gabbi's on the other. She picked it up, tracing the smiling faces with one finger. It had been such a happy day, full of sunshine and love and laughter. She swallowed a lump in her throat as she remembered catching Francesca's bouquet; how everyone had teased her and Rocco that they'd be next. She didn't set any store by the superstition, but nevertheless she'd believed they would be.

She was relieved that the conversation had moved on when she re-joined the family in the kitchen, and the subject of her boyfriend didn't come up again. Dinner passed pleasantly after that. Rocco's family were as warm and lively company as they'd always been, and Bea was as good a cook as Mimi remembered. The food was sublime – succulent roast chicken flavoured with preserved lemon, and a side dish of new potatoes with peas and coriander.

'It's all Ottolenghi,' Bea told her.

'Mum's latest obsession,' Gabbi said.

But delicious as the meal was, Mimi felt at odds the whole time and longed for it to be over. It was all just as it used to be, and yet nothing was the same. She was a guest here now, not one of the family like she'd been in that wedding photograph. She wouldn't be going home with Rocco at the end of the evening, laden down with parcels of leftovers to see them through the week. She wasn't an honorary aunt to Francesca's baby.

'I'm so glad you and Rocco are friends again,' Bea told her later as she saw her to the door.

'Me too. And thanks for dinner. It was amazing.'

'You're welcome. It's been lovely having you – just like old times.'

'Yes.' Mimi smiled sadly. Because it was nothing like old times. It was 'all changed, changed utterly'.

17

Rehearsals were proceeding briskly, and as they moved through the script, Mimi looked forward to her and Rocco's first kiss with a mixture of trepidation and excitement. Even though she knew it was coming and she tried to prepare herself, she still didn't feel quite ready when it happened. Her heart pounded erratically as Rocco took her in his arms and bent his head to hers. Then he kissed her passionately, his lips soft and warm, and achingly familiar. Mimi felt her body melt as she clung to him and kissed him back. It was tantalisingly brief, only a moment before Rocco had to lift his head and speak again. But for those few seconds everything else seemed to disappear and it was just the two of them. She forgot anyone was watching, the rest of the cast mere blurry figures in the background at the edge of her vision. Mimi was proud that even though her head was spinning, she was able to collect herself and deliver her next line with perfect timing. If she appeared a little flustered, it was in keeping with the scene, and she hoped Nina would see it as part of her performance.

As they moved into Act Two, rehearsals really hotted up, and Mimi had never been so happy to lose herself in a role. The relationship between the two main characters in *Private Lives* was intensely physical, the stage directions calling for lots of kissing, ardent embraces and lingering looks between the two leads, as well as a dance and a physical brawl. Nina was intent on ramping up the drama alongside the comedy, emphasising the irresistible sexual attraction between the couple and the ultimately destructive savagery of their passion. So one way or another, Mimi spent most of her time entangled with Rocco, whether she was snuggling up to him on a sofa, sitting next to him at the piano while they sang together, rolling around with him on the floor grappling with him, or tripping across the stage in his arms in a lively foxtrot.

It was sweet torture spending her days lying next to him while he gazed into her eyes and told her how desperately he wanted her, that they'd been mad ever to part, that he wanted her back more than anything. She got a twisted sort of pleasure from being able to say those things back to him without fear of consequences. Hiding behind her character, she could tell him out loud that she still loved him, that their break-up had been a mistake, without feeling exposed and vulnerable – because they were Amanda's words and sentiments, not hers. No one need know that she meant every word.

It gave her an illicit thrill to kiss Rocco at rehearsal in full view of everyone, knowing that no one would bat an eyelid or say a word about it, other than Nina perhaps suggesting one of them angle their head differently. When the show was up and running, she'd have a free pass to kiss him on stage six nights a week and every Wednesday and Saturday afternoon for two months. But it wasn't enough, because when rehearsals were over, she never wanted it to stop.

She didn't know if Rocco felt the same or if he was just throwing himself into his role, but their kisses were becoming increasingly heated as the days passed. Thursday morning found them lying together on a sofa sharing lingering kisses interspersed with lines of dialogue.

God, I love my job, Mimi thought as she cupped the back of his head, pulling him down to her again for another kiss. Rocco's eyes were heavy, dark with desire, and his voice was thick and throaty as he spoke his next line before leaning in again and kissing her passionately. She'd almost forgotten what an amazing kisser he was. Mimi startled a little as his tongue ran along her lower lip, but she smothered it, opening her mouth to him for the briefest moment before he had to speak again. She was sure his head blocked them from view and no one else would notice, but it still felt thrillingly dangerous and forbidden. She was flushed light-headed as Rocco pulled away and they carried on with the scene.

Too soon, rehearsal was over. Mimi felt a little dazed, still lost in the world of the play and struggling to focus as Nina gave them notes.

'Are you doing anything tonight?' Rocco's voice came from behind her as they broke up and she was packing her tote.

She turned around to find him pulling a messenger bag over his head.

'No, no plans.'

'Want to get some dinner?'

She looked to the door where the rest of the cast were

streaming out. Sam had left early to catch a flight to Manchester for a stag weekend.

'Just us?'

'Yeah, just us.' He smiled crookedly. 'Friends can have dinner together, right?'

'I suppose so.' Could they, though? She wasn't sure what was happening between them, still befuddled after their hot and heavy make-out session. Their make-believe make-out session, she reminded herself.

'I thought we could discuss the play.'

'Okay.' Mimi found herself agreeing, even though she knew she was treading on dangerous ground and no good could come of it. 'Just let me get changed and I'll be with you in ten.'

She ducked into one of the dressing rooms and changed out of the comfy sweats she wore for rehearsal and into a pair of cropped jeans and a soft white T-shirt. It was all she had with her – not very glamorous, but it would have to do. She touched up her make-up and arranged her hair in a messy up-style. Then on a last-minute whim she had a root through the rails of costumes to see if she there was something to jazz up her outfit a little. She found a beautiful full-length green kimono with a floral print and pulled it on as she went to join Rocco.

They went to La Cave, an old haunt of theirs – a subterranean late-night wine bar and restaurant hidden away behind a tiny door on Anne Street. A narrow flight of stairs led them down to the cosy interior, the soft lighting, red walls, and plush velvet seating lending it a warm, romantic atmosphere. It felt too intimate already just being there.

They were shown to a table in a little alcove.

'Shall we get a bottle?' Rocco asked as they consulted the wine menu.

'Bit pricy, isn't it?' Mimi murmured as she ran her eyes down the list.

'This is on me.'

'Thanks,' Mimi said, smiling up at him. 'I won't argue with that. Should we, though? We don't want to have heads on us tomorrow.'

'The good stuff doesn't give you a hangover.'

'I'll pretend I believe that,' Mimi said with a crooked smile. 'Because I do like the good stuff.'

'Anyway, I think we deserve it after what we've been through today.'

They'd spent the latter part of the afternoon working on the blocking for their big fight scene – screaming and slapping, hurling insults at each other, throwing things, and wrestling on the ground like children. It was draining, exhausting … and completely exhilarating. Mimi couldn't wait to do it again tomorrow.

Rocco ordered a wildly expensive bottle of Amarone that practically had the wine waiter bowing in respect.

'Wow, this brings back memories,' Mimi said, looking around when they'd ordered. The table was so small, their knees were touching beneath it.

'It does.' Rocco's eyes held hers across the flickering candle, and she shivered at the intensity in them.

'Although we never had wine like this back then.' She picked up her glass and took a sip. It was heaven.

She could see them now, sitting at the bar after a show, drinking red wine and picking at plates of cheese, kissing between mouthfuls. They'd be surrounded by friends and colleagues, but they'd only had eyes for each other, and it was as if there was nobody else in the room. After working themselves up at the bar, they'd practically run home to their little Dame Street flat to tear off their clothes and make love all night.

Mimi shook her head as if to clear it of the memories. 'I saw Nina with Mitch the other day when they thought no one was looking,' she said.

'No!' Rocco's eyes bugged out of his head, and Mimi laughed. She'd forgotten how much he loved gossip.

She nodded. 'They were stroking each other's hands. I'm sure they're having a fling.'

'I think Cara and Orla are doing it.'

'Really? What about Cara's girlfriend?'

Rocco shrugged. 'Maybe they broke up. Or she's cheating.'

'And of course you and Andrea are the talk of the town.'

Rocco gave her a patient smile.

'So, tell me about you and Willow,' she said, trying to establish a buffer between them.

He shrugged. 'Not much to tell. Like you said, you can read all about it in *Wow!*'

'You said they don't know everything.'

'Okay, what do you want to know?'

What did she want to know about the woman Rocco had chosen to share his life with? Nothing, really. She'd thought she'd use Willow as a shield, but now she was sorry she'd brought her up. 'Tell me something that isn't on the internet – something not fit for public consumption.'

Rocco flashed her a sly smile. 'I could tell you things that would shock and awe.'

'Go on, then.'

He shook his head. 'Not at liberty.'

She made an impatient face at him. 'You never used to be so coy.'

'Okay, I'll tell you this. Willow and I are ...' He looked

to the ceiling, pondering. 'Not what people think,' he finished.

'So what are you really? Vampires? Spooks? Undercover agents for the FBI?'

Rocco laughed, shaking his head. 'Something not fit to publish in *Wow!* magazine,' he grinned. He picked up a piece of bread and took a big bite.

'Hmm, kinky then?' she smirked.

'Not kinky. Just … let's say not exactly vanilla either.'

'I have no idea what that means, but I probably don't want to know.' She was finding this topic depressing.

'You might be interested to hear.'

'Maybe I would, but you realise you're not actually telling me anything?'

After a moment's silence he said, 'Okay, here's something. You know the story goes we bonded over pizza in her trailer on the set of *Waterfall*?'

'I did read something about that. Quite the scoop!'

'The pizza bit?' he said, grinning 'Not true.'

'I knew it!' She slapped the table triumphantly. 'I doubt Willow has ever eaten pizza in her life.'

'She's more of a quinoa salad girl.'

'She must find living with you a challenge,' she said and immediately regretted it. She didn't want to think about him and Willow living together. She was beginning to think it was a very bad idea coming here. It was only going to make her sad.

'We're not living together.' Rocco flicked a glance over her shoulder as if checking who was around, then he leaned across and lightly stroked her hand where it rested on the table.

'God, I've missed you, Mimi,' he said, looking at her with dark, hooded eyes.

Her breath caught, her heart hammering, but she

steeled herself against the melting effect of his words on her heart. 'Not enough to lift the phone and call me in four years.'

'I could say the same about you,' he said. 'Or maybe you didn't miss me?' He raised an eyebrow challengingly.

'I couldn't call. It hurt too much.' She was appalled by the raw honesty in her voice. She hadn't meant to say that.

'Same,' he said simply. For a long moment they just gazed at each other in silence. His eyes dropped to her lips, and for a breathless moment Mimi thought he was going to kiss her. She didn't know if the thudding of her heart was from fear that he would or that he wouldn't.

'You know, I always sort of thought you'd come over … to LA. I know it's daft, but the first few months I was there, I kept expecting you to turn up at my door, to be on the step waiting for me one day when I got home …'

'I thought the same about you – that you'd come back.' Her voice came out hoarse and throaty and she hated how pitiful she sounded. She hadn't meant to allow herself to be so vulnerable with him. But then she'd never expected him to say that he'd been pining for her. She hated to think of him waiting for her in LA, hoping every day that she'd turn up; his disappointment when she didn't.

'I'm back now.'

'You're too late.' God, his fingers were doing delicious things to her insides. But this was wrong. 'Anyway, I thought you wanted to talk about the play,' she said stiffly, pulling her hand away. She felt bereft.

'I'd rather talk about us.'

She shook her head. 'We shouldn't be here, Rocco. I shouldn't have come.'

'We're not doing anything wrong.'

'I doubt your girlfriend would agree.'

'Willow wouldn't mind. She's not the jealous type.'

Mimi frowned. What was he trying to say? He was definitely flirting with her. Were he and Willow in some sort of open relationship? Or drifting apart? Maybe they were going to break up? She gave herself a mental shake. Whatever was going on with them, it didn't matter. They were together, and she didn't do this.

She was relieved when they were interrupted by the arrival of the waiter with their food.

'Anyway, what about Cara and Orla?' she said when he'd gone, taking the opportunity to move on to safer topics. 'Do you really think they're running around together?'

Rocco laughed. 'Running around! I love the way you talk. And yes, I think they are.'

The mood shifted as they moved on to lighter topics, gossiping about the cast and Hollywood stars Rocco had met. There was no more reminiscing about their past. They talked about movies and plays and TV series they'd watched. Mimi told him about all the work they'd done renovating the theatre and putting on their first production. She felt on safer ground with him by the time they paid the bill and climbed the stairs back onto Anne Street. They were just friends, and that was fine – nice, even.

But halfway up the stairs, she stumbled over the hem of her kimono, and Rocco took her hand to steady her. He didn't let go, even when they reached the street. Mimi's heart pounded as they both looked down at their joined hands, her skin seeming to tingle beneath his. Her chest felt tight and she was transported back to other nights when they'd walked along these streets together, going home to their flat, to their bed, every nerve ending in her body singing with anticipation.

They didn't speak, Rocco's thumb gliding over the back of her hand as they walked towards Grafton Street to get a cab. Then suddenly he pulled her into a shuttered doorway.

'Mimi.' He breathed her name, his dark eyes full of intent, his face so close she could feel his warm breath on her skin. He lowered his lips slowly to hers, as if giving her time to pull away.

To her shame, Mimi didn't. Instead, she wrapped her arms around him, her legs going weak as they kissed hungrily, as if they'd never get enough of each other. Rocco's eyes fluttered open as his teeth grazed her bottom lip, and they were as heavy-lidded and dark with lust as they'd been this afternoon. But this was better than rehearsal. These kisses were for her, not Amanda. It was all for real when she parted her lips and he groaned deep in his throat as his tongue slid into her mouth. Despite knowing she shouldn't, Mimi couldn't bring herself to stop kissing him back, burying her fingers in his curls as she held him to her.

'I've missed you so much,' he murmured against her mouth, pulling her tighter against him.

'Stop!' she hissed, finally summoning up the will to push him away. 'What if someone sees us?'

'There's no one around,' he said breathlessly. It was late, the city slowly drifting into night-time and the only sounds were the distant footsteps of a few stragglers and the plaintive melody of a busker's violin.

'That's not the point. We shouldn't be doing this.' She pushed away from the wall and began walking away, angry with herself as much as him. 'You have a girl-friend,' she called to him over her shoulder as he followed her. 'And I have a boyfriend,' she mumbled as an afterthought.

'Sorry,' he said as he caught up with her. 'You're right. I shouldn't have done that. It won't happen again.'

God forgive her, but even though she knew it was the right thing, those words cut her to the quick.

They lived so close to each other, it would have made sense to share a cab, but Mimi insisted on calling her own.

'Don't trust me?' Rocco said jokingly. She didn't reply, but he must have seen the answer in her face. The truth was she didn't trust either of them to be alone in an enclosed space right now.

'Come on, there's no need for that,' Rocco said sadly. 'I'm sorry. It was … a moment of madness. I can behave myself.'

'It wasn't just you back there.' She was relieved when the phone in her hand pinged with a notification from the taxi app just as a car pulled up across the street. 'I'll see you tomorrow,' she said and ran across the street without a backward glance.

As soon as she was in the back of the cab on her way home, she burst into tears, overwrought from the conflicting emotions of the night – the thrill of being with Rocco again, back in one of their old haunts; the guilt of kissing him when he had a girlfriend; the spiralling lust their kisses had ignited that still gnawed at her gut; the aching longing to keep kissing him, to go to bed with him …

She had to tell someone, shameful as it was. Keeping this a secret would just give it more power and meaning. If she confessed, unburdened herself, it seemed like it would neutralize it somehow – make it not such a big deal, just a silly mistake, a momentary lapse of judgement. Reprehensible yes, but not something that had to be buried deep and never spoken of.

She hated the thought of telling Aoife, though. She

didn't want her worrying that she was going back to her old reckless ways, and she dreaded the thought of disappointing her. So she was relieved when she got home to find Aoife's bedroom door open, the room empty. She must have been spending the night at Jonathan's. There was a light on in Sive's room, though, creeping out under the door onto the landing. She knocked softly and opened the door. Sive was sitting up in bed, reading a script.

'Hi!' She looked up and smiled. 'Good night?' She put down the pages.

Mimi shook her head. 'Something terrible happened.' She sat down on the side of the bed and just blurted it out. 'I kissed Rocco.'

'What!' Sive gasped, sitting up straighter.

Mimi nodded. 'I know. I'm a terrible person. He has a girlfriend and—'

'You're not a terrible person,' Sive said earnestly, and it was just what Mimi had needed to hear – her absolution. She immediately felt better, cleaner. 'You just had a moment of weakness. Right?'

Mimi nodded. 'Yes, exactly. That's all it was.'

'How did this happen anyway? Did you kiss him, or did he kiss you?'

'He started it. But I joined in.'

'Where were you? Did anyone see?'

'No. There was no one else there. We went out to dinner together after rehearsal.'

'Just the two of you?'

'Yes.' It sounded so bad now, saying it out loud – so deliberate, as if she'd been inviting trouble. 'But we're friends now. I thought it would be okay.' Maybe they were kidding themselves that they could be friends.

'Well, now you know. You just have to be careful in

future not to put yourself into situations where something might happen.'

'Yes. You're right.'

'No more cosy dinners à deux.'

'Okay.' Mimi nodded.

'Now go forth, my child, and sin no more.'

Mimi smiled. 'Thank you.' She leaned forward and gave Sive a hug, and she went to bed feeling lighter, unburdened.

18

Avoiding one-on-one situations with Rocco wasn't easy, however, as the press tour for *Private Lives* swung into action the following week. The two of them were constantly thrown together outside of rehearsals – flitting between radio and TV studios for interviews, meeting journalists in hotel lounges, sitting in the back of cabs as they darted around town from one booking to the next. They posed together for photographs and perched side-by-side on the sofa of every chat show in the country.

Mimi was relieved that there was no lingering awkwardness between them about what had happened the other night. They'd fallen back into an easy dynamic as friends and colleagues, and they had a good double-act going as they talked up the show and fielded the same questions over and over – most of them aimed at Rocco.

'What is it about this play that appeals to you?'

'How long have you two known each other?'

'Why Halfpenny Lane?'

Mimi liked to think Rocco wasn't just being chivalrous

when he said that working with her had been a big part of the incentive for him. But she was under no illusions that Rocco was the story and she was surplus to requirements, mere set dressing to balance out the colourful chat-show sofas. She'd be asked a few polite questions about the history of Halfpenny Lane and its revival before the host inevitably turned their attention to Rocco and his glittering Hollywood career.

She didn't mind. It was great publicity for the play, and though she usually hated to be upstaged by anybody, in this case she was happy to take a back seat. She enjoyed talking about *Private Lives* and she got to wax lyrical about Coward's spiky wit while never missing an opportunity to slip in something about how sexy the play was. 'Considered so risqué in its day it was almost censored' had become her catchphrase – just in case anyone needed a further incentive to buy tickets for the live stream or get along to Halfpenny Lane when it opened hoping for returns.

She loved having a chance to talk about Halfpenny Lane and her Great-aunt Detta who'd founded the theatre. She was pleased when a couple of the older TV presenters who interviewed them remembered Detta and spoke of her fondly as a tour de force in Irish theatre and a great character. Rocco seemed to have picked up on it, and she was touched that now whenever he was asked why he'd chosen Halfpenny Lane for his return to the stage, he mentioned having known Detta personally, giving Mimi a cue to talk about the great-aunt who'd been such a big influence on her and her sisters.

On Friday they had a feature for a glossy magazine with an accompanying photoshoot at the Clarence Hotel, with a lunch laid on afterwards by the magazine. They were styled as their *Private Lives* characters, the art deco backdrop of the hotel lounge conjuring the appropriate air of glamour and sophistication, and they spent half the morning wrapped around each other on a velvet couch in various poses, gazing adoringly into each other's eyes, cocktails in hand.

Afterwards they were interviewed by a pretty young journalist named Joanna, who flirted outrageously with Rocco throughout. Mimi already knew the piece would start with lavish descriptions of his deep brown eyes and honey-gold skin kissed by the California sun. But it would all help sell the show, so she swallowed down her annoyance – and Joanna did make a noble effort to include Mimi, throwing her a bone every so often with a question about Halfpenny Lane or her own theatrical career.

They were joined for lunch at a nearby restaurant by a couple of editors and everyone who had worked on the photoshoot. Once again, Rocco was the centre of attention, and Mimi could tell the stylist seated next to her and gamely engaging her in conversation felt she'd drawn the short straw.

Mimi found it all rather wearing and she was relieved this was their final press engagement of the week. She knew the publicity circuit was a necessary evil, but she resented it eating into rehearsal time, and she found it hard to smile benignly and make small talk when she was itching to get back to work.

'Thank goodness that's over,' she said with a heartfelt sigh as she and Rocco walked back to Halfpenny Lane together for afternoon rehearsals. They'd both manfully resisted all offers of champagne at lunch, while the magazine crew laid into a couple of bottles.

'I've had worse gigs.'

'So have I. But I'd rather be rehearsing.'

'Me too.' Rocco smiled.

'Sive wants us to go shopping with her tomorrow, if you're free.'

'Us? What for?'

'Costumes for the play.' Sive was Halfpenny Lane's unofficial wardrobe mistress and costume designer. She was handy with a needle and thread, and they saved a lot of money on costume hire by trawling vintage stores for suitable clothes and adapting them to fit, as well as mending what remained of the theatre's old stock. It was another point in favour of *Private Lives* that there would be lots of clothes suitable for its 1930s setting available in the retro stores around town. Mimi and her sisters bought most of their own clothes from vintage stores and charity shops, so they knew all the best places to look.

'I have a house viewing in the afternoon,' Rocco said. 'Actually, I was going to ask you if you'd come with me.'

'Me?'

'Yeah, I'd like to get your opinion. It's always good to have another pair of eyes, isn't it?'

'True.' But if all he wanted was a second opinion, surely he'd ask one of his sisters or his parents. Still, she wasn't going to argue. She liked viewing houses, and she was curious about what sort of place he was looking for. Besides, she couldn't help the little surge of hope it gave her that Rocco wanted her back as more than a friend. Perhaps he and Willow were drifting apart, and his coming here to do this play was the beginning of the end. He'd sounded shifty and evasive at lunch when one of the editors had asked him if Willow would come over to see the show.

Besides,' Rocco said, 'I'd like to get your approval. Since we're friends now, you'll be spending lots of time wherever I live.'

A slow smile crept across Mimi's face. 'I might even need my own bedroom.' Or she might not …

'We could look into that, sure.'

'Okay, I'll come. We can go shopping with Sive in the morning?'

'Cool.'

'So where is this place? Millionaire Row?'

'Rathmines.' He took his phone out of his pocket, pulled up the listing on the estate agent's website and handed the phone to her.

'Nice!' It was a red-brick end-of-terrace Victorian house on a leafy square that Mimi knew well, and the asking price was just over two million euro.

'It's not far from you,' Rocco said.

'No.' But Mimi and her sisters could only afford to live where they did because they'd inherited the house from their parents. They'd never have been able to afford rent in their old neighbourhood on their meagre incomes.

'It's gorgeous,' she said, flicking through the photos.

'I'd have to make a few changes, obviously.'

'Don't tell me you'd think of removing the timber cladding on that bedroom ceiling?' Mimi said with mock horror.

'What can I say? I'm a philistine,' Rocco said with a laugh.

'It'd be like sleeping in a coffin.' Mimi shuddered. 'But apart from some dodgy décor, it's a great house.'

'The viewing's at three.'

'Will I meet you there?'

'Or we could get some lunch after shopping and go together.'

'Yeah, okay.' She shouldn't be so surprised at the suggestion. She had to keep reminding herself they were friends now, and it was perfectly normal and above board for them to have lunch together. Nothing untoward was going to happen at a house viewing.

19

———

'No Aoife?' Rocco asked when he met Sive and Mimi the next morning.

'No, she's doing a voice workshop,' Sive said. 'But she might join us later for lunch.'

'Or she might not,' Mimi said, knowing that Aoife would most likely opt to spend the rest of the day with Jonathan instead. He was working long hours in his new law firm, so time together at the weekends was precious.

It was a beautiful day, and the city centre streets were bustling with life as the three of them strolled through town. The pavement cafes were filled with groups of people enjoying the sunshine, eating breakfast and catching up with friends over coffee. Mimi was aware of eyes swivelling in their direction as people spotted Rocco, a few of them giving him a discreet nod of acknowledgement as they passed. A giggling trio of young girls stopped him for a selfie, and he willingly obliged, chatting with them briefly before carrying on.

They spent the morning trawling through all their favourite vintage clothing stores and had a lot of fun rummaging through the rails together and trying things on. They found a gorgeous burgundy silk smoking jacket for Rocco and a very glamorous eau-de-nil kimono with a peacock print for Mimi to wear in Act Two, which Amanda and Elyot spent lounging around in pyjamas and robes at Amanda's Paris flat. They also got Mimi a beautiful bias-cut evening gown in cream satin for Act One. Rocco's eyes widened appreciatively when she emerged from the changing room wearing it.

'Wow! No wonder I want you back.'

Mimi's breath caught as they locked eyes in the mirror.

'Cut that out,' Sive said lightly, swatting him out of the way playfully, 'and go try on that suit I found you.' She moved behind Mimi to get a closer look at the dress. Mimi was glad to have her there as a sort of buffer. She felt on safer ground with Sive around to keep the atmosphere light, and she could relax and enjoy the shopping trip knowing things weren't in danger of getting intense between her and Rocco.

'It's a little long, but I can easily hem it,' Sive said, head tilted to the side as she inspected Mimi's reflection. 'Otherwise, I think it's perfect, don't you?'

'Yes, let's get it.'

'How are you getting on in there, Rocco?' Sive called in the direction of the curtained changing room.

'Well … I've got it on … sort of.'

'Come on out and let's see you.'

'Prepare to have your world blown.' The curtain swept back and Rocco stepped into the shop. 'Behold,' he said, spreading his arms wide.

Mimi gave a shriek of laughter, and Sive collapsed in giggles. The suit was way too small. The trousers barely buttoned across his stomach and the jacket was so tight he couldn't put his arms down fully.

'You look like a reject from the sausage factory,' Mimi said through her laughter.

'Irresistible, right?' Rocco grinned. 'I mean, who doesn't love an overstuffed sausage?'

Mimi loved his lack of vanity and his ability to laugh at himself, despite being one of the most beautiful men she'd ever seen. 'I am fond of a Cumberland now and then,' she said. 'But I wouldn't want to marry one.'

'Why did they make people so small in those days?' Rocco complained, frowning at himself in the mirror. 'I mean, I'm not even fat! This isn't fair. I demand a recount.'

'Maybe I could let it out,' Sive said, chewing her lip as she eyed him in the mirror.

'Not enough to fit a whole other person,' Mimi said, wiping tears from her eyes.

'It's a shame. It's such a beautiful suit.' Sive sighed.

'I could go on a diet?' Rocco offered. 'Or play the whole thing arms akimbo.' He moved around stiffly, demonstrating.

Sive laughed. 'Maybe it would do for Mitch?'

Mimi shook her head. 'Mitch is skinny, but he's too tall. The trousers would be skimming his calves.'

'Okay, let's keep looking.' Sive's mouth twitched with laughter as Rocco turned and shuffled back to the changing room with difficulty, barely able to move for fear of ripping the seams. 'Be careful taking it off!' she called after him. 'We don't want to have to pay for it.'

They had a successful morning after that. They found another suit for Rocco, and Sive picked up an evening dress she thought would work for Sybil's second appearance in Act One. She hadn't taken Andrea's measurements yet, but she was well known at the shop and the owner assured her she could return it if it didn't work. She also bought some accessories – a beaded evening bag, some rhinestone jewellery and a couple of hats. She was always on the lookout for interesting bits and pieces to add to their stock.

While Sive was rummaging among handbags and gloves at their final stop, Mimi drifted off to rake through the rails of clothes. 'Ooh, look at this!' She called to Sive, pulling a gorgeous 1960s faux fur leopard-print coat off the rail. She inspected it from every angle, running her hand over the soft fur. It was in perfect condition.

She slipped it from its hanger, and Sive came to join her at the mirror as she pulled it on.

'It's gorgeous!' Sive said.

Mimi beamed, turning this way and that and checking her reflection. It really was beautiful, and she'd always wanted a coat like it. 'Oh, I love it!' It was so …

'It's so you,' Rocco said, coming up behind them and looking at her in the mirror. 'You should get it.'

'How much?' Sive asked.

Mimi turned over the tag hanging from the sleeve and her face fell. 'A hundred and fifty,' she said with a grimace.

'Oh, pity,' Sive smiled sympathetically.

'Oh, well, never mind,' Mimi said as she removed the coat. She hung it back on the rail. 'Are we ready for lunch? Because I'm starving.'

Armed with their purchases, they headed to a nearby Italian restaurant with outdoor seating and ate big bowls of pasta accompanied by crisp white wine. As Mimi had predicted, Aoife didn't join them. She texted to say she was going over to Jonathan's after her workshop, and she'd be spending the night at his place.

'I'm so glad you're moving back to Dublin, Rocco,'

Sive said, twisting linguini onto her fork. 'It's great having you here – the old gang back together.'

'It's great to be back.'

'You're like the brother we never had.' She laid her head on his shoulder affectionately. 'Except for Mimi, of course.'

'I should hope not,' Rocco said, his gaze flicking to Mimi opposite him. 'There are laws against that sort of thing.' His eyes darkened and Mimi felt heat creep up her face.

'Do you want to come and look at this house with us?' she asked Sive. She suddenly felt anxious about losing her chaperone for the rest of the day. 'If that's okay with you,' she added to Rocco.

'Of course.' He turned to Sive with a smile. 'The more, the merrier.'

'In that case, yes. I'd love to. Where is it?'

Rocco took out his phone and showed her the listing.

'Oh, I love those houses,' Sive said. 'I've always wanted to see around one.' She handed the phone back to Rocco. 'Are you going to buy it?'

'I haven't even seen it yet.'

'But you probably will, won't you? It looks perfect.'

'Unless that's trick photography and it turns out it's actually a kip – yeah, I probably will.'

Mimi experienced a twinge of envy. Rocco could talk about buying a house just like that, when she couldn't even afford to buy a second-hand coat she wanted. She knew that was largely down to the choices she'd made and she didn't regret them, but sometimes she couldn't help thinking it would be nice to just get whatever you wanted and not have to think about money.

'We'll practically be neighbours,' Sive said gleefully.

. . .

They lingered so long over lunch and had so many bags, Rocco decided they should get a taxi to the viewing. It was a beautiful well-preserved period house – two storeys over a basement, with steps up to the front door that was painted a cheery yellow.

The estate agent met them outside and shook hands with all of them, introducing himself as Tom. Mimi could tell that he was making a strenuous effort to act cool and professional, and not to appear starstruck by Rocco as he showed them inside. In the hall, he handed them all brochures and gave Rocco a brief rundown of the sale details before inviting them to look around for themselves.

Mimi couldn't help imagining herself living here as they wandered together from room to room. In a different life, she and Rocco might both be returning from LA triumphant and buying this place together. The house had been recently renovated, and the finish was impeccable. There were dark hardwood floors, a large kitchen/diner with midnight blue cabinets and marble worktops, and double doors leading out onto a sunny patio with steps up to a lushly planted garden. The big bay windows in the living room overlooked the gated park in the centre of the square, and the sounds of children playing drifted across the street.

There were a few things Mimi would change – she wasn't a fan of the tartan wallpaper in the study, and the wooden cladding on the attic ceiling would have to go. But otherwise, it was perfect.

'So, what do you think?' Rocco asked as Tom closed the door behind them and they skipped down the steps.

'I love it!' Sive beamed excitedly.

'Me too,' Mimi said. 'It's great.'

'That's unanimous, then,' Rocco said.

'Are you going to put in an offer?' Sive asked.

'I think I will.'

'It's so you,' Mimi said, echoing his earlier words. 'You should definitely get it.'

Rocco was getting a taxi to his parents' house where he was due for dinner, and they dropped Mimi and Sive home on the way. Mimi waved him off, pleased that they'd managed to spend a whole day together not at work without anything inappropriate happening. This friends thing might actually be doable.

20

'LAST DAY OF REHEARSALS,' Sive said to Mimi the following Friday as they ate breakfast together. 'Then it's hell week.' She gave a mock shudder. 'Though actually I don't know why they call it that. It's all heaven to me.'

Mimi smiled at her. 'Me too. I'm looking forward to it.'

'I didn't think you were a fan.'

Mimi shrugged. 'Maybe I've evolved. It's exciting seeing it all coming together.'

Tech week – also known not-so-affectionately in theatre circles as hell week – was when all the disparate elements of a show came together for the first time and the performance was rehearsed in its entirety with sets, lighting, sound, costumes and props all in place. It was thrilling seeing the production come alive, and all the hard work of rehearsals paying off. But tech rehearsals were also notoriously tedious, with lots of waiting around as scenes were repeated over and over until lighting cues and blocking were fine-tuned and any problems ironed out. It was a gruelling process, the stop/start nature of rehearsals leading to long hours, late nights and frayed tempers.

'Yeah, it's fun,' Sive said. 'I love seeing the set for the first time, and everyone's costumes – not to mention tripping over furniture that didn't use to be there, scrabbling around backstage for your props, trying to work out your route around the stage.' She laughed. 'At least you've rehearsed at Halfpenny Lane, so it won't be completely new to you.'

Mimi nodded. 'There are advantages to not being able to afford a separate rehearsal space.'

'We've made a virtue of our shortcomings.'

'Morning.' Aoife yawned as she shuffled into the kitchen. She flicked on the kettle and put a slice of bread in the toaster, then folded her arms and leaned against the counter. 'I suppose you won't be home for dinner tonight,' she said to Mimi.

'I don't expect so.' She'd been going out for post-rehearsal drinks with the cast and crew most evenings.

'Is everything set for next week?' Aoife asked Sive, turning her back to them as the kettle came to the boil and her toast popped simultaneously.

'It will be. We're building the set at the weekend.'

'*We?*' Aoife carried her tea and toast to the table and sat beside Mimi.

'You know you're a rubbish carpenter?' Mimi said. 'Sorry to be blunt, but it's *my* arse on the line. I don't want the furniture collapsing under me.'

Sive grinned, impervious to Mimi's insult to her skills. 'Don't worry, I'll just be painting flats and humping things around. It's all hands on deck.'

'All *stagehands*,' Mimi said dryly. 'I don't think it really befits one of the directors to be humping scenery around.'

'That's not the kind of operation we run and you know it,' Sive said, smiling happily.

'True.'

'Do you need any help?' Aoife asked. 'Jonathan and I could muck in.'

'Me too,' Mimi said. 'You know I was only joking. I like our bootstrap ethos.'

'You need to conserve your energy for tech week,' Aoife told her.

'Yes, you're the talent,' Sive agreed. 'And there's no need for you and Jonathan to help either,' she said to Aoife. 'Thanks for the offer, but Sam's rounded up plenty of volunteers.'

'Sam?' Mimi frowned. She didn't like the idea that Sive was working on the scenery because she wanted to spend time with Sam.

'You know he's been helping Cara a lot – and Nina and everyone.'

'I know he's very good at ingratiating himself.'

'That's mean!' Sive gasped.

Mimi felt a stab of guilt. Sive was right. Sam didn't deserve that, and she'd regretted the words even as she said them.

'He loves Halfpenny Lane almost as much as we do, and he really goes above and beyond. He's even acting as your pretend boyfriend. I don't know what you've got against him.'

'Don't you?' Mimi arched an eyebrow meaningfully. 'We almost lost Halfpenny Lane thanks to him.'

'But it all worked out in the end, didn't it?'

'No thanks to Sam,' Mimi said obstinately.

'Aren't you ever going to forgive him for that? You can't hold it against him forever,' Sive said plaintively.

'I don't see why not,' Mimi said with a flippant shrug. 'I'm good at grudges.'

'I do think we should move on from that,' Aoife said. 'Sam made some mistakes, and it ended up affecting us in a roundabout way. But he's overcome his problem, and you see how hard he's working at the theatre to prove himself.'

Mimi had to concede that was true. No one worked harder for Halfpenny Lane than Sam. He practically lived at the theatre these days. He set up the rehearsal space, made tea and coffee, bought pastries and organised the green room, assisted Nina and acted as Cara's right-hand man on top of his official usher job, tearing tickets and making the safety announcement for the evening performance. He'd happily spend his weekend painting scenery, hammering platforms together, marking out the stage with gaff tape and humping bits of scenery around. And he'd do it all with a smile on his face because he loved being part of it, which Mimi could relate to. He was a constantly cheerful, friendly presence, and never seemed to have a down day or to get annoyed no matter what he was asked to do. She liked Sam a lot when she thought about it. She just didn't like him for Sive.

'You're right,' she said, relenting. 'I'm not being fair. He's paid his dues, and I don't hold it against him anymore, honestly.'

Sive gave her a relieved smile.

'So we can all put it behind us?' Aoife looked at her hopefully.

'Well, if I was able to forgive *your* boyfriend for almost taking Halfpenny Lane from us,' she said teasingly to Aoife, 'I suppose I can find it in my heart to forgive mine.'

Mimi loved the rehearsal process. Sometimes she found it hard to say whether she enjoyed it more than the actual performance. But this time she was relieved it was almost over and they were moving into the next stage of the production. Working with Rocco so intensely on a daily basis was challenging, and she was looking forward to some respite. It was draining coping with her own heightened emotions on top of throwing herself into her role. And while the chemistry between them was great for the show, leaning into it day after day was messing with her head, blurring the lines between fiction and reality.

When rehearsals finished, she never wanted the kissing to stop, and she felt dizzy and disoriented leaving behind the cocoon of Amanda's glamorous Paris flat, the warmth of Rocco's arms around her, the heat of his body against hers. She could happily have lived in that world forever, sniping at Rocco, making out with Rocco, listening to him say how much he wanted her. It was equal parts torture and bliss, because then the scene would end and she'd be abruptly thrust back to reality with a thud.

The final rehearsal went brilliantly. Everyone was on fire, spurring each other on to up their game, and the heat between Mimi and Rocco was palpable. Mimi was wired as they walked off the stage together that evening, fizzing with a particular blend of adrenaline. It itched under her skin, leaving her edgy and agitated. She knew all that would ease it was to kiss Rocco again, to feel his hands on her, to tear at his clothes. Then he turned to her, his eyes burning into hers, and she knew – she just *knew* – that he felt the same.

They'd barely got into the wings when he glanced behind him, then grabbed her hand and pulled her into the tiny cubicle they used for quick changes, kicking the door shut behind them. They moved together with equal urgency, as if by silent agreement. Mimi took Rocco's face in her hands, pulling his head down to hers as he pressed her against the wall of the tiny space. Then his mouth was on hers and her arms were around his neck, her fingers raking through his hair. They kissed fiercely, hungrily, while their hands roamed, clutching frantically at each other.

'What if someone comes in?' Mimi breathed between kisses.

Rocco lifted his head a fraction. 'We're rehearsing,' he panted back, his breath hot on her lips.

She nodded, burying her fingers in his hair as he kissed her again.

'How was that?' he murmured, barely lifting his mouth from hers.

'Good.' She nodded. 'But needs work.'

Wordlessly, he pulled her closer and bent his head to her again.

'Better,' she said breathlessly.

'Do you think we should …' Mimi's senses leapt as he ran his tongue along her lower lip.

'It would make it more authentic?' Her eyes clung hungrily to his mouth, greedy to have it back on hers.

He pulled her closer, his hands firm on her waist. She melted against him as his mouth opened over hers, her hands roving over his back and tugging at his shirt, seeking the heat of his bare skin. Their breathing became ragged as they kissed on and on. Mimi ran her hands over the muscles of his shoulders and nuzzled her face against the stubble on his cheek, loving the rasp of it against her skin. She was consumed by him and still she couldn't get enough. She moaned as his hands slid down to her waist and he pulled her against him.

'I don't know where they've got to.' Andrea's voice, followed by her tinkling laugh, shocked Mimi to her senses.

With a gargantuan effort she pulled away. 'What are we doing?' She blinked up at Rocco.

'Rehearsing, remember.' His eyes were hungry, focused only on her mouth as he reached for her again.

She stepped back, shaking her head. 'I think that's enough rehearsing for one night.'

He closed his eyes, wiping at his mouth with the back of his hand as he released her. 'Are you sure?'

She wasn't sure at all, but one of them had to call a halt. This thing between them was getting out of control. 'I don't think we should rehearse again without Nina.'

He sighed heavily. 'You're probably right.'

'I mean, what about Willow?'

Rocco gave her a pained look. He opened his mouth as if he was about to say something, but then closed it again.

'And Sam,' Mimi mumbled as an afterthought.

'Yeah, you're right. Sorry.' Rocco hung his head, hands on his hips.

'They're looking for us.' She nodded to the door of the cubicle. They couldn't be seen coming out together or it would be obvious what they'd been doing. She put her ear to the door but heard nothing. 'I'll go out first,' she said smoothing her hair. She pressed her palms to her face to cool her cheeks. Then she checked her reflection in the mirror and stepped out into the wings on shaky legs.

'Where did you get to?' Andrea asked, narrowing her beady little eyes at Mimi as she walked into the green room. She was lounging on the sofa with Mitch. Nina and Orla were sitting in the armchairs. 'Sam was looking for you.'

'I had to make a call,' Mimi said, flopping onto the sofa beside Mitch. 'Where is Sam?'

'He's gone on to the pub with Cara and the others. We were waiting for you and Rocco. Where is he?'

Mimi shrugged. 'I don't know. I thought he'd be in here.' She prayed the bloody girl would let it go.

'Ah, here he is,' Andrea said, looking to the door as Rocco came in. 'At last!'

Mimi was relieved he didn't look dishevelled – not at all like he'd just had a make-out session in a cubicle.

'All off to the pub, then?' Andrea said, standing.

'Definitely!' Mimi jumped up and joined the throng heading for the door, grateful for the safety of numbers. She was jittery after her encounter with Rocco, and she needed to decompress in the easy company of her colleagues.

Cara and Sam were already in the pub waiting for them. Mimi took a seat beside Sam and was wedged in on the other side by Mitch, relieved that Rocco wasn't within touching distance. Sam put an arm around her casually when she sat down, and she gave him an affectionate smile that wasn't entirely fake.

She relaxed over drinks as the light-hearted chatter and laughter flowed around her. Everyone was on a high after the rehearsal and looking forward to tech week with a mixture of dread and excitement.

'I can't wait to see the set on Monday,' Andrea said.

'You can have a preview if you want to come and help out at the weekend,' Sam said to her with a cheeky smile.

'No, thanks. I'm planning to stock up on sleep before next week.'

'Any other takers?' Sam looked around the group. 'Mitch?'

Mitch shook his head. 'Sorry. Andrea's got the right idea.' He picked up his pint and drained it.

'Another?' Rocco asked, nodding to the empty glass.

Mitch shook his head. 'Thanks, but that's me done.'

'But it's only nine o'clock,' Mimi protested. 'And it's Friday night!'

'What can I tell you?' Mitch said good-humouredly as

he stood. 'I'm an old man. I need my sleep. And there's a shepherd's pie at home with my name on it.'

'Obviously we can't compete with that,' Sam said.

'I'll come with you,' Nina said to Mitch, pulling on her jacket. 'You've reminded me I'll hardly see my bed next week.'

You're not going to see it tonight either, Mimi thought as she watched them go. She'd been right about them.

'I'll have to love you and leave you,' Sam said when he'd finished his drink.

'You're going?' Mimi asked, alarmed.

'I'm meeting a few of the lads,' he said, standing. 'I told you, remember?'

'Oh yes, the lads. Well, have fun … honey.'

'Thanks.' He leaned down and put an arm around her, then dropped a quick kiss on the top of her head.

'Don't stay out too late,' Cara said to him. 'We have an early start tomorrow, and it's going to be a long day. There's lots to do, and you don't want to be dealing with a banging head.'

'Don't worry, I'm just going for a quick one. I'll be tucked up in my bed by ten, like a good little boy.' He waved cheerily to everyone, and blew a kiss to Mimi, then turned and left.

'Aw, that's so adorable,' Andrea said, hand on her heart.

To Mimi's dismay, it wasn't long before everyone started to murmur about going home.

'We should probably have an early night ourselves,' Cara said to Orla.

'You're helping with the set tomorrow?' Mimi asked Orla. 'You don't have to do that, you know.'

'Oh, I don't mind.' Orla blushed as she smiled at Cara.

'You're going too?' Mimi asked as Andrea stood and

started pulling on a jacket. She didn't think she'd ever be wishing for Andrea's company.

'Sorry. I have a dinner to get to,' Andrea said. 'It's a friend's birthday.'

'I suppose I should think about getting something to eat myself,' Mimi said, swirling the dregs of gin and ice in her glass. 'I'm starving.'

There was a flurry of goodbyes, and suddenly it was just her and Rocco at the table. Mimi swallowed the last of her drink. 'It seems we're the only ones not rushing home to get in an early evening bonk,' she said and regretted it immediately. Thankfully Rocco didn't say anything. She felt him looking at her, but she avoided his gaze.

'Do you want another?' he asked.

'No thanks. I'd better be off myself.'

Rocco finished his pint and they walked together to the door.

'Do you want to get something to eat?' he asked as they stepped outside. The street was busy, the night air filled with a cacophony of boisterous shouts and laughter, the thumping beat of music pouring from open doorways and the distant wail of sirens.

Mimi knew she should say no. She should go home and eat there. She looked at him uncertainly, trying to decide where things were between them now.

'Just dinner,' he said.

'Yeah, why not.'

'Great! Let's see if we can get into Trocadero.'

It was a busy Friday night, and the restaurant looked full when they went in, the maître d' frowning down at his seating plan when Rocco said they didn't have a reservation. But magically, somehow, they got a table – probably down to Rocco, Mimi thought as they were led into the depths of the cosy restaurant. Fame could be a very useful superpower to have.

'We're going Dutch this time,' she said when they were settled with water and menus. 'This time' unnerved her as soon as she'd spoken the words – as if this was a regular thing they did.

Rocco nodded. 'Fair enough.'

She was glad he didn't argue, even though it was an extravagance for her. Men who always insisted on paying on dates annoyed her. It felt so infantilising. Not that this was a date, she reminded herself.

They both ordered pasta, and they got a bottle of red wine. As an afterthought, Mimi decided to order a starter. 'Want to share some deep fried brie?' she asked Rocco. 'I need the soakage.'

'Sounds good,' Rocco said, smiling at the waiter as they handed him their menus.

'It's a while since I've been here,' he said, looking around when the waiter had gone.

The restaurant had a long association with Dublin's theatrical community. Stars of stage and screen had flocked to it over the years, and photographs of many of its famous patrons lined the walls. There were so many familiar faces, Mimi felt like she was surrounded by friends and family. There was a photograph behind Rocco of a much younger Sir Peter Bradshaw, a hell-raising star of Old Hollywood, who'd helped with the fundraising for Halfpenny Lane – as had Margaret Brennan, the Irish theatrical legend and national treasure who was further along the wall.

'I suppose *you'll* be up here the next time I come,' Mimi said, nodding to the photographs.

'*You'll* probably have your picture up here before I do.'

She shook her head. 'I don't bring the same bragging rights.'

She felt slightly light-headed. She hadn't eaten enough and she shouldn't have had drinks at the pub on an empty stomach. When the starter arrived, she fell on it greedily.

She was glad that the earlier tension between her and Rocco seemed to have dissipated, and they chatted easily as they ate, keeping the conversation light. Then, when they'd moved on to coffee and just as Mimi was congratulating herself for having got away with it, Rocco had to go and ruin everything.

'Sorry about earlier,' he said, looking down at his cup.

Mimi shrugged. 'No biggie. A moment of madness.'

'Or a moment of clarity?' he murmured, so softly she had to strain to catch the words.

'What?' Her heart leapt in her throat. This felt dangerous again – wrong. They shouldn't be here, they oughtn't to be having this conversation.

'You know, I think you were right about me having an ulterior motive in coming here.' His gaze was fixed on the table where he was tracing patterns on the tablecloth with one finger. 'Maybe I wanted to test out a theory – prove something to myself.'

'That you could still cut it on the stage?'

'That. And … that I was really over you.'

Mimi's breath stilled, her chest tight. Her mouth was so dry she felt like she was choking. She didn't want to ask, but the words spilled out before she could stop them. 'And what was your conclusion?' She attempted a casual, teasing tone.

The silence stretched out so long she thought he wasn't going to answer. She began to wonder if she'd even said it out loud. Then he looked up and his eyes held hers.

'That I can still cut it on the stage.'

Her sharp intake of breath was audible. 'You shouldn't say things like that to me.' But when he reached across the table and put his hand over hers, she didn't pull away. 'You have a girlfriend.' She left a gap, waiting for him to contradict her, to tell her he was breaking up with Willow, or that their relationship was just a publicity stunt. But he said nothing. 'And I have a boyfriend,' she finished defeatedly. So that was it – he just wanted a fling with her while he was here? When the cat's away … but she didn't want to play with him, not like that.

Rocco nodded, but his fingers continued to play with hers on the table.

'We're friends, remember?' she said desperately, heat building inside her as he turned her hand palm up, his thumb stroking over her wrist.

'Yeah, sorry.' He pulled his hand away.

Mimi felt bereft, longing for him to touch her again. 'Let's get the bill,' she said, signalling to the waiter.

They didn't speak as they finished their coffee and Mimi paid the bill, but there was an air of urgency about them both as they left the restaurant, and Mimi's heart was racing in anticipation as if it had already decided what was going to happen. Once outside, Rocco took her hand and led her into the shadows of the dark alley beside the restaurant. He pulled her into his arms, and for a moment, Mimi gave into the mindless pleasure of his mouth on hers, the heat of his body enveloping her. Then, with a Herculean strength of will, she wrenched her lips from his. She didn't want this, she told herself, even as her treacherous body said otherwise.

'We can't do this,' she breathed, one hand on his chest, holding him away.

He blinked rapidly, his eyes heavy as they dropped to her mouth.

'We *can't*,' she repeated, stepping back.

He raised his eyes to hers and nodded, sighing as he ran a hand through his hair. Her fingers itched to do the same. She clasped them behind her back to stop herself reaching for him again.

'I'm not that person, Rocco. I don't do this. And neither do you. At least you never used—' She broke off as an awful thought struck her. She felt all the muscles of her face drop, along with her stomach. 'You never cheated on me, did you – when we were together?' Her voice was barely more than a whisper.

'No!' He frowned. 'Of course not.'

She realised he wouldn't admit it if he had. But the vehemence of his response, coupled with her gut instinct, told her it was the truth.

'Look, there's something I should tell you about me and Willow. I shouldn't be saying this, but—'

'Then don't. I don't want to hear it. Unless it's that you're breaking up with her.' She looked at him for what felt like minutes, but he said nothing.

'No, I didn't think so. I'm going to call a cab.' She turned on her heel and walked away without looking back.

21

MIMI FELT REFRESHED after a weekend away from the theatre and Rocco. She hadn't told her sisters what had happened on Friday because she was too ashamed to admit it to them. But she'd had time to sort out her feelings in private and to give herself a good talking to. She arrived for the first tech rehearsal on Monday with renewed determination to focus on the work and not let Rocco derail her. They couldn't be more than friends now, and that would have to be enough for both of them.

As usual she arrived well ahead of the scheduled rehearsal time. She was irritated to once again find Andrea already there ahead of her when she walked into the green room.

'Oh my God, have you seen this?' Andrea lifted her head from the newspaper she was poring over.

'No, what?' Mimi asked without real interest as she rummaged in a cupboard for a mug.

'Is this true?'

Mimi turned, irritated. But she almost dropped the

mug she was holding when she looked at the paper Andrea had laid open on the table and was faced with a picture of her and Rocco outside Trocadero on Friday night. Her heart pounded, her breath catching in her throat as she scanned the page. She felt a modicum of relief that there was only the one picture, and it had been taken as they were going in. She and Rocco were walking separately, side by side. But it didn't stop her feeling sick when she thought how damning it *could* have been. She gulped, prickly heat creeping up her neck.

She turned back to the coffee machine and filled her mug as she tried to school her features before facing Andrea again.

'It's true Rocco and I had dinner together on Friday, if that's what you mean' she said casually. 'I didn't realise it was headline news.'

'Everything Rocco does is headline news,' Andrea murmured behind her.

When Mimi turned back, coffee in hand, Andrea was reading the article. Mimi sat beside her and scanned it along with her – she might as well know the worst. The piece was full of speculation about Rocco's relationship with Willow, saying there were rumours of a split, and that he'd been seen 'stepping out in Dublin with former flame Mimi Carroll'.

'Oh, for goodness' sake!' Mimi huffed. 'We weren't "stepping out", we had dinner after the pub, that's all.'

'But it's true you used to be a couple? You told me so yourself.'

'Yes, they got that bit right. But it was a long time ago.'

'Four years, it says here,' Andrea pointed to the article. 'You broke up with Rocco when he moved to LA?'

'That's correct. But we are not "stepping out".' She frowned crossly.

'I'm not even sure what that means.' Andrea gave a tinkling little laugh that grated on Mimi's last nerve. 'You have a funny way of talking sometimes, if you don't mind me saying so.'

'And if I do mind?'

Andrea frowned in confusion.

Mimi heaved an exasperated sigh. 'It means dating. And that,' she nodded at the paper, 'was definitely not a date. We're just friends now – two old friends who are working together.'

'Hmm.' Andrea shot Mimi a sceptical look.

'You went out for lunch with him yourself.' Then she remembered that Andrea *had* considered that a date. She decided a friendly dose of reality might be in order. 'You know what Rocco's like. He's just super-friendly with everyone. Sometimes people take that the wrong way ... read more into it.'

'I suppose.' Andrea lifted her chin, blushing.

'But I've known him long enough to know he's just being friendly and it doesn't mean anything.'

When Andrea got up to make more coffee, Mimi turned the paper towards herself and read the whole piece properly. They'd devoted half a page to the non-story. She was relieved that it focused mainly on speculation about Rocco and Willow's relationship. It said he'd been seen out and about in Dublin with his ex-girlfriend, actress Mimi Carroll, who he was in rehearsals with for *Private Lives* at Halfpenny Lane Theatre. At least it was free advertising for the play, Mimi thought.

Meanwhile, the article stated, Willow seemed to be enjoying the single life in LA and had been pictured out and about with 'gal pal' Kim Harper, further fuelling speculation that the couple were drifting apart. There was a picture of Willow and Kim coming out of a restaurant near Willow's home in Los Feliz, and another of them playing with Kim's dog at the beach.

Mimi was relieved that the piece was so bland. She shuddered to think how much worse it could have been if they'd been snapped leaving the restaurant. How could they have been so reckless? As it was, it was just a photograph of two colleagues going to dinner together. Nothing to see here, folks. They'd got away with it, but they'd been lucky. She wouldn't risk that again.

But contrary to her blasé dismissal of the article to Andrea, she harboured a secret feeling that there might be some substance to it. It would explain a lot about Rocco's behaviour. She knew he wasn't a cheater, and he'd been about to tell her something about his relationship with Willow last night before she cut him off. Maybe the rumours of a break-up were true, and he didn't want to say anything about it before it was official. It would only be respectful to hold off until he'd spoken to Willow in person.

The idea took root and blossomed inside her, and it felt like the sun coming up, throwing new light on everything that had passed between her and Rocco in the last few weeks. The more Mimi thought about it, the more likely it seemed that he wanted her back, and all she had to do was wait …

Tech rehearsal began with everyone in high spirits. The actors spent a bit of time admiring each other's costumes and walking around the stage exploring the set, opening and closing doors, planning their routes around furniture and finding their path from one side of the stage to the other, while mumbling lines under their breath. Sive was on hand to take care of the wardrobe and oversee costume changes. She flitted around backstage helping everyone get ready, and she'd stay for the rehearsal up to the final costume change to see how the clothes worked under the lights and make notes of any adjustments that would be required.

Mitch and Rocco looked very debonair in beautifully cut suits, and Andrea was wearing a pretty floral summer dress with a short-sleeved jacket that Sive had made herself and a little hat she'd found on their shopping expedition. Mimi felt somewhat underdressed in the filmy negligee she wore for her first appearance in Act I.

'Oh wow, this is gorgeous!' Andrea breathed, her face lighting up as she stepped out onto one of the twin terraces where Act I took place.

Mimi smiled across at her from the adjoining terrace, sharing in her excitement. Gillian, the set designer had managed to conjure all the glamour and sophistication of a ritzy hotel in Deauville on scant resources, and the carpenters and team of volunteers had done a wonderful job of bringing her vision to life.

Rocco walked onto the terrace behind Andrea, and Mimi's heart skipped a beat as he glanced across at her and their eyes locked.

'You look amazing,' he said.

'Thank you, darling,' Andrea said playfully in Sybil's accent, turning to him with a coquettish smile.

Mimi blushed, knowing Rocco had been looking at *her* when he'd said it. Her mood lifted by the minute as she continued to familiarise herself with the set, buoyed up by the growing conviction that Rocco was still in love with her, and it was just a matter of time until they'd be together again.

She walked on and off the balcony a few times, opening and closing the French windows, and then she went to find her props backstage. Sam and the stagehands had been busy over the weekend, marking out the floor with gaff tape and setting up the props table in the wings. The table was marked out in blocks, with a space for each item, and each block neatly labelled so that everything could be easily found and put back where it belonged.

'Good job, Sam!' she said, looking up to find him standing beside her.

'Thanks. I'm rather proud of it.'

'Hold onto this guy,' Cara said as she passed, clapping Sam on the shoulder. 'He's a gem.'

Sam grinned, his face flushed with pride.

The production was as much Cara's baby now as Nina's, and she was bustling around, liaising with designers and technicians, managing the stagehands and delegating tasks. She was responsible for running the show – calling the cues, keeping track of timings and coordinating all the disparate elements to make sure the performance ran smoothly.

'I intend to,' Mimi called after her as she strode away. 'Really, well done, Sam.' She threw her arms around him in an excess of emotion, suddenly feeling the need to hug *someone*.

'What's brought this on?' he laughed, rearing back in surprise.

'Can't I be a proud girlfriend?' She smiled at him. 'Cara's right, you're a keeper.'

'If you two can stop canoodling for a minute, I'd like to find my props.' Andrea's teasing voice came from behind Mimi.

'Sorry.' She released Sam, and turned to find Rocco

standing beside Andrea, scowling at the floor. He was jealous, she realised – because he thought this thing with her and Sam was real. Maybe that was what stopped him being more forthright about declaring his feelings. But it was fine; it only made her more convinced she was right. She could set the record straight about her and Sam later. She was itching to talk to Rocco and thrash it all out between them, but there was no time now. She just had to be patient.

Rehearsal was intense, and Mimi had no opportunity to talk privately to Rocco. But it was running through her mind all morning, going over how she'd introduce the subject and give him an opening to come clean about his relationship with Willow. They'd have to clear the air at some stage about what had happened on Friday night, so that would give her a way into the conversation. However, she got the impression Rocco was aware they needed to talk but wanted to put it off as long as possible. He was throwing himself into his role with as much energy as ever, but when their scenes were over, he was keeping a professional distance, and he always seemed to be occupied with someone else in their downtime.

She finally got her chance when she stepped out onto the fire escape for some fresh air during an afternoon break to find Rocco already there. He was standing with his eyes closed, his face tilted to the sun.

'Sorry about the paper,' she said quietly as she closed the door behind her.

He turned to her and smiled. 'It's not your fault.' He shrugged. 'No biggie. I'm used to it.'

'Well, I'm not. I don't know how you stand it, having

people watching your every move like that, sticking their noses into your private life, making up all sorts about you—'

'It's the price you pay, unfortunately.'

'I hope Willow wasn't upset about it,' she said tentatively. 'If she's seen it, that is.'

'Nah, she'll be cool with it. She's used to people writing crap about her. She'll take it with a pinch of salt.'

'Oh. Good.' Mimi nodded. That hadn't got her very far. 'Look, I think we need to talk – clear the air.'

'I'm sorry about Friday,' he said quietly.

She shrugged. 'Not your fault. There was a pair of us in it. But—'

'It won't happen again.' She wasn't sure from his tone whether it was a statement or a question.

She took a deep breath. 'The thing is, about me and Sam—'

He frowned, and opened his mouth to say something, but he was interrupted by his phone ringing. 'Sorry,' he mumbled, looking down at the screen. 'I need to take this.'

She nodded, as he put the phone to his ear.

'Hey, sweetheart,' he said as she pulled open the door to go back inside.

He had his back to her, and she knew she shouldn't, but she lingered a moment on the other side of the door, listening to his side of the conversation.

'Don't worry,' he was saying. 'It's not what you think … I know, but … no, we're still good … Willow, I promise you … believe me, nothing's going to happen … that's all over, she's with someone else now … I'm all yours … as long as you need …'

Mimi's heart sank as she listened. She was such an idiot, giving credence to that stupid newspaper article. Obviously, it was just a load of hogwash, and she should have known better than to buy into it. And it didn't sound like Willow was cool about it at all, she thought as she made her way back to the auditorium. Thank goodness she hadn't come out and told Rocco her relationship with Sam wasn't real.

'Are you okay?' Sam frowned at her in concern as she passed him in the corridor.

'Yeah, I'm fine.' She blinked tears from her eyes, aware that she must look upset. 'Just annoyed about that stupid thing in the paper.'

'Ah, don't let that get to you.'

She stepped closer to Sam as she heard the fire escape door open and close behind her. 'What would help is a kiss from my boyfriend right about now,' she whispered in his ear.

Sam pulled her into his arms without hesitation and kissed her, while Mimi heard Rocco's footsteps as he passed them, returning to the auditorium.

'Better?' Sam grinned, lifting his head.

Mimi nodded. 'Thanks.' She didn't feel better really, but at least she hadn't completely humiliated herself.

'You know, I think this fake boyfriend thing is working,' Sam murmured. 'Rocco didn't look like a happy chap earlier when Andrea accused us of canoodling. He's definitely jealous.'

Maybe. But he was just being a dog in the manger, Mimi thought defeatedly. He'd as good as told her last night that he wasn't over her, and maybe it was true he still had feelings for her. But Willow was the one he was committed to. He was all hers.

. . .

'Sorry we got interrupted earlier,' Rocco said to her when they were alone again. He'd followed her out to the fire escape in their next break.

'It's fine.' She shrugged. 'I think we'd said everything we need to say.'

'Had we?' He frowned. 'You were about to say something about you and Sam …'

'Just that I don't want to hurt him.'

Rocco nodded. 'He's a good guy.'

'I love working with you, Rocco, and I'd like if we could be friends. But that's all it can be. We've both moved on. We're with other people.'

He nodded, smiling sadly.

'That photo was a wake-up call. We were lucky they took it when they did. If it had been later—'

'I know.'

'I won't cheat on Sam. And it's not just about getting caught. Even if no one found out, *I'd* know, and it's not what I want. I can't have a fling with you.'

He frowned. 'That's not what—' He broke off and sighed heavily. 'That's not what I want either.'

'Good. So we stop this now before anyone gets hurt. Agreed?'

Rocco nodded. 'Agreed.'

Mimi returned to rehearsal with a heavy heart, all her hopes of this morning dashed. Still, at least she'd managed to saved face. It wasn't much consolation, but it was something.

'I suppose you saw the "news" about me and Rocco?' she asked her sisters that night as she joined them for a glass of wine in the kitchen. It was after ten when she'd got home and she was exhausted, emotionally and physically drained, but still too wound up to go to bed. She knew she wouldn't sleep.

'That you're stepping out together?' Sive said playfully.

'That he's cheating on Willow with you?' Aoife joined in.

'It's such a load of nonsense!' Mimi fumed, unable to laugh about it. 'Honestly, can two people not have dinner together without—'

'Hey, it's okay,' Sive said, putting a calming hand on her arm. 'We're on your side. We'd much rather Rocco went out with you than Willow Bell.'

'But I'm not going out with him!' Mimi said crossly.

Sive flashed her a look. She didn't say anything, but Mimi knew she was thinking of her confession about kissing him.

'You want to, though, don't you?' Aoife asked, her eyes full of understanding.

Mimi shrugged. 'It doesn't matter what I want,' she said, lifting her chin. 'We broke up and he's moved on. I just have to accept that.'

'Are you sure there's no truth in that article?' Sive asked.

'No!' Mimi frowned, turning to her. 'We were just having dinner.'

'Like when you went to La Cave?' Sive said, giving her a meaningful look.

'What?' Aoife gasped, eyes wide as she turned to Mimi. 'Did something happen between you?'

Mimi blushed. 'Okay, full disclosure, we kissed,' she admitted. 'But that's all, I swear! I called a halt.'

'What about Friday night?' Aoife asked.

'Um … same thing.' Mimi dropped her gaze, unable to meet her sisters' eyes.

'So maybe it's true,' Sive said. 'Maybe Rocco and Willow really are drifting apart.'

Mimi shook her head. 'It's just journalists trying to manufacture something out of nothing because they got some photos. I mean, a woman hanging out at the beach with her friend is hardly the scandal of the century, is it?' She didn't want to admit how much she'd let the article raise her hopes. She'd so wanted it to be true. It was just wishful thinking, she realised now.

'I suppose you're right,' Sive conceded reluctantly. 'When you put it like that.'

'Anyway, I as good as asked him the other night if they were going to break up.'

'Why would you ask him that?' Aoife gasped.

'Because … he said things that made me think he wanted us to get back together. He pretty much said straight out that he's not over me.'

Aoife frowned crossly. 'He shouldn't say things like that to you if he doesn't mean them.'

'How do you know he doesn't?' Sive said. 'He did kiss her after all.'

'It was just a moment of madness,' Mimi said. 'It won't happen again. We agreed.'

'But you want it to, don't you?' Aoife asked, looking at her carefully.

Mimi felt her face crumple, and suddenly she couldn't hold back the tears that were streaming down her cheeks. She nodded, unable to speak for the sobs that were clogging her throat. 'Oh god, I'm still completely in love with him!' she sobbed.

Aoife and Sive put an arm around her on either side as she sobbed helplessly.

'Ugh, sorry!' She shook her head, regaining control.

Aoife handed her a tissue and she wiped her eyes. 'I don't know what came over me.'

'You've obviously been holding that in for a while,' Sive said. 'You needed to let it out.'

'It must be hell for you working with him every day,' Aoife said.

'I suppose it is.' She hadn't realised what a strain she'd been under the past few weeks, trying to fight her feelings for Rocco, battling the passion that had flared up between them whenever they were alone together, dealing with the guilt afterwards for giving into it. 'Heaven too, in ways.' She smiled. 'But mostly hell.' She wiped her eyes with the tissue. 'I thought I could be all grown-up and professional about it, and I'd be fine with being friends with him. But it turns out—'

'You're not,' Aoife finished for her.

'No. Not even a little bit.' She sighed. 'I'm a mess.'

'You could still pull out,' Sive said gently.

Aoife nodded. 'Andrea would be only too happy to step into your role, and we wouldn't mind. No judgement. If that's what you need—'

'And do what? Take to my bed with a broken heart like some tragic heroine from an opera? No,' Mimi said firmly, looking at her sisters in turn. 'No way. I'm not letting this stupid obsession with Rocco ruin everything.'

'Are you sure?'

'Absolutely.'

'But how do you know Rocco doesn't feel the same way as you?' Sive persisted. 'You haven't told him you're still in love with him, have you?'

'Of course not.' Thank goodness. She shuddered to think how close she'd come to doing just that. 'He's with Willow. It would be wildly inappropriate – not to mention humiliating. Anyway, I heard him on the phone to her this afternoon. It sounded like she was upset about this "story", and he told her she had nothing to worry about, that there's nothing going on between us.'

I'm all yours. His words echoed in her head. 'He's definitely not breaking up with her.' She took a big gulp of wine. 'Anyway, it's all great publicity for the play,' she said staunchly. 'That's the main thing.'

'True,' Aoife said. 'Every cloud …'

ANY LINGERING HOPES Mimi was harbouring that Rocco wanted her back were dashed as soon as she picked up her phone a couple of days later. Her obsession with Rocco had led her to stalking Willow online – obsessively checking out her social media, poring over articles about her, hunting for clues. As a result she was now promptly served up all sorts of content relating to her. And this morning there was a lot.

It seemed she'd posted a story on her Instagram during the night – early evening in LA. It was something bland about enjoying the end of a day on the beach, her hand around a wine glass, the main focus of the photo the view of the ocean in front of her. But eagle-eyed followers had zeroed in on her hand and the sparkling diamond on her ring finger. The story had been removed, but not before several people had taken screenshots, and it was now being widely shared across the internet, along with an avalanche of speculation about the story behind it.

Mimi had been about to get up, but instead she sank back against the pillows, scrolling miserably through social media. Willow's mundane caption had now been replaced with the news that she and Rocco were engaged as people added their own narrative to the photo.

'Tell us you're engaged to the hottest guy on the planet without telling us you're engaged to the hottest guy on the planet' one fan posted.

Obviously, this hadn't just happened. They must have got engaged before Rocco had come to Dublin – who knew how long before – and they'd just been waiting to announce it. Mimi felt sick, paralysed, completely poleaxed as she thought back to what Rocco had said the other night. God, she was such a chump. She'd asked him if they were breaking up, when *this* was what he'd wanted to tell her about their relationship. It was what he'd been hinting at all along – *Wow! magazine doesn't know everything … I could tell you things that would shock and awe …* And she'd chosen to believe it was that they were splitting up, because she'd wanted to so desperately. She'd even given serious consideration to Andrea's theory that they weren't a real couple. He must have been trying to break it to her gently because she'd made it so painfully obvious she was still in love with him.

Well, she couldn't stay in bed all day wallowing, she thought, throwing back the duvet with a determination she didn't really feel. But she'd just have to go through the motions and get on with things.

As soon as she went into the kitchen for breakfast, she knew Aoife and Sive had already seen the story. They were sitting at the table and eyed her warily as she entered the room.

'I suppose you've seen the news?' she said, determined to confront it head-on and get it over with. They'd done enough pussyfooting around over the last couple of years where Rocco was concerned.

'Yeah, we saw.' Aoife gave her a gentle smile.

'So, they're engaged,' she said, turning her back to them as she made coffee. She couldn't bear their pitying looks.

'It looks like it,' Aoife said.

'But looks can be deceiving,' Sive said as Mimi joined them at the table.

'I did tell you they weren't breaking up.'

'I can't believe he's engaged to Willow Bell, of all people!' Sive said.

'I don't know why that's so surprising,' Mimi said, keeping her voice even. 'She's his girlfriend, after all. She seems like the logical person for him to get engaged to if you ask me.'

'It's just … I really thought you two were going to get back together.'

Me too, Mimi thought. She'd only realised how deep her delusion ran when she saw the news about his suspected engagement. She was taken aback by what a blow it was. It didn't make sense. She knew he and Willow were together, and he'd told her flat out they weren't breaking up. But somehow this was on another level. It felt so final.

'Are you okay?' Aoife asked her.

She nodded, tears springing to her eyes. She clenched her jaw to staunch them. 'I'm fine.' She lifted her chin. 'It's just a bit of a shock. I suppose I didn't realise it was this serious between them.' Even as she said it, Mimi heard how absurd she sounded. After all, she knew nothing about Willow and Rocco's relationship really – no more than all these people avidly gossiping about them online.

'They haven't actually *said* that they're engaged,' Sive pointed out. 'Maybe it's just a stupid rumour.'

'Maybe,' Mimi said dully. Amid all the conjecture,

there were plenty of people theorising that there was no engagement, forensically examining the nature of the ring and which hand it was on, pointing out that Willow wasn't given to posting about her private life online and was unlikely to announce her engagement in an oblique Instagram story.

But either way, it was a reality check for Mimi. Engaged or not, Rocco and Willow were a couple. They were committed to each other – *I'm all yours* – and if he *was* going to propose to anyone, it would be to Willow. She'd been living in a fantasy, as deluded as those fans who were acting as if Rocco's engagement was a personal betrayal. At least she had closure now, and she could move on once and for all. There'd be no more wondering and hoping and speculating. She knew exactly where she stood with Rocco – firmly in the past.

'Oh god,' she groaned, burying her head in her hands as a thought occurred to her. 'You know the worst thing about this?'

'What?'

She lifted her head. 'Bloody Andrea. She's going to be unbearable about it.'

Andrea didn't disappoint.

'I suppose you've seen the news?' she asked Mimi as soon as she stepped into the green room later that morning. Inevitably she was there before everyone else. She always was. She was sitting on one of the sofas, scrolling through her phone. Mimi didn't even have to glance at it to know that she was referring to the story about Rocco and Willow's engagement.

'Yes, I saw it,' she said tightly. She bent to take a mug from the cupboard, feigning indifference. Her back to

Andrea, she busied herself making coffee, and Andrea fell silent.

When she turned around, Andrea's head was still bent over her phone, her thumb scrolling.

'Did you do anything last night?' Mimi asked brightly, hoping to steer the conversation away from Rocco. No such luck!

'Can you believe it?' Andrea wailed as Mimi flopped onto the sofa beside her and put her mug on the coffee table.

'It's a bit of a surprise all right,' Mimi said blandly, trying to play it down. She took a sip of coffee, wishing it wasn't too early for something stronger. This was going to be a long day.

'I can't believe he'd do this to me!'

'Sorry, to *you*?' Mimi asked, startled into engaging. She really didn't want to talk about bloody Rocco, but she couldn't help herself. What was the silly woman going on about now?

'Yes, to me. You know we … had a thing?'

'Did you?' Mimi frowned, confused.

'I told you, remember? I asked if you were okay with it.'

'Yes, but I didn't think—'

'He asked me to his party, remember?'

'He invited all of us.'

'But I was sort of a co-host.'

Mimi gritted her teeth and said nothing. She knew Andrea had volunteered to go early and help Rocco set up. Somehow in her mind that made them a couple?

'And we went out together – just the two of us. I can't believe he was stringing me along all this time.'

'All this time? It was one lunch – and it wasn't a date. I thought I'd explained that. Rocco is just a friendly person. You know men and women can be friends, right?'

'Yes, but … it felt like more than that. I really thought we had something, you know – a real connection? It may have just been one date, but—'

'For god's sake, it *wasn't a date*!' Mimi said through clenched teeth. 'And even if it had been, if he was cheating on anyone, it was her.' She nodded to the photo of the shiny, smiling Willow on Andrea's phone. 'She's the one who should be pissed off about it if he *was* leading you on – which I really don't think he was.'

'I just … I know it was just lunch, but I thought it was the start of something.'

'Oh, cry me a river!' Mimi snapped, losing her patience.

Andrea gasped, her eyes filling with tears.

'Sorry,' Mimi said, her tone not in the slightest conciliatory. 'But you went on one date with the guy – if you insist on calling it that. How do you think *I* feel?'

Andrea blinked at her in bewilderment. 'What do you mean? Was he coming on to you too?' Her eyes were wide with shock.

'No, of course not,' Mimi said briskly. 'But we were together for *four years* – in a proper relationship, living together and everything.'

'Sure, but … that was all over ages ago, right?'

'Yes, but—'

Andrea's eyes widened. 'Did you think you were going to get back with him? Did something happen between you … here?' She pursed her lips. 'It seems he's been leading us both a merry dance.'

'No! Nothing happened.' Mimi jiggled her foot under the table, feeling irritated and impatient, not just with Andrea but with herself. Her own reaction to the news had been just as nonsensical, really. She'd fooled herself into believing she and Rocco might get back together. 'It just took me by surprise, that's all. But neither of us has any reason to be upset with Rocco about this. We're both just being silly. Did he kiss you when you went on your … when you had lunch together?'

'No, but—'

'Did he sleep with you?'

'Of course not.' Andrea gave a harsh little laugh. 'We were in a burrito bar.'

'There you are, then. He behaved like a perfect gentleman. He didn't do anything wrong.' Mimi was shamefully aware that the same couldn't be said for her dinner with Rocco.

Andrea opened her mouth to protest.

'And no, going for burritos with someone is not cheating. The man has to eat, after all.'

'Actually, I had a Paleo box,' Andrea said smugly.

Of course you did, Mimi thought.

'But he led me to believe it was something more.'

'More than a Paleo box?'

Andrea giggled. 'No, that there was something more between us.'

'How so?' Mimi frowned. 'Did he touch your leg under the table? Hold your hand? Play with your hair? Ask you back to his place for the night?'

'No, none of that.' She frowned, and Mimi could tell she was mentally going back over the lunch and reframing it in her mind. 'It was just like having lunch with a friend or colleague really, I suppose,' she said, as if seeing it for the first time. 'There was no more action than if I'd gone out with you. No offence.'

Mimi blinked, not sure what 'no offence' was supposed to mean in the context. 'So, no harm done, then.'

'I suppose not,' Andrea said grudgingly.

Mimi was relieved when Mitch breezed in, putting an end to the tortuous conversation.

'Willow's coming over next week,' Rocco told her later that day.

They were sitting side by side in the auditorium, speaking in low murmurs. Andrea, Mitch and Orla were on stage running through the opening of Act Three over and over, while a lighting cue was adjusted.

'She is?' Mimi blushed at how alarmed she sounded.

'Don't worry, it's not to beat you up,' he said with a crooked smile.

Of course not – as if Willow Bell would be threatened by *her*.

'She wants to see the play. She'll be here for opening night.'

Mimi smiled. That would be great publicity for the theatre. 'So she wants to check you out on stage?'

'And to spend time with her boyfriend, of course.' He grinned.

'I'm sure your family are dying to meet her.'

He was silent for a moment. 'I'm not engaged by the way,' he said then, darting a look at her. 'In case you were wondering.'

'You're not?' She hated how relieved she felt. It didn't change anything, she told herself firmly.

He shook his head. 'Willow just happened to post a photo where she was wearing a ring.' He rolled his eyes. 'Do you think I need to make an announcement?'

'Maybe let it be known. Andrea's acting like a jilted bride.'

'Well, Willow coming over here should clear up any misunderstandings.'

Mimi knew Rocco probably didn't intend it that way, but that felt like as much of a dig at her as Andrea.

'And hopefully it'll put paid to all these stupid rumours.'

'Won't her coming here to see you rather confirm them?' She frowned.

'Not about our "engagement". I mean the rumours about us drifting apart.'

'Right. They're definitely not true, then?'

He gave her a strange look. 'They're about as true as what that article was implying about you and me.'

Mimi held his gaze, not sure how to take that. He looked away first. 'Well, she seems lovely.'

His features relaxed into a wide smile that twisted her heart. 'Yeah, Willow's great. You'll like her. She's really funny and warm and sweet.' Her insides twisted at the fondness in his voice, the way his face softened when he talked about her.

So the opposite of me, she thought with a pang. Okay, she could be funny, but she couldn't see anyone describing her as warm or sweet. She had more of a cool and acerbic kind of vibe going on.

'I think you'll get on well.'

'I'm sure we'll be braiding each other's hair in no time.'

'And there'll be lots of press while she's here. It'll be great publicity for the show.'

'Won't you be trying to avoid all that?'

'Willow's quite keen to scotch all these rumours, so we're going to play into it a bit – let them get their photos of the loved-up couple.'

· · ·

As it turned out, Rocco didn't need to announce anything. At some point in the day, Willow posted on her Instagram laughing the whole thing off as nonsense. She explained that it was her mother's engagement ring she was wearing in the photo. She'd tried it on after having it cleaned and resized, and she'd simply forgotten about it when she took the picture. It certainly wasn't meant to be taken as some kind of signal or oblique announcement.

By the end of the day the story had completely fizzled out. But Rocco still got a lot of good-natured teasing about it throughout the day, with lots of back-slapping and congratulations, and everyone jokingly asking when the big day was, so they could save the date. He accepted it all in good humour, graciously joining in the laughter.

The only one who didn't see the funny side was, of course, Andrea. 'I feel sorry for him,' she hissed in Mimi's ear. 'I bet Willow posted that picture deliberately to try and push him into proposing to her for real.'

23

'I FEEL like I could sleep for a week,' Mimi said as she and her sisters left the theatre together on Friday evening. Aoife and Sive had come to watch the dress rehearsal, which had gone well – almost unnervingly so, since it was an old theatrical superstition that a bad dress rehearsal meant a hit show.

But after the rigours of tech week, Mimi was wiped out. She'd felt her eyes drooping while Nina gave notes to the cast, and she'd noticed Mitch dropping off and jerking awake a couple of times. She'd barely summoned the energy to change out of her costume and hang it up. Thankfully everyone else seemed as keen to get home and into bed as she was, and there'd been no suggestion of post-rehearsal drinks.

She was looking forward to a weekend of resting, eating and sleeping, recharging for the week ahead. She might exert herself to hold a book open or to go for a short walk … or she might not. Above all, it would be relaxing to have two whole days without seeing Rocco.

'Just don't forget you have to get up for dinner on Sunday,' Sive said.

'Oh, yes! The wanderer returns.' Sive's boyfriend Ben was finally back from his travels, and she'd invited him over for dinner to celebrate.

'Jonathan's coming too,' Sive said. 'And your boyfriend, of course,' she added with a mischievous smile.

'Sam doesn't have to come. Rocco won't be there, so he's off duty.'

'It'd be mean to have Jonathan and leave Sam out. Anyway, he's not just your fake boyfriend. He's like one of the family now. He's our …' she twisted her lips, musing. 'Boyfriend-in-law?'

'So not a thing.'

'Anyway, you can stay in bed until dinnertime, if you want. All you have to do is turn up and eat. We'll do all the cooking and everything.'

'Speaking of food, I'm starving. Should we get a takeaway?'

'No need,' Sive said. 'I made macaroni cheese for tonight.'

'Oh, you genius!' Mimi threw an arm around her. 'That's perfect.' She'd barely have to chew.

After a soothing supper of macaroni cheese and a couple of glasses of wine, Mimi went to bed, and stayed there for most of Saturday, only getting up to eat and to lie in the garden for a while with a book.

By the time everyone was gathered for dinner on Sunday, she was thoroughly reinvigorated and looking forward to getting back to work. It had been another hot, sunny day and they ate in the garden.

'This is nice.' Sam grinned when they were all seated

around the table and Ben had been introduced. Aoife had made a piri-piri chicken tray bake with lots of peppers and baby potatoes, and there was salad and a bowl of tzatziki on the side.

Sive's boyfriend was the strong and silent type, and rarely said anything unless he was asked a direct question. Trying to get him to chat was like drawing blood from a stone. But he always seemed perfectly happy to sit in silence and let the conversation go on around him, and he had a smiling, friendly demeanour, so his silence didn't generally make people uncomfortable.

Nevertheless, his relationship with Sive was a bit of a mystery to Aoife and Mimi. They liked him well enough, but he seemed such an unlikely match for their lively, outgoing sister. They had so little in common. Ben was an outdoorsy type, with a solid build matching his personality. He was always hiking and climbing mountains, and he'd spent the last year travelling the world working as a trekking guide.

'So, Ben. How was ... the world?' Mimi asked him. 'Did you have a great time?'

He nodded. 'Yeah, it was good.'

Mimi waited for more, but seemingly that was it. He'd travelled to Vietnam, India, Nepal, Morocco and all over Europe, and that was all he had to say about it? It was 'good'? She'd forgotten what hard work he could be.

'What was your favourite place?' Aoife tried.

He shrugged. 'I don't know. Vietnam maybe.'

'Vietnam is amazing,' Sam said. 'I was there on my gap year. Did you go to the Cu Chi Tunnels?'

'No, I was just in the north – in Hanoi and trekking in Sapa.'

'One of the scariest experiences of my life,' Sam said. 'You're in this tunnel with your face basically in the arse of the person in front. I was wedged behind this American woman who started freaking out and wouldn't move. Meanwhile the guides kept trying to move us on, pushing me deeper and deeper into her butt cheeks. Then she farted!' He laughed, shaking his head. 'I was lucky to escape with my life.'

They all started sharing their funny travel stories of hair-raising bus rides, dodgy hotels and scary food. Jonathan told them about the time he got into a fight with a baboon in South Africa – 'the baboon won'.

'The baboon always wins,' Sam said sagely. Then he launched into a story about a trip to Morocco involving a long bus ride, a bad case of food poisoning and no toilet paper. 'All I had was some dirham notes. So I improvised.'

'Talk about devaluing the currency!' Jonathan laughed.

Then there was the time when Sam was in Spain and giving it a go with his schoolboy Spanish. 'It was boiling hot, and I kept telling the taxi driver *"estoy caliente"*. I wondered why he was giving me such funny looks. I only discovered afterwards I was telling him I was horny. He thought I was coming on to him!' He laughed. 'In future I'll stick with the international language of mime.'

'You're not always safe with that. Remember the time we were in Crete,' Aoife said to her sisters, 'and I was trying to mime to this waitress who was pushing more food on us that I was full. She thought I was trying to say I was pregnant, and she snatched away my wine and wouldn't let me have any more.'

'And there was the night we went for a drink in that local "taverna",' Mimi said.

'We'd come across this little place on the way back to our hotel one night,' Aoife continued the story for their guests. 'So we decided to have a nightcap. There were just two tables, and an old couple were sitting at one with a bottle of ouzo. So we took the other one. It was ages before the woman got up from the other table and asked us what we wanted.'

'Well, she didn't speak any English,' Sive put in. 'We presumed that was what she was asking.'

'So we pointed at the bottle of ouzo,' Mimi continued. 'She went inside, brought us out three glasses, and poured us drinks from their bottle – with very bad grace, we thought.'

'Yeah, we weren't impressed with the service at all,' Aoife said, laughing.

'Anyway, we sat there having our drinks, and when we'd finished, she came over with the bottle and offered us more. So we had another round.'

'She was friendlier by then,' Aoife said. 'She seemed to have warmed up to us a bit.'

'Then when we got up to leave,' Mimi said, 'we signalled to her that we wanted to pay, and she just kept shrugging and shaking her head. She and her husband – we presume – cleared up our glasses and took everything inside. She still hadn't brought us the bill, so we hung around for a while waiting. Every so often one of them would peep out the window, checking if we were still there. Then eventually the woman appeared in the doorway and made a sort of shooing gesture at us and shut the door.'

'And that was when we realised,' Sive said. 'It wasn't a taverna at all. It was just their house.'

'And they'd been sitting there minding their own business, having a quiet drink before bed, when we show up demanding some of their ouzo.'

Everyone laughed.

'There was no signage or anything. I don't know what made us think it was a taverna,' Mimi said. 'They're probably still talking about the rude Irish girls who barged into their house demanding drink.'

Inevitably the talk eventually turned to the show.

'Are you coming to the opening night?' Sive asked Ben.

He shrugged. 'I don't know. What night is it on?'

'Wednesday.' They were having a couple of previews on Monday and Tuesday prior to opening.

'I don't think so. There's a reunion with some of the crowd who were on my Annapurna trek.'

'Oh, pity.' Sive's face fell for a split second, but she quickly covered it with a smile. 'Well, you can come some other night.'

'You should,' Sam said. 'It's a terrific show. You don't want to miss it.'

'I don't mind. I'd go if you were in it,' Ben said to Sive. 'But it's not really my thing, is it?'

'Not a Noël Coward fan?' Jonathan asked.

'Not a fan of theatre in general,' Ben said shyly. 'I prefer TV.'

Sam shot him a look of utter horror, as if he'd just blasphemed in a house of worship. Mimi had to admit, that was how it felt to her too.

'I'd forgotten what a live wire Ben is,' Mimi said to Aoife later as they cleared up. Their guests had left, and Sive had gone to stay in Ben's house for the night.

Aoife laughed. 'He'd make a great spy. I think he might have spoken a total of two sentences all evening.'

'And one of those was to say he doesn't like theatre!' Mimi rolled her eyes. 'I mean, read the room.'

'Do you think they might be having problems?'

Mimi shrugged. 'I don't know. It's hard to tell what's going on with them, isn't it?'

'Sive was so excited about him coming home, but now that he's here, she seems … I don't know. A bit subdued?'

'I know what you mean. I do sometimes wonder if he's right for her.'

'She seems happy with him. And he's a nice guy … as far as we know.'

'Yeah.' Mimi gave a little laugh. 'It's not that I don't like him. I just … don't feel I really know who he is. Do you think Sive does?'

'I suppose she must. Surely he talks more when it's just the two of them.'

'God, you'd hope so. All I know is the more I see of Ben, the more I get what she sees in Sam.'

24

MIMI ARRIVED at the theatre on opening night with mixed emotions. She was excited about the performance, but also aware that this was the beginning of the end. Once the show opened, the clock would start running down to the final performance – and when the run was over, she'd no longer have an excuse to kiss Rocco or run her fingers through his hair or tell him out loud that she loved him. She wouldn't be working with him every day or cavorting around on a stage with him every night, doing what she loved best with the man she loved most.

She brushed her gloomy thoughts aside as she climbed the stairs to the backstage area and they were soon forgotten as she greeted the cast members and crew who were milling around, all keyed up for the performance. Tonight was just the beginning, she told herself. She still had two months of this show, and she was going to enjoy every single moment.

Before going to her dressing room to get ready, she walked around distributing gifts to the cast and crew. First night gifts were a cherished theatre tradition that Mimi loved. She enjoyed trawling websites for swag, trying to find the perfect mementos for a particular show. They didn't have to be expensive – they usually weren't since theatre workers tended not to have much cash to splash – but that was all the more reason to make them thoughtful, considered. She treasured the collection of buttons, badges and handwritten cards she'd collected from various productions over the years, each one bringing back fond memories and marking a significant stage in her career.

For *Private Lives* she'd decided on fridge magnets of the show poster. She liked to give everyone the same thing, so no one felt slighted or undervalued. Detta had impressed on her and her sisters the importance of treating every member of the cast and crew with equal respect, from the biggest star to the lowliest stagehand. Each one of them was a vital cog in the machine that made the whole thing work.

In turn she received a framed group photo of the cast from Rocco, a pin in the shape of a cocktail glass from Nina, several buttons and cards, and a photobook from Andrea with behind-the-scenes photographs from rehearsals. Mimi was touched. It was a lovely keepsake, and Andrea had obviously put a lot of thought into it. Cara had made a batch of brownies and left them in the green room, and Mitch gave everyone a bag of his home-made fudge.

The dressing room she shared with Andrea was filled with flowers, and there was a large squashy parcel on Mimi's dressing table that looked intriguing. She was just about to open it when Andrea came in and she decided to leave it. It obviously wasn't something that everyone had been given, and she didn't want there to be any bad feeling. Instead, she started opening her cards, reading the messages and chuckling over the in-jokes about things that had happened during rehearsal.

'I have something for you,' Andrea said, sitting next to her and bending down to rummage in her bag.

'Oh, you already gave me the photobook,' Mimi said, lifting it to show her. 'It's lovely. Thank you.'

Andrea shook her head. 'There's something else. Hang on.' She found whatever she was looking for and sat up. 'I wanted to give you something special,' she said, handing Mimi a small, wrapped package. 'To say thank you for being so generous with your time and advice. You've been such a great mentor to me.'

'Oh!' Mimi exclaimed, startled. 'I don't think I've done anything—'

'It's been such a great experience working with you, and I can't tell you how grateful I am for the opportunity.'

'Well … thank you.'

'And I've loved our little chats in the mornings when it's just the two of us here. It's meant a lot to me, really.' Andrea gave her a kind smile.

'Me too,' Mimi said, deciding this was one of those occasions when insincerity was justified. She wished she hadn't thought so meanly of Andrea now – but at least it seemed she'd been oblivious to it. 'It's been a pleasure working with you, Andrea. I'm sure you'll go on to great things.' She was relieved that at least she could say that and mean it.

'Oh, this is lovely,' she said as she opened the gift. It was a silver bracelet with a drama mask charm dangling from it. 'Thank you so much.'

Andrea smiled, obviously pleased with herself. 'Aren't you going to open that one?' She nodded at the bulky parcel on Mimi's dressing table.

'Oh, I was going to leave it for later.'

'Go on, I won't be jealous.'

Mimi was glad of the permission, because she couldn't wait to open it and see what it was. 'I must admit, I am curious.' She picked it up and opened it carefully.

'Wow!' Andrea's eyes widened as Mimi pulled out a vintage leopard-print coat – the one she'd tried on when she'd gone shopping for costumes with Sive and Rocco. 'That's gorgeous.'

Mimi picked up the card inside. There was just a printed message – 'Break a leg!' – and no signature. But she knew who it was from.

'Somebody loves you,' Andrea said as Mimi stood and pulled on the coat, admiring it in the mirror.

'They do,' she said, her eyes blurring with tears. Then she quickly pulled it off again and hung it on the back of her chair. 'Okay, that's enough of that. Time to get ready.'

The play went brilliantly, the audience laughing in all the right places and clapping enthusiastically at the end of each act. Mimi couldn't have wished for a better performance. Her heart swelled with pride as she and Rocco waited in the wings as first Orla, and then Andrea and Mitch took their bows. Then it was their turn. Rocco took her hand, and the applause reached a crescendo as they ran onto stage together. The audience rose to their feet, cheering and whooping, and Mimi blinked tears from her eyes as she looked out over the auditorium, picking out some individual faces and feeling the waves of appreciation rolling towards her. Rocco squeezed her hand, his thumb rubbing over hers.

Then they turned to each other, he put his arms around her, and the crowd whooped as he bent her over in a theatrical kiss. She cupped her hand around the back of his head and buried her fingers in his hair as his lips lingered longer than they should have. She was so glad they'd decided to include the kiss in their curtain call. Nina had thought it would be amusing, God bless her – and Mimi could kiss her right now for thinking of it. This was her favourite moment of the show, and she'd get to do it again, night after night for two months. She tried not to think of Willow out there somewhere in the audience watching.

Rocco seemed as reluctant to break the kiss as she was, and the audience laughed as it went on and on, assuming it was part of the act. In her peripheral vision, Mimi saw the rest of the cast coming back onstage. She was breathless, her chest heaving as Rocco lifted his head and released her, feeling dazed as Mitch, Andrea and Orla joined them and the four of them held hands and took their final bows.

She felt bereft as they walked off into the wings and Rocco dropped her hand. It's just the play, she told herself. It's just Amanda, it's not me.

The show had gone without a hitch and Mimi knew her performance had been flawless – better than that, it had been brilliant. She was on a high from the applause and very pleased with herself as she made her way off stage.

But now she had to face the green room, and she was less confident about how she'd handle that performance. She dawdled over doing her make-up and changing out of her costume, putting off the moment when she'd have to join everyone for the after-show party – and meet Willow Bell.

Finally, she couldn't put it off any longer and she made her way to the green room. She paused for a moment to compose herself before she opened the door and stepped inside. The room was already buzzing with the hum of conversation and the clink of glasses. The first person she saw was Rocco – because of course it was. Her eyes just gravitated to him automatically, like metal to a magnet. He was surrounded by his family, who'd all turned out to see him, and Willow Bell was with them, standing close beside him.

'Mimi!' Sive called to her from the other side of the room, waving her over. She was with Aoife, Sam and Jonathan.

Mimi picked up a drink and went to join them. She clinked glasses with everyone and took a sip. 'Real champagne,' she said, smiling. 'I'm impressed.'

'Don't get used to it,' Aoife said. 'But we thought we could splash out this once in view of our famous guests.'

'And the revenue they'll bring in,' Jonathan added.

'We wouldn't want Halfpenny Lane to be shown up in front of the Hollywood contingency.'

'We figured we could afford it thanks to Rocco,' Sive said. 'And you should get a bonus for delivering the cash cow. Or is he a cash bull? Is that a thing?'

Mimi laughed.

'Plus you deserve it,' Sive said. 'You were amazing! That was a champagne-worthy performance.'

'Hear hear!' Aoife said. 'You were incredible.'

Sam and Jonathan agreed, and she basked in the praise as they all told her how marvellous she was.

'Thank you. And thank you for my coat,' she said to Aoife and Sive. 'Though you really shouldn't have. It's very extravagant.'

'Coat?' Aoife frowned.

'The opening night present you left in my dressing room.'

Sive and Aoife looked equally puzzled.

'The leopard-print coat I found the day we went shopping for costumes,' she said to Sive.

'Someone bought that for you?' Sive gasped. 'It wasn't us.'

'No,' Aoife said, shaking her head.

'Oh.' They all knew there was only one other person who could have given it to her.

'Mimi!' She turned to see Bea beckoning her over to their family group.

She sighed. 'I'd better go and say hello.' She took a gulp of champagne. 'Time to face the music.'

Sive and Aoife gave her compassionate smiles.

'Come with me,' Mimi said, grabbing Sam's hand. She arranged her features in a serene smile as they crossed the room together.

'Congratulations,' Bea said, pulling her into a hug. 'You were amazing!'

'You were, both of you,' Mia said. 'You were so funny. The play was brilliant.'

'This is Willow,' Rocco said, beaming with pride as he introduced her to Sam and Mimi.

She looked smaller in real life, but just as stunning as she was in photos. She was tiny, with delicate fine-boned features and big blue eyes framed by impossibly long lashes. Her dark blonde hair was cut in a close-cropped feathery style that emphasised her overall elfin appearance, and her pale, almost translucent skin was a perfect foil for Rocco's swarthy olive complexion.

She congratulated Mimi on her performance, sweetly fulsome in her praise. 'And I love this theatre. I watched the live stream of *Three Sisters*,' she said. 'I'd love to have been here to see it live. It was so wonderful – it really blew me away. It must have been great for you and your sisters to be in it together.'

'Thank you. And yes, it was.'

'Have you been to Ireland before?' Sam asked her politely. He wasn't even trying to hide his boyish excitement at meeting such a major Hollywood star, his eyes sparkling.

'No, this is my first time. But I love it already. I'm so envious of the theatrical tradition you guys have here. No wonder this guy is so brilliant,' she said, nudging Rocco, who smiled at her affectionately. The way they looked at each other was tearing Mimi up. Their obvious affection, and their ease and familiarity around each other clawed at her gut.

'Hopefully I'll be back soon for a longer visit,' Willow said, smiling up at Rocco.

'Will you be moving here, then?' Sam asked. 'I know Rocco's been looking at houses.'

Willow's smile faltered as she glanced at Rocco. 'I'm just here for a flying visit this time,' she said. 'I'm going back to LA on Monday.'

'Nothing's decided yet,' Rocco said.

'It's a bit tricky to arrange anything when we're in different places. It's hard enough when we're in LA; we both have such busy schedules.'

Did that mean Rocco might not be moving back to Dublin after all, Mimi wondered. For all her gushing about the place, Willow didn't sound keen.

'Are you an actor too, Sam?' Willow asked him.

'Not yet, but I'm hoping to be. In the meantime, I'm working here in Halfpenny Lane.'

'Oh, what do you do?'

Sam shrugged. 'General dogsbody,' he said cheerfully. 'Usher, stagehand, man-of-all-work – I step in wherever I'm needed.'

'Sounds like a great way to learn the trade.'

'It is. I love it – best job I've ever had.'

'But you do act?'

He nodded. 'I'm not classically trained or anything—'

'Oh, me neither,' Willow said with a smile. 'I learned on the job. Though of course I've taken lots of classes since then. If you ever find yourself in LA, I could recommend some great teachers.'

'That's really kind, thank you. I haven't been in anything yet, apart from college productions.' He gave Mimi a meaningful glance.

'It's so hard to get a start in this business, isn't it?' Willow said kindly.

'I imagine it's the same in LA,' Sam said. 'Worse probably.'

Willow nodded. 'So much of it is about connections, who you know …'

'Well, I don't have to worry about that, now that I'm going out with this one.' He gave Mimi a squeeze. 'I'm expecting to make my debut at Halfpenny Lane soon – sleeping my way to the top in the grand old tradition of showbiz.' He guffawed, while Mimi felt heat creep up her neck. She gave him a discreet dig with her elbow.

'Sorry,' he said. 'Stupid joke.' His face flushed. 'The truth is, boyfriend or no boyfriend, Mimi wouldn't let me set foot on the stage here if she didn't think I could cut it.'

'You got that right, buster,' Mimi said, and everyone laughed.

'It's so cool what you guys have done with this place,' Willow said, looking around the green room. 'I'd love to have a nose around backstage,' she said to Mimi. 'If that would be okay?'

'Of course!' Mimi said. 'Would you like the full tour?'

'Yes, please.' Willow looked genuinely thrilled at the idea.

They put their drinks down and Mimi led her out of the green room. Willow showed a keen interest in everything as Mimi showed her around the poky dressing rooms and the backstage area, telling her about the restoration work they'd done. As they stepped out onto the stage, Willow looked around wonderingly at the little auditorium. Then she took a deep breath and strode to the apron of the stage, and Mimi knew she was imaging herself standing there in front of an audience. She'd done the same thing often enough in her childhood.

'Gosh, I envy you being able to do this,' Willow said, turning to Mimi.

'Sure you do,' Mimi scoffed, joining her.

'No, really. I haven't done any theatre work since Junior High – a production of *The Wizard of Oz*. Least said about that the better.'

'You were Dorothy, I presume?'

'Yeah.' She smiled. 'It was fun. But the nerves … I'd be terrified to go on stage now. I'm in awe of anyone who can do it.'

Maybe there could be a silver lining in this great fat thunder cloud after all, Mimi thought. If she could persuade Willow to give live theatre a go … somewhere so small and obscure, it wouldn't matter if she fell flat on her face …

'Ever thought about going back to it?' she asked.

'No. I have too many commitments now anyway. At least, that's my excuse. Truthfully, I don't think I'd ever have the courage. I really admire Rocco for doing it.'

Great! That was, what … a whole five minutes before they were talking about Rocco?

'Yeah, he's a real hero,' Mimi said dryly.

'Seriously, though, I admire you so much – all of you. Whenever I go to the theatre, I'm blown away by the actors who go through the same show night after night and keep it fresh every time. It gives me a bad case of imposter syndrome. It's so brave, putting yourself out there like that in front of a live audience … it kind of takes my breath away. It makes me quite teary, actually.'

Mimi could relate to that. It was exactly how she felt in the audience at the start of a show, before anything had even happened. It never failed to move her that people put so much effort and energy into doing this thing for an audience – making them laugh and cry and relate and feel something, wringing emotions from them as if it was the most important work in the world.

'Well, if you ever want to give it a go, you'd always be welcome here.' Mimi wiggled her eyebrows like a fairground hustler.

Willow laughed. 'Thanks, but I think I'll stick to hiding behind the camera – for now at least. Maybe some day, though. Never say never.'

Willow sat down on the stage, dangling her legs over the edge, and Mimi sat beside her.

'It must have been amazing to have all this around you growing up.'

Mimi nodded. 'It was. My sisters and I used to play here all the time. We'd put on little shows for our parents and Detta.' She smiled fondly at the memory.

'Obviously I never saw your great-aunt on the stage, but I loved her in the movies – not that she made many.'

'No. Theatre was her great love – and this place especially.' Mimi nodded to the auditorium.

Willow laid her hands on the stage floor behind her and leaned back. 'So how long have you and Sam been together?'

There was something in the super-casual way she asked

the question that rang false. 'Not long – just a couple of months.'

'But … it's serious?'

Mimi frowned. Why was Willow fishing about her relationship with Sam? 'Who knows?' she said with a shrug. 'Like I said, it's early days.'

'Sorry, am I being weird?' Willow chuckled.

'A little bit,' Mimi said, smiling back at her. 'Look, Rocco and I are over, if that's what you're trying to ask me.' She thought about the phone conversation she'd overheard. Maybe Willow was more insecure than she appeared – or than she had any reason to be. 'That's all in the past. We're friends now, but that's all.'

'Are you sure?'

'Yes! I swear.' Mimi was aghast that Willow didn't believe her – and that she'd confront her about it so directly. Surely Rocco hadn't said anything about their indiscretions?

'Hey, I'm not accusing you of anything.' Willow held up her hands, palms open in a calming gesture. 'I just thought … I don't know. I get the feeling there's unfinished business between the two of you. I mean, you only split up because you didn't want to move to LA, right? And now Rocco's moving back to Dublin …'

'You're not planning to move here with him?'

'No, I'm not. Much as I love it, I can't see myself living here. Besides, I have too many ties in LA.' Her smile faltered and she had a faraway look in her eyes.

'So you'll do the long-distance thing?'

'I suppose so. In our business you have to get used to doing long distance anyway, what with location shoots and everything. It's hard to find time to be together.'

'I'm sure you'll work it out,' Mimi said.

'What if we don't, though?'

'Sorry?' Was she trying to hint that she and Rocco might split up?

'What if I wasn't on the scene and Rocco was unattached … do you think you'd get back together?'

Mimi blinked at her, unsure how to answer.

'Sorry, I'm being weird and inappropriate again,' Willow said. 'Ignore me.'

'Look, maybe Sam isn't "the one",' Mimi said, sketching quote marks in the air. 'But nothing's going to happen between me and Rocco. I've seen the way he looks at you – the way you are together. It's obvious you love each other.'

Willow smiled. 'We do,' she said softly. 'That's true.'

'And even if I hadn't seen it for myself, I read it in *Wow!* magazine,' Mimi said, hoping to lighten the atmosphere.

'Don't believe everything you read,' Willow said with a grin. 'The bit about bonding over books was true, though. Rocco is so well-read, it's scary!'

'Tell me about it.'

'I did an English lit degree, but he made me feel so ignorant sometimes.' She smiled wistfully. 'Actually, people would be very disappointed if they knew what was actually going on in our trailers on that set. It was mostly me being a basket case and Rocco trying to hold me together.'

Mimi raised an eyebrow.

'I'd lost my mom shortly before the shoot,' Willow said, a cloud passing across her features.

'Oh, I'm so sorry.'

'Thanks. Rocco told me you lost your parents at a young age. So you know what it's like.'

'Yeah. I went a bit bananas at the time. I gave poor Aoife an awful time when she was trying to hold us all together.'

'You were lucky – to have her I mean,' Willow added quickly. 'To have both of them. I wish I had a sister.'

'You don't have any siblings?'

'No. Only child.' She smiled. 'But Rocco was a really good friend to me. I don't know how I'd have got through that shoot without him. He pretty much carried me the whole way – covered for me when I was flaking out, ran interference with the press ...'

'Yeah, he's a good guy to have in your corner.'

'There you are.' They both turned to see Rocco walking onto the stage behind them. 'I wondered where you'd got to.' He sat down beside Willow. 'Talking about me, I suppose,' he said with a grin. 'Swapping notes about what a great boyfriend I am?'

'Of course. And friend.' Willow smiled at him. But Mimi noticed an odd look pass between them.

'Well, sorry to break up that conversation, but we need to go shortly.'

'Are you coming?' Willow asked Mimi.

'Mum's having some people back to the house,' Rocco told her. 'You're welcome to come. But you probably have plans.'

'I do. But thank her for me.'

Willow and Rocco stood.

'Oh, and Rocco,' Mimi said, suddenly remembering her manners. 'Thank you for my present.' She smiled up at him. 'I love it.'

'You're welcome.' He held out a hand to help her up.

She shook her head. 'You go on. I'll be there in a few minutes.'

She watched them go, glad of a moment alone to gather her thoughts. Rocco was right – Willow was lovely. Funny, warm, down to earth – all those things he'd said and more besides. She was bright and kind, and so easy to talk to. In other circumstances, she was just the sort of woman Mimi would want to be her friend.

But much as she liked Willow, she was glad she'd be returning to LA and they'd probably never meet again. It would be painful enough to see her and Rocco in movies and on magazine covers, a constant reminder of what she'd lost. In time, she might even have to endure the tastefully curated photos of their wedding splashed all over the internet – endless close-ups of the happy couple beaming lovingly at each other, living monuments to love and happiness and good luck.

Whenever she thought about it, one thought kept nudging back into her head: *it should have been me*. She railed against the unfairness of it all, even as she knew she had no one to blame but herself. If she'd gone to LA with Rocco, maybe now it *would* be her. It'd be *their* 'lovely home' in *Wow!* magazine. She'd had her chance and she'd blown it – and she was fine with her decision, she really was. It was just all this proximity recently that had dredged up her old feelings. Soon the run of the play would be over, and Rocco would no longer be a constant presence in her life. Maybe he'd go back to Hollywood. Or he'd move to Dublin and they'd be friends.

Either way she'd be fine. She had the theatre and her work, she had family and friends, and maybe one day someone would come along and she'd even fall in love again. Or maybe not – and that would be okay. She didn't need a man to make her life complete. Detta had shown them that. She'd been single all her life and she'd been happy. She could follow in her footsteps and become a marvellous old broad, focusing on the theatre, with the occasional love affair thrown in to spice up her life.

The show's the thing. She heard Detta's voice in her ear as clearly as if she was sitting here next to her. *The show's the thing, darling girl.* She swallowed hard, blinking tears from her eyes. She knew what she'd meant by it now, and she'd never felt Detta's presence so strongly as she did in this moment. The theatre had been Detta's answer to everything – the distraction from every heartache, the cure for all ills, and the consolation for all of life's disappointments. The show was the thing you could always rely on; an anchor when you were adrift, a lifebuoy to cling to when you were drowning in a sea of troubles, a guiding light showing the way when you were lost. It had been her saviour and refuge, and it would be Mimi's too.

'The show's the thing,' she murmured to herself, a new sense of peace descending on her as she stood and went to join her sisters in the green room. And Rocco or no Rocco, the show would go on.

25

'WE'RE ON ALL the front pages!' Sive gasped the next morning, combing through the pile of papers on the kitchen table. Aoife had gone out early to get all the first editions, so they could read the reviews over a celebratory breakfast of coffee and croissants.

More accurately, Willow and Rocco were on all the front pages. If Rocco's presence on Halfpenny Lane had caused a fuss, it had turned into a full-on frenzy with Willow added to the mix. They'd all left the theatre together last night, and when they'd stepped outside it had been to the clicking of cameras and the shouts of photographers asking Rocco and Willow to turn this way or that, yelling for them to put their arms around each other or 'give us a kiss'. Mimi and her sisters had stood to the side, watching in dismay as the laneway lit up with camera flashes.

It had been Mimi's first real taste of that level of fame, and she didn't like it. She felt for Willow, recalling what Rocco had said about wanting to be famous for your work, not who you were going out with. She'd hate to garner this sort of attention simply for having a boyfriend, and she understood why they'd wanted to keep their relationship under wraps for as long as possible.

Still, it was all grist to the mill, she supposed, and Willow had handled it with aplomb. She'd managed to maintain a good-natured smile while giving the paps enough to satisfy them without dragging it out too long, somehow keeping it brief without appearing brusque. It was a skill she'd clearly honed over years of experience, a poignant reminder that she'd been dealing with this kind of thing since she was a child.

She had Rocco looking after her too, Mimi thought, her gaze falling on the broadsheet in front of her. He had an arm around Willow's shoulders, pulling her closer as the photographers swarmed around them. He was so protective of her, she thought wistfully. But why wouldn't he be? She seemed so delicate and vulnerable; Mimi felt quite protective towards her herself – which was annoying.

Anyway, the important thing was it all gave more visibility to the reviews, which were glowing. She was pleased to see there was as much critique of her performance as Rocco's. She had to admit she'd been anxious that his star power would overshadow the whole production and make him the sole focus of attention. Of course, he was the headline, and there were a couple of short reviews in the tabloids devoted almost entirely to him, with the rest of the cast merely mentioned as an afterthought, credited for providing 'able support'. She was glad that a couple of reviewers singled Andrea out for special mention, 'making much of her turn as the insipid Sybil'. Whatever her faults, Andrea deserved that.

'Oh, this one's a bit mean,' Sive said, frowning. 'Not about any of the performances, though – more about Nina's direction.'

'Show me.'

Sive slid the newspaper across the table to her.

'Ugh, she basically misunderstands the whole play,' Mimi said, scanning the piece. 'She seems to think we should have turned it into some dreary kitchen-sink drama about domestic violence to make it relevant for modern audiences. What tosh!' She tossed the paper away from her.

'Well, she's a lone voice crying in the wilderness,' Aoife said. 'Everyone else gets it. Listen to this …'

They passed the papers around, reading snippets to each other as they ate their breakfast, and marking quotes they could use for advertising. There was praise for Rocco's charm and charisma, Mimi's self-assurance and comic timing (which one critic pronounced 'miraculous'), and Nina's skilful balancing of the comedy with the darker themes of the play.

'"With its stellar inaugural production of *Three Sisters*",' Aoife read, '"and now this pitch-perfect rendition of Noël Coward's timeless classic, the Halfpenny Lane Theatre is shaping up to be an exciting addition to Dublin's cultural life that punches well above its weight."'

'That's one to cut out and keep,' Mimi said, grinning.

Aoife smiled, closing the paper. 'I think it's safe to say we've got a success on our hands.'

Mimi didn't see much of Rocco for the rest of the week outside of performances. He and Willow were keeping a low profile while she was in town, and she didn't blame them. But Willow came to the green room after the Saturday afternoon matinee to say goodbye to everyone.

'You should look me up if you're ever in LA,' she told

Mimi after they'd hugged. 'I'd love to see you. Let me give you my number.'

'Oh! Okay …' Mimi pulled out her phone. She had no intention of calling Willow but exchanged numbers with her out of politeness.

She was surprised when her phone rang that evening as she was cooking dinner with her sisters, and she saw it was Willow calling. She picked it up, presuming it was a butt dial.

'Mimi, hi! I was wondering if I could see you before I leave – just the two of us.'

'Oh, really? I'm not sure if …' She racked her brain for a polite excuse.

'Please? I'd really like to talk. And you might hear something to your advantage,' she said with a little laugh.

'Well, now you've got me intrigued. All right.'

'Could you come over here tomorrow, around six?'

'But won't Rocco be there?'

'No, he's got a family thing – a cousin's wedding – and he won't be back until late.'

There was always some cousin getting married in Rocco's family. 'Okay. I'll see you then.'

She ended the call to find Sive and Aoife looking at her curiously.

'Oh god, Willow wants to talk to me. In private – just the two of us.'

'Why?' Aoife gave a concerned frown.

'I don't know. She was being a bit mysterious. She wants me to go over there tomorrow while Rocco's out at a wedding.'

'Do you think she knows?' Sive said. 'That you snogged Rocco?'

'No. She couldn't, could she? It's not like he's going to

tell her. Anyway, she said I might hear something to my advantage, so it can't be that.'

'Oh, that sounds exciting!' Sive beamed. 'Maybe she wants to be your benefactor and she's going to give you a million dollars.'

'Yeah, that's probably it,' Mimi said dryly.

'What are you going to do?' Aoife asked.

'I have to go, don't I?'

'It would look suspicious if you said no,' Sive agreed. 'Like you have something to hide.'

'The trouble is I do have something to hide. I *have* sometimes felt like she's watching me and Rocco when we're together, as if she suspects something.'

'Do you think she could?'

'I don't know. But she has no reason to. There's nothing going on between us, not anymore.'

'But why would she want to see you on your own, without Rocco? She hardly knows you.'

'And why not just tell you on the phone, whatever it is?'

'I have no idea. But I guess I'll find out tomorrow.' Mimi sighed. 'God, I hope she doesn't want us to be BFFs.'

26

'THANKS FOR COMING TO SEE ME,' Willow said, ushering Mimi inside.

'Yeah, no worries.' She followed as Willow led the way down the hall and into the living room. Barefoot, in a white vest top and a pair of wide-legged silky lounge pants, she looked heartbreakingly at home in Rocco's house.

It was a warm evening and the doors to the terrace were thrown open. Willow waved Mimi to a sofa. 'Would you like a drink?'

'I'd love a white wine, please, if you have it,' Mimi said, suspecting she was going to need it.

Willow left the room and returned with two large glasses of white wine.

'Sorry to have been so cloak and dagger,' she said, handing Mimi one. She sat on the couch opposite, curling her legs under her.

'Rocco doesn't know I'm here?'

'No. There's something I've been wanting to say to you, but he didn't want me to.' Willow looked down at her hands and smiled to herself. Then she raised her eyes and caught Mimi's gaze. 'It's about me and Rocco.'

There was a flash of something bright as Willow raised her glass to her lips – a ring on her finger catching the light. With a stomach-churning sense of inevitability, Mimi's gaze fell on Willow's hand and the sparkling diamond she was wearing. Oh god, they were really engaged after all. She took a big gulp of wine.

'It's fine,' she said, waving a hand dismissively. 'You don't have to ask my permission or anything.'

'Sorry?'

'If you were going to ask me for his hand in marriage or whatever. Rocco's a free agent. I have no jurisdiction over him, so do whatever you want.'

'Um … I know?' Willow gave her a bemused smile – which was fair enough. She hardly knew what she was saying herself.

'Sorry. It's just I've had some weird conversations like that – girls asking if it's okay with me if they date him. Not that he did anything about it,' she added hastily, realising she was talking to his fiancé about him dating other women. 'I'm sure nothing happened.'

'Well, that's not what this is about. The thing is … we're not together.'

'Oh! You've broken up?' Mimi frowned. She hoped Willow wasn't going to blame it on her.

'No.' After a pause Willow took a deep breath and said, 'You have to promise not to tell anyone this, but we never were together – not like that.'

Mimi frowned. She was beginning to regret sipping the wine so quickly. Her head felt fuzzy already. 'I don't understand. You were just pretending to be a couple?'

'Yes.'

Then light dawned – those fandom conspiracy theories

were true! 'So … it was just a publicity thing? I didn't think stuff like that really happened.'

'You'd be surprised,' Willow said with a rueful smile. 'But that's not what this is – much as the studio would love it.' She took a sip of wine. 'The thing is, I *am* in a relationship, but not with Rocco. I have a girlfriend – Kim.'

'Oh!' Mimi tried not to appear shocked, in case it would come across as homophobic, but she could hardly be blamed for being a bit flummoxed. 'But didn't you use to go out with Mark Farrell? And Jason Cole?' She realized she was showing a worrying knowledge of Willow's dating history. She'd read way too much about her recently, thanks to those damned internet algorithms.

Willow gave a little smile. 'Well … God loves a trier,' she said with a shrug.

Then Mimi remembered the photos – Willow and her 'gal pal' Kim. So there'd been some substance to those stories after all.

'There were always reporters nosing around trying to find out what was going on in my private life,' Willow said. 'There'd been rumours about me, but I wasn't ready to come out publicly – especially not then, when I'd just lost my mom. I was under all this pressure from the studios and the media, and I just couldn't deal with it on top of that. Plus, I didn't want to put Kim through it all. It's hard enough for me to cope with, and I'm used to it. It's even more difficult for people who aren't in the business.'

'And she's not?'

'No. She's a photographer.' She looked down, running a finger along the stem of her glass. 'Honestly, I was afraid it would scare her off. All that stuff puts so much pressure on a relationship, and I wanted it to be just between us – at least for a while.'

Mimi nodded. 'I get that.'

Willow heaved a sigh. 'So, in the end I decided it'd be easiest to give them what they wanted. I already told you what a great friend Rocco was to me. When I said we love each other, that's the truth. He wasn't seeing anyone at the time, and he agreed to be my pretend boyfriend, to give me and Kim some breathing space. I think he was happy to get everyone off his back too about who he was dating.' She smiled. 'We had a laugh fooling everyone – it was kinda fun feeding them all this BS and watching them gobble it up.'

'You even got a ring.' Mimi nodded to her hand.

'Oh no, that's from Kim.' A warm smile suffused Willow's features as she stretched out her hand and gazed at the ring lovingly. 'I really am engaged.'

'Oh, wow! Congratulations!'

'Thanks.'

'Well, your secret's safe with me. But I still don't get why you're telling me all this?'

'Because I've seen the way you and Rocco look at each other. I know how he feels about you, and I'm pretty sure you feel the same way about him. I don't want to stand in your way if there's a chance of you getting back together.'

Mimi's heart started racing at 'I know how he feels about you'. 'How do you think he feels about me?'

'Oh, I don't think, I know – believe me. It wasn't just me crying on his shoulder in that trailer – it was also him crying on mine. About you.' She took a sip of wine. 'It was me who persuaded him to come here, you know. I could see he was still in love with you, and he told me how things ended between you. I thought he should give it another shot – get closure, at least, if nothing else.'

'But what about your fake relationship?'

'We were going to call it quits on that soon anyway. I

told him if something happened between you, I was happy to bring our break-up forward.'

'But Rocco didn't want you to tell me this – that you're not really together?'

'No. At first, he was all for it. He was going to tell you himself – he had my blessing. But then he got here, and you were with ...' She circled her hand in the air as she tried to come up with the name.

'Sam,' Mimi said dully.

Willow nodded. 'So he figured you'd moved on. I felt so bad for sending him here, getting his hopes up. I tried to persuade him he should try anyway, if there was a chance you felt the same way. After that photo came out of the two of you outside that restaurant ... I thought maybe something had happened.'

'It was just dinner,' Mimi said meekly, feeling her cheeks flush.

'Yeah, I know – perfectly innocent. And Kim and I were just walking her dog on the beach that day.' She shot Mimi a sly smile. 'Thank goodness there are no photos of what happened later after we got home.'

Mimi laughed. 'Touché.'

'I tried to convince Rocco then that he should tell you how he felt anyway, but he insisted there was no point. You were with someone else, and you were happy; he didn't want to interfere with that. So he said he'd continue with our little charade for as long as I wanted.'

Mimi thought of the conversation she'd overheard, seeing it in a whole new light. *I'm all yours ... as long as you need ... she's with someone else, nothing's going to happen.* He hadn't been reassuring a jealous girlfriend. He'd been telling Willow that he'd be her fake boyfriend for as long as she needed him to be.

'Well, I guess this explains why I felt like you were

watching me and Rocco all the time – and all your questions about my relationship with Sam.'

'Sorry.' Willow laughed. 'Was I that obvious?'

'I thought you were suspicious that something was going on between us.'

'I was – but I was actually hoping I was right, for his sake.'

'You really think he's still in love with me?' Mimi couldn't suppress the big grin that spread across her face. Then she remembered Sam and felt guilty. She should try not to look so pleased.

'I know he is. And you feel the same, right?'

Mimi nodded. 'He's the one. He was always the one.'

'And Sam?'

Mimi lowered her eyes, playing with the stem of her wine glass. 'Okay, don't laugh. Sam and I aren't real either. He's my fake boyfriend, like Rocco's yours.'

'Oh!' Willow exclaimed, eyebrows raised. 'Plot twist! I did not see that coming.'

Mimi gave her a sheepish smile. 'I know. Crazy. But Rocco was with you, and I wanted him to think I'd moved on too.'

'I get that.'

'So … what now?' Mimi asked.

'That's up to you, I guess. But feel free to carry on having innocent dinners with Rocco – or whatever else you want to get up to.'

'But what if we're caught?'

Willow shrugged. 'It'd be the perfect explanation for me and Rocco breaking up.'

Mimi frowned. 'I'm not sure I want to be the one to come between you. Everyone would hate me.' Willow was so beloved, and their fans so invested in them as a couple, she'd never be forgiven for causing their split. 'I'd be public enemy number one.'

'You're right.' Willow grimaced. 'It wouldn't be fair to Rocco either, making him out to be a cheat when he's been such a loyal fake boyfriend. Sorry, bad idea.'

Mimi shook her head. 'Don't worry about it. I'm just not prepared to deal with that kind of notoriety. We can wait until you and Rocco have officially broken up.'

'I'm the one deceiving everyone, and if anyone's going to be made to look like a cheat, it should be me.' Willow swirled the remaining wine in her glass. 'When I go back to LA, I'll stage some PDA with Kim and be careless about getting caught …' She smiled. 'It could be fun.'

'Don't feel you have to do that on my account. You'd get a lot of hate for cheating on Rocco.' She didn't like to think of Rocco's fans turning against Willow. Some of them seemed alarmingly unhinged. 'You can take your time.'

'No, it'll be okay. People will be more forgiving because it's a gay relationship. They won't be so censorious because they'll be afraid of looking homophobic. In fact, they'll probably cheer me on. I know it's hypocritical, but it's true. We might as well use it to our advantage.'

'But I thought you weren't ready to come out yet? Wasn't that the whole point of your fake relationship with Rocco?'

'Yeah, but I'm feeling a lot stronger now. I was in a bad place then. I couldn't deal with all the hoopla on top of Mom dying. Now it's time to fess up and be honest about who I am. Apart from anything else, it's not fair on Kim. She doesn't complain, but I'm sure she's fed up with all the hiding and sneaking around. She deserves her spread in *Wow!* talking about our romance and showing off her engagement ring. I bought her one too.' Willow's eyes took on a dreamy look as she twirled the diamond ring on her finger.

'How did it happen?' Mimi asked. 'Who proposed to whom?'

'She did.' Willow smiled. 'She went down on one knee and everything. It was so romantic. She's a lot braver than I am. She's put herself out there again and again, and I've held back as if I'm ashamed of our relationship.'

'I'm sure she doesn't think that.'

'Well, it's not true. I'm so proud of her.' She drained her glass and put it on the side table. 'So it's time I owned up to what kind of relationship I'm actually in — a bloody brilliant one with an awesome woman who's way better than I deserve — and damn what anyone else thinks about it.'

'She sounds amazing.'

'She is. I don't know why she's put up with me for so long.'

'I'm sure she understands, though. She must see what it's like for you, living in the public eye all the time. It's not like just coming out to friends and family — you'll be coming out to the whole world. It's pretty daunting.'

'God, when you put it like that, it does sound terrifying!' Willow laughed.

'But there's no rush. Rocco and I can wait. We've been apart for four years already. What's another few months?'

'I think you two have wasted enough time already. Besides, I want to do this for Kim.'

Mimi finished her wine. 'Maybe you should wait a week or two at least.' She suddenly felt nervous for Willow, her protective instincts kicking in. 'Give people time to get used to the idea of you and Rocco drifting apart. His moving here would be a natural separation for you anyway. That way no one has to be the bad guy.'

'Maybe.' Willow's eyes twinkled. 'But I'm kind of excited about doing it now.' She sighed. 'God, I'm going to miss Rocco, though.'

'You can always visit – and I'd love to have somewhere to crash in LA,' Mimi said with a cheeky grin.

'Well, you're welcome any time.'

'And the offer of a spot at Halfpenny Lane is always open.'

Willow laughed. 'Thanks, but that sounds even scarier than coming out to the whole world.' She stood and stretched. 'Anyway, you have all the information now. What you do with it is up to you.' She picked up their empty glasses. 'More wine? Why don't you stay for something to eat. There's some picky stuff in the fridge, or we could get a takeout.'

'Picky stuff sounds great.' Mimi made to stand.

'I'll get it,' Willow said. 'You stay there and plot your next move.'

27

'You're back in one piece anyway,' Aoife said when Mimi got home later that night. 'How did it go?' Aoife and Sive were sitting at the kitchen table, drinking wine.

'It was actually lovely.' Mimi sat down and poured herself a glass. 'Willow's really nice.'

'Are you hungry?' Aoife asked her. 'There's veggie chilli in the fridge. Sive went over to Ben's for dinner, so there's plenty left.'

'Thanks, but I ate with Willow.'

'Get you with your famous friend,' Aoife said teasingly. 'So, tell all – what happened? She clearly didn't want to beat you up.'

'What makes you think that? Maybe I won.'

Aoife laughed, and Sive gave her a thin smile.

'Come on, tell us what really happened,' Aoife said.

'Okay, but you have to promise not to repeat a word of it.' She paused, making sure her audience were primed for the big reveal. 'It turns out Willow and Rocco aren't together at all.' A wide grin spread across Mimi's face as she spoke. She was so overflowing with happiness, she couldn't stop smiling. Willow had given her permission to tell her sisters the whole story, as long as she swore them to silence.

'Willow's gay?' Aoife said wonderingly. 'And that engagement ring was for real?'

'Yeah.' Mimi smiled fondly. 'She posted that photo on Instagram the day they got engaged, and she forgot to take it off.' Willow had told her she'd been so drunk on champagne and giddy with happiness, she'd snapped the photo and posted it without thinking.

'Wow. So …'

'Rocco's all mine.'

'Does he know she told you?'

'No, she left that up to me. He doesn't know I know.'

'This is starting to sound like that episode of *Friends*,' Aoife said dryly. 'But you're going to tell him?'

'Yeah. But maybe I should make him sweat a bit first – get him back for making me feel like a scarlet woman.'

'Poor Rocco! It sounds like he's been sweating it out enough.'

'But he could have told me, instead of making me feel like I was a terrible person, and pretending he didn't want to be with me.'

'He was being a good friend to Willow. You can't hold that against him. Besides, you were doing the same to him. He thought you were with Sam.'

'True.' She couldn't really blame Rocco for being loyal to Willow and keeping her secret. 'Still, he could have given me some hint—'

'Sticking his tongue down your throat at regular intervals wasn't enough of a clue for you?' Aoife said.

Mimi laughed.

'Or saying he wasn't over you?'

'Okay, okay. But I thought he just wanted a fling. I did think his relationship with Willow was real, remember.'

'I still think you should put him out of his misery.'

Mimi nodded. 'You're right. I will. I just need to break up with Sam first. Then, once Willow goes public about her engagement, we'll both be single and free to do whatever we want without looking like a pair of bounders.'

'It sounds like quite the evening,' Aoife said.

'It was.' Mimi and Willow had chatted easily as they drank more wine and picked over a platter of antipasto. Mimi was surprised how much they had in common, and she liked Willow a lot. She could see why Rocco was so fond of her. Even though she'd only known her a short time, they'd bonded quickly, and she'd miss her.

'What about you?' she asked Sive as she topped up all their glasses. She'd noticed Sive seemed strangely subdued. It wasn't like her to be so quiet, especially when Mimi had such exciting news to impart. 'What did you have at Ben's?'

'Oh, just … burgers.' Sive's hand shook as she picked up her glass and she put it down again.

'Are you okay?' Mimi frowned, concerned.

'Not really.' She gulped, her eyes brimming with tears.

'Oh my god, what's wrong?'

'Sive?' Aoife put an arm around her. 'What is it?'

She swiped at her eyes. 'Ben broke up with me.' Her voice cracked and tears spilled down her cheeks.

'Oh no!' Mimi gasped. Privately, she was amazed Ben was capable of getting enough words out to break up with anyone. 'Why didn't you say something, instead of letting me prattle on about Willow?'

Sive choked back a sob. 'You were so happy; I didn't want to spoil it.'

'Don't be silly.' Mimi leaned across the table and took her hand. 'What happened?'

'He—he met someone else on that stupid Annapurna trail.' She sniffed.

Mimi found it even harder to imagine Ben engaging enough to get it on with someone else. She'd always felt part of the reason he'd been with Sive for so long was because he could only make that kind of effort once in a lifetime.

'She was one of the guides. He said they just clicked from the start. They have so much in common.'

Was she the strong and silent type too, Mimi wondered. She exchanged a look of thin-lipped, narrow-eyed fury with Aoife, both of them ready to wring Ben's neck.

'Is she from here?' Aoife asked.

'No, she's Portuguese.' Sive drew a ragged breath. 'He's moving there in a couple of weeks.'

'Wow!' When Ben finally made a move, he didn't hang around.

'Anyway, I'm going to bed.' Sive brushed tears from her eyes and stood. 'I'm wiped out.'

'Sleep well – or try to,' Mimi said. She knew how exhausting heartbreak could be.

'Let us know if you need anything,' Aoife said.

They both looked after her worriedly as she shuffled out of the kitchen.

'God, I feel like such an idiot now for banging on about Rocco.'

'It's not your fault. You weren't to know.'

'Bloody Ben! Where does he get off dumping her anyway? She's the best thing that ever happened to him.'

'At least she has her show starting next week to keep her busy and take her mind off things.'

'Yeah.' The new TV series Sive had got a part in was

starting shooting on Tuesday. 'God, I could happily strangle Ben, though.'

'I'd happily hold him down while you did it.'

'Do you think she'll be okay?'

Aoife nodded. 'She'll bounce back. You know Sive. And maybe it's a good thing in the long run. We never thought he was right for her.'

'That's true. And they were so young when they got together. It's surprising it's lasted this long really.' Mimi drummed her fingers on the table. 'Maybe it was more of a habit than anything.'

'Who knows? Anyway, now she has a chance to find someone better suited to her.' A smile played around Aoife's lips. 'I mean, there's always—'

'Don't even say it.'

Aoife grinned. 'There's always Sam.'

28

'Could we have a word?' Mimi asked Sam as soon as she arrived at the theatre the following evening. She'd come early so she could get him alone before anyone else arrived.

'Sure.'

She led him into the green room, and they sat side by side on the sofa. 'So, I think it's time to call it a day,' she said. 'You've been great, but your services will no longer be required.'

Sam blanched, his jaw dropping. Then light dawned, relief flooding his features. 'Oh, you mean us? The whole fake boyfriend thing?'

'Of course. It's time for us to break up.' She frowned. 'What did you think I meant?'

He put a hand over his heart. 'For a second there I thought I was getting the sack from my job.'

'Never! Although Cara did ask me if we could make you her assistant – officially, I mean.'

'Really?' Sam beamed with pleasure.

'I know you're already doing that, but we could make it your main role, if you're interested. It would be a bit of extra money, so we'd have to look at the budget, and it wouldn't be much—'

'Well, you know I'd do it for free.'

'You seriously need to work on your negotiating skills,' Mimi said wryly, but she couldn't help smiling at his enthusiasm. 'Anyway, we can discuss that another time. Right now, I'm here to break up with you.'

'Gosh, this is a bit sudden,' Sam said, grinning, clearly enjoying himself hugely. 'I can't say I'm surprised, but … I know we've had our problems, but don't you think we could give it another try, old thing?' The last part was delivered in a stiff-upper-lip English accent.

'No, I don't.' Mimi rolled her eyes. 'And I am not your "old thing".'

'I suppose you don't need me now that Willow's gone back to America.' He pouted.

'Exactly. Our relationship has outlived its usefulness.'

'I knew it! You were just using me to make her jealous,' he flung at her accusingly. He looked so hurt and anguished, Mimi was almost taken in for a moment.

'Give it a rest, Sam. You've played your part, but the show's over. Take your bows and exit stage left like a good boy.'

'We always knew this time would come,' he said wistfully. 'But it's still sad when it happens.'

'Careful, you're in danger of tipping over into melodrama, and you're still on audition, remember.'

'Aw, but I had a whole bit with a wobbly chin and quivering bottom lip that I haven't done yet.'

Mimi sighed, pursing her lips. 'Okay, you can show me your wobbly chin.'

Sam obliged and Mimi had to admit it was pretty effective – he actually looked as if he was biting back tears.

'Very nice. Very Celia Johnson in *Brief Encounter*.'

'Thanks,' Sam said, brightening up immediately.

'Anything else you'd like to throw at it before we continue?'

'Sorry?'

'We've had accents, tears … I thought maybe you'd prepared a dance or a song.'

'No, that's me done,' Sam said cheerfully. 'So, what's the story?' he asked, rubbing his hands together. 'Why are we breaking up? Give me all the gory details.'

'No major drama – there was no cheating or anything horrible like that. We just realised we're not that into each other. We broke up yesterday, and it's all very amicable, so there's no awkwardness or hostility between us.'

'Sounds great! Easiest break-up I've ever had anyway.'

'Me too.' Mimi smiled.

'Well, since I suppose this is sort of my exit interview, how did I do?'

'Very well.' Mimi nodded. 'Apart from almost losing it just now, but you pulled it back. I'll put your name in the hat for Young Scrooge when the time comes.'

'Thank you. I appreciate it.' Sam stood. 'Well, I'd better get back out to front of house.' He held out his hand and Mimi took it. 'It's been a pleasure doing business – or whatever you'd call this – with you.'

On his way to the door, he turned around. 'And if you know any other women in need of a fake boyfriend—'

'I'll be sure to recommend you.'

Mimi confided in Andrea about her break-up with Sam as soon as she arrived in their dressing-room that evening, knowing she could rely on her to spread the news. Sure enough, by the time they all left the theatre that night, the entire cast and crew were up to date on Mimi's relationship status.

Mimi didn't say anything to Rocco about what Willow had told her, however. She didn't want anything to happen between them until he was officially single, and the best way to make sure of that was to continue acting as if his relationship with Willow was real. The temptation might be too much for them if they both knew they were free, and she didn't want them to be caught 'cheating' before Willow made her announcement.

Fortunately, she didn't have to wait long. True to her word, Willow didn't waste any time announcing her engagement once she got back to LA. The story broke two days later, and as Willow had predicted, the response was largely positive and supportive. She said she hadn't intended to mislead anyone; she'd simply wanted to keep it to herself for a while. When asked about Rocco, she said their split was amicable and he remained one of her very best friends.

'What did I tell you!' Andrea crowed that evening when they were in the dressing room. 'I bet it was fake all along, and Rocco was just her beard.'

'I think that's a bit far-fetched, don't you?'

'That sort of thing happens all the time in Hollywood,' Andrea said.

As if you'd know, Mimi thought.

'I mean, she's gay! What would she be doing with Rocco?'

Mimi shrugged. 'I suppose she's bi. She's dated guys before.'

'Or has she?' Andrea said mysteriously, leaning forward and squinting into the mirror as she applied mascara. 'It explains the vibe I got off her anyway.'

'Vibe?' Mimi side-eyed her. 'What sort of vibe?'

'You know – that feeling you get when you know some-one's checking you out.'

'You think she *fancied* you?'

'I thought I must be imagining it at the time, but—'

'You don't think so now?' Mimi asked, aghast. Was there no end to the woman's narcissism?

'Anyway,' Andrea said, putting down her mascara wand and smiling at her reflection in the mirror, 'the good news is that Rocco's available now.'

'Oh! And you intend to make a play for him?'

'I sure do,' she said, smiling confidently.

'Andrea, could I ask you a favour?' Mimi turned to her and leaned forward confidingly, deciding to play to her vanity.

'Of course.'

'Could you not?' She put a hand on Andrea's knee.

'Not … what?'

'Remember you asked if it was okay with me if you went out with Rocco?'

Andrea nodded, covering Mimi's hand with her own. 'And you gave me your blessing.'

'Well, can I take that back?' Mimi made a pleading face.

'Oh!' Andrea's smile faltered for a second, but it was back in a flash. 'Of course!' she beamed, obviously flat-tered that Mimi needed her to step aside. 'Who am I to stand in the way of true love?'

'Thank you.' Mimi smiled beatifically. 'You're so sweet. I won't forget this.'

'No problem.' Andrea sprang up and smoothed down her skirt. 'Just don't forget to invite me to the wedding!' she called over her shoulder as she went to the door.

. . .

Having spent so much time pushing Rocco away, Mimi wasn't sure how to go about giving him the green light now.

'I suppose you heard about me and Sam?' she asked him later when they were sitting in the green room during the interval.

'I did. And obviously you've seen the news about me and Willow.'

'It was hard to miss. So, I was wondering if you fancied going out for a bite to eat after the show?'

'To commiserate with each other?'

'Yes. We can drown our sorrows and eat our feelings.'

'Sounds good.'

Act Three beginners to the stage, please, Cara's voice came over the intercom.

'And maybe practise our stage kisses,' she added, abandoning the subtle approach as Mitch, Andrea and Orla left the room. She was suddenly bursting with impatience to put her cards on the table and get things cleared up between them.

Rocco's eyebrows shot up. 'I'm game for that.' He smiled. 'They definitely need work.'

Mimi grinned. If he was supposed to be playing the heartbroken jilted lover, he was making a very poor job of it.

'A lot of work', she said, getting up as they were called to the stage. Her stomach fluttered with excitement as they made their way to the wings. For once she couldn't wait for the show to be over.

Nothing more was said, but it was as if they had a prearranged plan for the rest of the evening. Their curtain call kiss lasted a little longer than usual, and they put more into it than ever before. They both dawdled over getting changed, waiting until the other actors were gone so they wouldn't be seen leaving the theatre together – though Mimi didn't escape without getting a meaningful wink from Andrea as she said goodnight. They went out by the stage door to avoid Sam who would be clearing up front of house. It wasn't as if they were doing anything wrong, but it would seem like indecent haste in the circumstances, if anyone were to see them. Outside they threw themselves into a taxi and when the driver asked them 'where to', they turned to each other and both said, 'La Cave?' simultaneously, then nodded in agreement.

It was like old times when their choreography was in perfect sync and nothing needed to be said. But Mimi wasn't going to make that mistake again. This time she wanted everything to be clear between them. She'd say out loud how she felt and what she wanted, so there could be no misunderstandings.

'Sorry to hear about you and Sam,' Rocco said when they were ensconced in the restaurant with a bottle of wine and a cheese platter.

'Are you?'

He grinned sheepishly. 'Not really. I'm relieved, actually – not least because I'm pretty sure I saw him eyeing up your little sister.'

'Oh god, poor Sive!'

'She could do a lot worse. I like Sam.'

Mimi shook her head. 'I don't mean that. Ben broke up with her at the weekend.'

'Oh no! Poor Sive. I hope she's not too heartbroken.'

'She's pretty gutted at the moment. But hopefully she'll get over it quickly.'

'You don't seem too upset about you and Sam.'

Mimi shrugged. 'I'm fine. We were only together a

short time and it never got serious. We realised quickly it wasn't working.'

Rocco sighed. 'It seems to be catching – first me and Willow, then you and Sam, and now Sive! Everyone's breaking up.'

'I know about you and Willow,' Mimi said, lowering her voice in case they'd be overheard. The tables in this place were so close together.

Rocco gave a wry smile. 'Like you said, it'd be hard to miss.'

'No, I don't mean that. I know you weren't really in a relationship with her.'

Rocco frowned, looking cagey.

'It's okay, Willow told me.'

'She did? When was this?'

'Last Sunday when you were at your cousin's wedding. She invited me over.' She smiled. 'You were right about her. She's lovely.'

'I knew you two would get along.'

'Anyway, she thought I should have all the facts, in case I wanted to do anything about it.'

Rocco dropped his eyes, watching his finger trace patterns on the tablecloth. 'Is this why you broke up with Sam?' His voice was so soft she barely caught what he'd said.

'It may have had something to do with it, yes.' She reached across the table and put a hand over his, stilling it. When he looked up, she whispered, 'I'm still in love with you, Rocco. I never stopped being in love with you.' She lifted her hand and leaned back. 'And god knows, I tried,' she said with a laugh, feeling the need to lighten the atmosphere.

'It was the same for me.' He leaned across the table,

speaking in a hushed voice. 'It didn't work. I never stopped being in love with you either.'

'So, we both have all the facts. What do we do now?'

Rocco leaned back, considering. 'I propose we pay the bill, get out of here and go back to my place.' He signalled for the waiter as he spoke. 'Get some kissing rehearsal in — maybe even pull an all-nighter on it?'

'We are a bit rusty.'

'And after that ...' He drummed his fingers on the table. 'Maybe we could ... I don't know ... live happily ever after?' His face was suffused with happiness. 'Just throwing it out there. I'm open to suggestions.'

Mimi grinned. 'Happy ever after sounds good to me.'

'I suppose we should leave a decent interval before we let it be known we're together,' Rocco said the next morning.

It was almost midday, and they were lying side by side in bed in his house. Mimi had a deep sense of contentment and satisfaction that she hadn't experienced in years. She felt like she was finally back where she belonged.

'Willow won't mind, will she?' Mimi turned on her side to face him.

'No, not at all. She's happy for me to move on as soon as I like.'

'There you are, then. And as far as the public's concerned, she's the one who cheated and dumped you. I'm sure no one would blame you for seeking consolation in the arms of another.'

Rocco shifted closer on the pillows, and Mimi drank in his face. He was so ridiculously beautiful, yet so reassuringly familiar. He reached out and traced a finger across her cheek, brushing a tendril of hair behind her ear. 'Does everyone know about me and Willow? That it wasn't real?'

'Just Aoife and Sive, and they're sworn to secrecy.

Willow said I could tell them.' She smiled. 'It was really nice, what you did for her.'

Rocco shrugged. 'She's a good friend.' After a pause he said 'But what about Sam? It's a bit soon after your break-up with him. We don't want to humiliate him.'

'Oh, Sam won't mind.'

'I know your break-up was mutual, but still—'

Mimi sat up and leaned against the headboard, holding the sheet to her chest. She realised they still had a lot to say. There'd been no time for talking last night – or this morning. 'Look, I might as well tell you. The thing about me and Sam is … we weren't really together.' She blushed. It seemed so idiotic now.

'What do you mean?' Rocco sat up beside her, frowning in confusion.

'We were faking it, like you and Willow.'

'But why? If you're going to tell me you're gay—'

'Because you were coming here with Willow, and I didn't want to be poor little left-behind Mimi while you were parading around with your movie-star girlfriend.'

'So you roped in Sam?' Rocco grinned. 'He wasn't kidding when he said his title was "general factotum" and he called his job description "fluid".'

'He's very obliging.' Mimi pouted as if she was put out with him for laughing at her, but she couldn't help smiling.

'We're a right pair, aren't we?' Rocco laughed.

'Yes. Made for each other – because who else would put up with us?'

'I must say Sam was very convincing in the role of your boyfriend.'

'He was, wasn't he?'

'So much so that I frequently wanted to punch him.'

Mimi grinned, laying her head on his shoulder and

nuzzling against his face like a cat. 'You know he wants to be an actor?'

'He told me. Though why he'd want to leave behind the honour and glory of dogsbodying for you, I don't understand.'

'What can I tell you? He's got the bug. Nothing I say will put him off.'

'Well, I think he could be very good. You should give him a chance.'

'Oh, we intend to. Unless I'm very much mistaken, I think you'll be seeing him making his debut this winter in the role of Young Scrooge.'

Rocco's phone buzzed, vibrating on the nightstand. He shifted away from her and picked it up, smiling as he looked down at the screen. 'I put in an offer on that house we saw,' he said, 'and it's been accepted.'

'So it's yours?' Mimi squealed. 'Congratulations!'

'Unless you don't like it?' He turned to her, eyebrows raised. 'We could keep looking …'

Mimi's heart skipped a beat. '*We*? You mean … did you just ask me to move in with you?'

Rocco grinned. 'I suppose I did.'

'Well, the answer is yes!' She leaned in and planted a kiss on his mouth. 'I love that house, and I love you.'

'That's settled then.' He tossed his phone on the bed and his eyes darkened, dropping to her lips as he pulled her closer. 'Now, how long have we got before we need to be at the theatre? Because I think we should get some more rehearsal in.'

'Absolutely,' Mimi said, wrapping her arms around his neck. 'After all, practice makes perfect.'

A NOTE FROM THE AUTHOR

Thank you for reading *Stage Kisses on Halfpenny Lane*. I hope you enjoyed it.

If you'd like to hear more about me and my books, and keep up to date with my writing news, you can sign up for my mailing list at:

www.subscribepage.com/clodaghmurphy

I will never spam you, and you can unsubscribe at any time.

You can also visit my website or find me on social media.

www.clodaghmurphy.com

ALSO BY CLODAGH MURPHY

<u>The Halfpenny Lane Series</u>
The Little Theatre on Halfpenny Lane

The Disengagement Ring

Girl in a Spin

Frisky Business

Scenes of a Sexual Nature (novella)

Some Girls Do

For Love or Money

The Reboot

Dingle All The Way (novella)